To Ceri,

C000184967

TWO SCOOPS, TOO MUCH

TERRI BOAS

Thank you again for taking
the time to read and
review Two Scoops, Too
Much ♥.

I hope you enjoy the
continuing stories of Briony,
Lauren and Natalie.

With love

Wrate's Publishing

Terri
Boas

and best wishes,

xxx

First published in 2021 by Wrate's Publishing

ISBN 978-1-8383400-6-3

Copyright © 2021 by Terri Boas

Edited and typeset by Wrate's Editing Services

www.wrateseditingservices.co.uk

A CIP catalogue record for this book is available from the British Library.

To my bub, Portia.
It always seems impossible, until it is done.

Chapter One

The backing music stopped and the pub fell silent. Everyone was enraptured by the women who had just sang so passionately to each other on the slightly raised stage next to DJ Steve's booth.

The confessions and declarations that Briony and Lauren had made to each other only minutes earlier in the cellar had sent love, warmth, oxytocin and passion pulsing through their veins. Lauren pulled Briony into a tight hug. Meanwhile, the pub's patrons waited in anticipation of their next move.

Lauren looked over Briony's shoulder with an excited smile on her face and seductively brought her microphone to her lips. Ever the performer, she winked at her audience. "Shall I kiss her?" she asked, knowing full well she'd receive a positive response. She had full confidence in how well girl-on-girl kissing went down in a boozy pub environment.

Flo was the first to react and immediately rang the bell behind the bar. "You go, girls! Slippery nipples on the house." She smiled at the women as she began spreading empty shot glasses across the bar.

The pub erupted with cheers and encouragement, and DJ Steve played *I Kissed a Girl* by Katy Perry.

Even though free shots were being prepared for them at the bar, no one moved. They looked on as Lauren cupped Briony's face and pressed her lips against her mouth. Briony pulled Lauren in closer, wrapping her arms around her and gently running her hands through her hair. Then she put her hand behind her neck and pulled her in even closer. The passion between the women was electrifying.

Aware of not overstepping the mark and making the audience uncomfortable, Lauren pulled gently away from Briony, who, clearly hoping for more, still had her eyes closed and her mouth open. "I love this woman more than she'll ever know," she announced over the microphone. A cheer echoed around the pub as if England had just won the World Cup.

Briony snapped back into the room and felt the blood soaring to her cheeks. She shut her mouth and looked over at the many people grinning back at her and Lauren. She was reminded of when Mary Poppins tells one of her charges, "Close your mouth, please, Michael, we are not a cod fish." Whilst singing with Lauren, she hadn't paid any attention to her audience – she had been far too preoccupied thinking about what Lauren had told her in the cellar only moments earlier.

When Lauren had revealed to Briony that she loved her more than a friend, Briony hadn't needed to consider her reaction. Instinctively, she knew that she cared for and loved Lauren just as much. Although she felt exhilarated by the evening's events, she also felt confused about how things would change moving forward. And all the while this had been going on in her head, she'd had to remember the lyrics and harmonies to their favourite karaoke ballad, *I Know Him So Well*, by Elaine Paige and Barbara Dickson. Only now did she notice all the staring eyes and leers, and she wondered how on earth she had missed them.

Lauren tenderly squeezed her hand. "I kissed a girl, and I liked it," she sang. As her stunning voice blended with Katy Perry's blasting from the speakers, she motioned for their audience to get on the dancefloor.

Briony let Lauren get on and do her thing. She observed the punters watching her sing and wasn't surprised that they couldn't take their eyes off her best friend. She paused amid that thought. Was Lauren still her best friend, or was she now her *girlfriend*? She scrunched her face up while considering the label. It wasn't one she was particularly keen on.

Just then, she felt a familiar arm slip around her waist. "Bri, I am so happy for you and Lauren. For as long as we've been friends, there has been something special between you two, but I guess until now none of us really acknowledged it."

Briony turned around and threw her arms around Natalie's neck. "I'm so glad you're here," she said, holding her friend in a tight squeeze, before fully digesting what she'd just said. "Do you think the thing between Lauren and me was *that* obvious?"

"Yes, totally, and it's just perfect. I'm over the moon that you've finally got it together."

Natalie watched her friend's eyes glaze over as she fought to hold back the tears.

"I love you so much," Briony gushed.

"I love you, too, Bri. So, so much."

As the tears spilled from both the girls' eyes, Natalie grabbed Briony's shoulders and looked her square in the face. "Alright, enough of this. There'll be no more liaisons with douchey Jason the spin instructor for me, and Bri, no more drunken dates with Mani, the looser son of your American boss. No one who tries to orchestrate a threesome with you and Lauren is worth your time. Let's get a shot in." Then she added teasingly, "Maybe you're onto something. I'm really excited about this slippery nipple."

Briony giggled, blushed and turned to look at Lauren on the stage. She had moved into doing a full Katy Perry set and was now singing Briony's favourite, *Hot n Cold*.

Natalie pulled Briony by the hand to the bar, which was busy with pub goers swiping at the now full shot glasses. Despite the frenzy, as always, Flo was in control and ensuring that it was one drink per customer. Briony wondered again how the landlady had known what had happened in the cellar with Lauren.

"Right, that's it, no more shots," Flo eventually shouted at her customers. "If you can't be trusted to only have one, no one is getting any."

She spoke to them like they were animals and they duly retreated.

"However, Briony, Natalie and Lauren – when she stops entertaining – must have theirs."

She expertly placed a cherry on top of the three shot glasses she had reserved for her favourite patrons. "I guess you wanna know how I knew?" she said to Briony.

Briony's cheeks turned pink. "Yeah, Flo, I really do. You didn't come down, did you? Oh my gosh, how embarrassing."

Her cheeks went a deeper crimson at the idea that Flo had witnessed them smooching in the cellar.

"I saw Lauren pull you past the toilets," Flo started to explain, "and the only place to go after that is upstairs, to the flat, or down to the cellar. Your Lauren looked troubled, but she had hold of your hand, and I just had a feeling. I'm pretty intuitive, you know, and, well, there's always been something between the two of you. It was only a matter of time."

Briony threw the shot to the back of her throat, swallowed hard and then chewed the cherry. "What is it that I've missed? Natalie said the same."

4

Flo smiled back at Briony, her gaze turning to Lauren as she approached her friends from behind and wrapped her arms around them both. "It's been such a special night, and I am so happy you're here to share it with us, Nat."

The girls pulled in tighter. Lauren's touch was electrifying to Briony, and the spark made the hair on her arms stand on end.

"Is there a shot for me, please, Flo?" Lauren asked.

"Of course there is, Lauren, need you ask? It's right there in front of you."

Lauren didn't need to be told twice and fired the shot down, just the same as her friends had done. "Is there a chance you have three more? Pretty please," she asked, while chewing the cherry.

"As you asked so kindly," Flo replied with a wink, "and because you have provided the entertainment this evening. You're lucky, I rescued a load from the animals only a few minutes ago. Here you go."

Lauren, suddenly feeling uncharacteristically bashful, turned to Briony. "I'm sorry if I embarrassed you earlier," she said.

Briony had to think for a moment about what Lauren was referring to. "Oh, so I guess you're apologising for kissing me live on the stage, in front of a pub full of people?"

Lauren raised her shoulders and smiled her sexy smile. For effect, Briony purposely left a pregnant pause. "No, babe, I'm not embarrassed at all. My cheeks did rouge up a bit because so many people were watching, but it really didn't matter because it was you, and I thought it was really romantic."

"Oh, you girls, stop it." Natalie pretended to wave away her tears. "Let's get drunk!" She grabbed Lauren's hand, while Lauren took hold of Briony's. They skipped over to the empty booth where they had begun their night. Three half-drunk glasses of red wine welcomed their return.

"What? Wait, Nat," said Briony. "I've got work in the morning and Mani will be there. I'd better not drink any more."

"Fuck him!" said Natalie. "You wouldn't be here if it weren't for him secretly inviting Lauren to his dad's *Downton Abbey* room and asking for a threesome. So, any hangover will be all on him." Natalie poured the last of the red wine into the three glasses.

Agreeing with Natalie, Lauren leaned in and pushed Briony's hair away from her ear. In her one-shoulder dress, Briony could feel her friend's warm breath over her bare skin. She felt a tingle flurry through her insides.

"Babe, I've been thinking," said Lauren. "Why don't you just resign? You won't have to work with or see Mani ever again. I've saved up a bunch of money through working on the ships and only contributing to the bills when I'm at home with you. You don't have a mortgage, so we would be OK for a bit. Maybe we could travel together or something."

Briony's tingle erupted into a kaleidoscope of butterflies. *Is this what real love feels like?* she wondered to herself. She linked arms with Lauren, pulling her in closer and breathing in her distinctive Yves Saint Laurent Opium perfume, or, as Lauren referred to it, Yves Saint *Lauren* perfume. Then she lurched forward, retrieved her three-quarters full glass of red and held it aloft across the centre of the table. "To the future!" she said.

Lauren and Natalie cheered and repeated her line.

"Tits and arse!" they then added in unison. The wine glasses were clinked together at the top and the bottom, and right on cue the girls burst into peals of laughter.

Chapter Two

Natalie peeled away from Briony and Lauren and set off for home just around the corner. For the first time since being down in the cellar, the two girls were alone. Lauren's left hand found Briony's right and they instantly intertwined their fingers. As they walked, they kept bumping against each other, either from the alcohol or because they wanted to keep confirming to each other that they were present and aware that their relationship had changed. Each time their bodies collided, they giggled like schoolgirls.

As they made their way up to their building's communal entrance, Briony accidentally stepped her heel into the flowerbed and tripped, pulling Lauren down with her. The security light flashed brightly as the women laughed and rolled around in the soil, inadvertently flattening the tulips and daffodils, for which Briony paid a monthly garden maintenance fee. Briony picked up a handful of soil and threw it at Lauren. It crumbled over her hair and fell down her face and chest, slipping into her dress.

Briony couldn't control herself, and from the girls' alcohol-induced peals of laughter, it was clear that neither of them were giving any consideration to their neighbours.

Lauren straddled Briony, who was now fully lying in the flowerbed, her electric purple dress raised high up her thighs. Teasingly, she smothered Briony's face with soil and shook her head, sending a flurry of it all over her chest. Just then, the security lights turned off, bringing them sharply back to reality. Lauren let go of the soil and shook the remnants from her hand. She then leaned into Briony and gently wiped off the clumps of mud she'd dropped onto her face.

Briony loved the thrill that Lauren's tender skin-on-skin touch gave her. She so wanted a kiss, but as much as she wanted to show her that she did want more, she wasn't brave enough to initiate one. Instead, she pushed Lauren's shoulders so that she fell backwards. The two girls sat facing each other in the flowerbed. Lauren tucked some of Briony's loose hair behind her ear and cupped her cheeks, just as she had done earlier down in the cellar. Briony remembered the enjoyment she had felt when Lauren held her face with such affection. Slowly and gently the girls made out.

When they finally drew away from each other, Lauren pulled Briony to her knees, and the tingling she felt intensified. She hadn't realised just how much she loved Briony and was so far beyond happy to learn that her old friend felt the same. She was confident that Briony could never love her as much as she loved Briony, and she knew she would always protect her. "Let's get out of the mud and go upstairs," she suggested. She began to pull Briony up.

"Do we have to?" Briony protested, trying to pull Lauren back down, which made her burst out laughing and crumble to the floor. The girls giggled and drunkenly rolled once more in the mud. Lauren was now on top of Briony. She stopped moving and this time tucked Briony's hair behind both of her ears. As she pressed against her, their laughter stopped. Both women were aware that they had been this close many times throughout their lives, as they play fought or hugged, but the attraction they felt for each other was now significantly stronger.

Eventually, Lauren pulled Briony from the floor and they carried each other to the porch and up the stairs. Briony opened the door to her flat and the women stumbled in, clip-clopping their heels noisily across the laminate floor into the lounge. The flat felt like home to the girls now more than ever; it was their private space to be together.

Lauren went into the kitchen to make them both a calming herbal tea. She also poured out two glasses of water to ease their pending hangovers. Since Briony was going to have to face Mani in the morning, she wanted to help her feel as alert as possible. The idea of him and Briony together made her shudder.

Earlier that evening, Mani, the son of Briony's boss, had enticed Lauren into a room at his dad's mansion, where he had requested a threesome with Briony. As far as Briony was aware, she and Mani were exclusively seeing each other, but Lauren had followed her instinct about the slimeball and had managed to film the scene on her phone. She was livid with how he had used Briony. In her mind, the footage she had captured of him revealing his true colours wasn't nearly enough to teach him the lesson she reckoned he deserved. But the amount of red wine, cosmopolitans and slippery nipples she had consumed throughout the evening clouded her mind, and she knew she wasn't capable of plotting her revenge tonight. She carried the two steaming mugs of tea into the lounge and found Briony fast asleep on the sofa. It appeared that she was sleeping with a smile on her face, which sent a rush of warmth through Lauren's body. Placing the mugs on the coffee table, she went into Briony's room to retrieve her duvet and pillow. Fortunately, Briony's sofa was deep, and once the back cushions were removed there was enough room for two. They had fallen asleep on it many times after a night out, and at other times just because it was warm and comfy and they couldn't be bothered to move.

Carefully, Lauren removed the bigger cushions, before slotting Briony's pillow in front of her and rolling her head onto it. She moved her body into a comfortable side-sleeping position and covered her with the duvet. Then, in true Lauren tradition, she went to the bathroom and removed all her face paint. After years of wearing stage make up while performing on the ships, she'd made it a habit to always take her face off before bed, otherwise it wasn't pretty in the morning. She slipped into her pyjamas and sat cross-legged on the floor in front of Briony. As best she could, she removed her make up, too. She didn't follow her normal routine of facial wash, serum and moisturiser, she just used a make-up remover wipe. Briony stirred a little when the cool cloth touched her face, but it wasn't enough to wake her from her alcohol-induced slumber.

Lauren finished by gently applying a dab of moisturiser to Briony's face. She was happy to see her still sleeping soundly. She drank her tea, gulped down some water and then climbed in next to Briony under the duvet. Normally, it was Briony's arm that wrapped across Lauren's tummy as they fell asleep, but tonight Lauren's arm slid over Briony's and pulled her in. Almost instantly, she drifted off.

* * *

I'm wide awake.

The beginning of Katy Perry's song *Wide Awake* hummed from Briony's phone on the lounge floor. She'd uploaded the ringtone as her alarm thinking it was funny. Lauren was the first to move and she leaned across Briony to turn the noise off.

Briony groaned from underneath Lauren's body, and Lauren could tell she was feeling rough. "You OK, babe?" she asked. She rolled back over Briony and lay next to her awaiting a response. Slowly, Briony opened her eyes, revealing her bloodshot but still pretty blue peepers. Lauren's heart sank; she had a bad feeling about Briony's day ahead at work, and from the look of her, her hangover was just the beginning of a post-thirty, four-day recovery.

"I feel pretty shit, but from what I remember it was a good night, so feeling like this is worth it." Despite her tired eyes, Briony still managed to shine a sweet, caring smile at Lauren, who responded with a wink.

"It really was a fab night, Bri," Lauren replied, "but now I have business to attend to."

Briony envied Lauren's frivolity, but rolled over with a groan, not wanting to engage with whatever her friend was cooking up. Her personal energy was limited, and she couldn't expend it unnecessarily, especially with a full day of work ahead of her.

On the other hand, Lauren was relatively hangover free, and she was now able to devise a winning plan to make Mani pay. It all started with Briony. "There's a pint of water on the table, babe," she told her. "Please drink it and I'll get you some Nurofen, a cup of coffee and a couple of pieces of jam on toast. Then I need you to shower and pick out something extremely inappropriate and damn sexy to wear to work."

Briony raised her left eyebrow, revealing a glimmer of interest in the rest of what Lauren had to say, but she still didn't speak. Lauren climbed over her unmoving body and went off into the kitchen to complete the first stage of her scheme.

Briony's head felt stuffy, heavy and tired, but she was flooded with excitement. It had felt different waking up next to Lauren this morning, and she loved it when her friend was in planning mode. Life was never boring when Lauren was around, and Briony had a good feeling about whatever she had in store for her.

By the time she had pulled herself up, Lauren had waltzed in with a white coffee with two sugars, two slices of white toast with butter and jam, two Nurofen tablets and a mischievous smile painted across her face. Despite the depth of cotton wool that filled Briony's head, she couldn't wait to hear what she had to say. Lauren sat on the coffee table opposite Briony and watched her slug down the water and tablets, before proceeding to sip at the piping hot coffee.

"Bri, babe. Look, I'm not gonna lie, the thought of you having to work alongside, or even underneath, Mani – excuse the pun – makes me sick."

Briony snorted, remembering that she had been the one on top of Mani during their impromptu sex session in the work kitchen. She hadn't been underneath him at all. She looked up at Lauren, who didn't look amused. "OK, I'm sorry, it's just . . ."

"No, don't do that," Lauren said.

Briony's high plummeted and she wished she could take back her snort. Lauren's eyes were blue like hers, but they were more of a navy than the bright blue of her own. And when she looked into them, she saw that they were hurting, causing her own eyes to moisten. She dropped to her knees and clutched Lauren round her waist, sobbing into her pyjama bottoms.

Lauren held her close, and she too began to cry, which was most surprising to her. The girls' bodies shuddered together as their tears spilled, encouraged along by last night's booze and their lack of sleep.

12

Lauren pulled Briony back onto the sofa, and this time they laughed. "Oh my word, what a couple of dicks!" she said.

The girls wiped each other's faces free from tears. "I bet I look like a panda," said Briony. "As always, Laur, babe, you look pristine in the morning."

Lauren blushed. "I took your make up off last night whilst you were sleeping," she explained, sending love surging through Briony's veins.

"You did what? That's the nicest thing anyone has ever done for me."

Lauren's smile returned. "I didn't strip you down and get you into your pyjamas, though."

Now it was Briony's turn to blush. She looked down at her Primark dress; it was riding high up her legs, and she pulled the duvet up to cover her modesty.

"Right, OK, like I said last night, we have a lot to talk about," Lauren said. "But all that can wait, because right now, I have a plan."

Briony leaned in with her coffee, totally engrossed in Lauren's step-by-step scheme for her morning at work.

"Have a shower," said Lauren, "and I'll write your resignation."

Chapter Three

Natalie's keys jangled as they hit the door. Inside, Martin was ready and waiting for her. As quiet as Natalie thought she was being, it was a pissed quiet, and as she shut the front door, took off her shoes and placed her keys on the glass-top table by the stairs, it was clear that a brass band would have made less of a racket.

There weren't any lights on, so she assumed everyone was in bed. Switching on the hall light, she 'tip-toed' into the kitchen, banged around in the cupboard to get a glass for her water, turned the tap on full and smiled to herself as she overfilled the tumbler. She'd had a good night and was genuinely happy for Briony and Lauren. They complemented each other on so many levels and made a good match. She shared with them their 'new relationship' excitement and could imagine the thrills they were both feeling. She smiled and looked up the stairs, to where her husband was sleeping. He had to be her one. He was a good guy, a good dad and a good provider. He had even managed to forgive her for her betrayal. But despite all that, he didn't excite her the way Jason had at the beginning of their fling, and she'd never looked at him the way Briony and Lauren looked at each other. Despite counting all her blessings, Natalie didn't like the feeling that something was missing. She'd told Martin she wanted to make it work and she really did, but what if the hole in their relationship just kept getting bigger?

She shook her head. *It's just the drink talking, it'll all be fine in the morning,* she silently decided.

Natalie chuntered away to herself as she made her way up to bed, running her handbag against the wooden spindles of the staircase. She clattered in a most unladylike fashion into the bathroom; the short walk home and fresh air having only increased her drunken state. As she reached for the bathroom light, she felt someone come up from behind and awkwardly push her into the room until she was bent over the sink. Her perpetrator stepped away and she heard the door close behind them. It wasn't slammed shut, so she knew she wasn't in any real danger. Whoever this was didn't want to wake the sleeping children . . .

It was dark apart from the distant streetlamp shining through the bathroom window. All that could be heard was the heightened breathing of Natalie and her pursuer.

"Mart, is that you?" she laughed.

He waited and then exhaled. "Yes, yes, it is. I wanted to surprise and seduce you, but you're much drunker than I thought you'd be for a Tuesday night."

Natalie laughed again and turned to face her husband in the dark. "You'll never believe what happened," she said. Wanting to witness Martin's reaction to her big news, she stumbled past him and reached again for the light cord by the bathroom door. As the bulb illuminated the room, Natalie took in the sight before her. Martin had put on his handcuffs, and the key to them was hanging around his neck on a thin, black ribbon. He was naked save for a pair of unusually tight orange and black striped pants. Natalie gasped as she noticed

15

that there was a picture of a tiger's face stretching across her husband's package. Martin cowered slightly, lifted his head and looked back at his wife. "Rooooaaaar," he said, but it wasn't the roar of a tiger in its prime.

Natalie tried her hardest not to smile, but then a loud, drunken guffaw got the better of her. Soon she was crying with laughter.

"OK, stop it now, please, it's not that funny. I thought you could let the beast loose and we could carry on from where we left off the other night."

Is he for real? Natalie thought to herself, and she fell about laughing once again.

"Mart, I know you have a tiger tattoo, but I've been looking at that since you got it on your 21st birthday. Can't you see how amusing all this is? Did you really think your get up would get me in the mood?"

Her husband shifted uncomfortably, looked down at the faded tattoo on his right shoulder, and nodded his head. "Can you unlock me, please?" he asked, pushing his chained hands over to Natalie.

"Come here, you silly sod," Natalie giggled.

Martin bent down so she could lift the key over his head, but she hesitated as he started to talk and lost track of what she was doing.

"I'm really trying, Nat. I can't lose you."

She could see the hurt she had caused by getting sexually involved with her spin instructor. Mart was trying, but his behaviour made her realise that she couldn't just walk back into her marriage. She needed to repair the damage she had caused, and she needed to stop thinking about what their relationship lacked. With his wrists still cuffed, Martin moved to sit on the edge of the bath, while Natalie sat cross-legged on the floor in front of him. "I'm so sorry, Martin," she said. She looked up to meet his gaze, enjoying the warmth of his love. Quite unexpectedly, she also started to feel turned on. She caressed his ankles, working her way up his calves and running her fingers through his fair curls, before kissing his inner thigh, all the way up to the tiger. "How about we have a shower together?" she suggested.

Resting her hands on his legs, she pushed herself up to a standing position and turned on the shower. The hot water flowed fast, and it didn't take long for the glass to steam up. Still tipsy, she tugged at her clothes, which in a sober state would have slipped off much more seductively. She then grabbed the key around Martin's neck and pulled him into the shower.

In retrospect, trying to unlock the handcuffs while under the influence and with water gushing down both their bodies wasn't as smooth and as sexy as she had hoped, but Martin's continuous excitement proved that the fumbling hadn't hindered him in any way. Finally, their bodies slipped into a rhythm as they moved against the glass of the shower door. Martin had to bite his lip; he desperately wanted to bring Natalie to orgasm before he finished himself. Fortunately, the idea of another man pleasuring his wife helped him control himself.

* * *

Natalie woke to find her husband placing a mug of coffee on the bedside table next to her. She smiled inside; he looked so very pleased with himself. He'd covered up his nakedness with an old dressing gown that had probably seen better days, though Natalie had never witnessed them. She'd tried to throw it away many times, but Martin was thrifty and refused to part with it.

"Good morning, baby, did you sleep well?"

Natalie cringed. "Baby? When on earth have you ever

called me that? I'm not twenty or in *Dirty Dancing*, and, no offence, Mart, you're no Patrick Swayze."

Martin sat down next to her. "Yeah, you're right, it didn't sound convincing to me, either. No offence taken. Last night was good, though, huh?" He raised both his eyebrows at her.

She reached for her coffee and nodded. "Yes, it was, but we don't have to go on about it. I think you should get rid of the tiger pants, though."

Martin looked her in the eye and nodded his agreement.

"Oh, I didn't get round to telling you last night, but you'll never guess what happened at the pub. Briony and Lauren only proper snogged on the stage after singing karaoke. Lauren declared her undying love to Briony over the mic. It was so lovely."

She could see Martin's cogs turning as he imagined the two women kissing. "You're kidding?" he eventually replied. "That's a right turn-up for the books. You've always said there was something different between those two."

Natalie changed the subject to something that had been on her mind for a while. "So, I was thinking that when Milo starts school full-time in September, I want to start making some money of my own. I was thinking of training as a PT."

Natalie watched the blood drain from her husband's face. In retrospect, she realised that her words were incredibly thoughtless, considering that Jason was a PT as well as a spin instructor. She knew that Martin's attempt to seduce her last night was provoked by his insecurity over her sleeping with Jason and getting pregnant by him. He'd been sympathetic when she told him she'd lost the baby, but she also saw the relief in his eyes. Now the torment had returned to them.

"Oh, Mart, I'm sorry, it's just I've been thinking about getting a job for a while now."

She expected him to say, "You don't need to work," but he refrained and waited for her to continue.

"I've been talking to the mums at school, and some of them say that going back to work saved them. I really get that. I've been lucky in that we could afford for me to stay at home and care for Bethany and Milo, but from September they'll both be at school, and I want to start bringing in some money of my own."

Martin nodded. "You know you don't have to work," he predictably suggested.

"Yes, but come on, Mart, you know me. I need something to do. Since college and before the kids came along, I pretty much always had two jobs on the go. I gave up my cashier position at the bank and my as-and-when job behind the bar at the Red Lion when I had Bethany, and I haven't worked since. That was almost eight years ago."

She could see that she was chipping away at Martin's defences. "I got chatting to this mum at the school gate, Holly. She picks her son Seb up in a flash BMW, has fabulous, highlighted hair and looks great in sports wear because she's in such good shape. Anyway, it turns out she works as a personal trainer."

"But you've got a brand-new Audi Q8. I only bought it for you a couple of months ago," Martin pointed out.

Natalie recognised that her husband had a point. She considered her answer before replying and softened her voice. "You're right, Mart, I do have the best car on the school run, and I love it, I really do." She paused and leaned in close enough so that he could feel her body heat. "But you bought it. I want to make my own money to pay for my own things, just like I used to."

She knew he couldn't fight her on this. "I reckon I would make a great PT."

Martin shook his head to stop her from continuing. "Why a PT? Why can't you go back to the bank? I'm sure they'd take you on again in a flash."

Natalie was starting to lose her patience. "Why not a PT? It'd be great to work around the kids and it pays well. I also enjoy getting fit and seeing my body change, and I'd like to help other women feel the same. Maybe I could work with postpartum mums, you know, helping them to get their bodies back after giving birth."

Martin shook his head again. "But what about him?"

Rather insensitively, Natalie rolled her eyes at her husband. "This has nothing to do with Jason," she said.

Martin squirmed upon hearing the name of his wife's ex-lover.

"I wouldn't have to go anywhere near the gym," Natalie reasoned, remaining close to Martin's body and breathing her words across his shoulder. "I could train online, get my own equipment and work independently."

"It's clear that you've put a lot of thought into this," Martin replied.

Natalie could feel that he was becoming uncomfortable, but she knew that despite his protests, he would have no choice but to give in to the woman he loved.

In a flash, Martin took her completely by surprise by putting his hands on her shoulders and pushing her back on the bed, before straddling her and holding her down. Natalie gasped; she was completely unprepared for this level of dominance and wasn't sure she enjoyed the power shift.

"I'll tell you what I want to do," Martin said, his venomous-sounding words making Natalie shudder. "I want to smack you for being so naughty."

Towards the end of the sentence, Martin's words turned playful, but Natalie couldn't help wondering whether there was some truth behind them.

Thankfully, one of the children screamed from downstairs and distracted Martin, who climbed off Natalie as if nothing had happened. She recognised it was Milo, and that the cry was more attention-seeking than one of hurt. She was in too much of a state of shock to move or speak. She'd just seen a side to her husband that she'd never been privy to before. She watched him tie the belt of his dressing gown. He looked back to normal again as he gallantly went to the aid of their son.

Natalie got up and looked at herself in the mirror, considering whether Martin would have smacked her. She was 99.9 per cent sure that he wouldn't have done, but this was the first time the remaining 0.01 per cent had even been a possibility.

Chapter Four

Briony pulled Gina, her E-reg, red Escort, into the car park of Schwartzberg Finance Ltd. She could see that Keith, her line manager, and Mr Schwartzberg were at the office already. She parked in her space, filled her lungs with air and exhaled in preparation for what was no doubt going to be a game-changing day.

Looking in the rear-view mirror, she checked that her smoky and sexy eye make up hadn't smudged. It was a little overdone for work, but she'd let Lauren do her face that morning. She applied a little extra pink lip gloss and was ready to go. Chanel No 19 sailed around her as she shook her mane of loose curls – which she normally wore in an up-do for work – and climbed out of Gina. As she stuck her leg out, she revealed the emerald, lace trim of her black stockings. She wasn't wearing the full garter and suspenders get-up, these had never been her thing, but Lauren's hold-ups still made her feel super sexy.

As she stood up, she shook out her infamous pinafore dress to remove the creases that had formed while sitting in the car. She had worn this dress just last week to impress

Mani, when, leaving the house in a rush, she'd accidentally left the zip at the back half undone. In his dad's office, Mani had suggestively pulled it up from her shoulder blades to her neck, marking the beginning of their brief, flirty non-relationship/relationship. The dress was black and clung tight to her curves.

She balanced on her black, strappy, suede heels, which crisscrossed around the bottom third of her leg, and fidgeted to find the calmness she needed to walk into the office. Her head was still a little stuffy, but the Nurofen, water, toast and coffee had eased it slightly.

She looked up at the building and could see Keith peering down at her from one of the windows. He was pointing at her outfit, clearly questioning why she was wearing that dress again, why her hair was down and why she was wearing shoes designed for the dancefloor rather than the office floor. Briony simply looked behind her, as if he was pointing at something else, and shrugged her shoulders. She smiled as he turned in a huff. She knew he was heading straight for the staircase. It was time to put phase one of the plan into action.

* * *

Briony sauntered through the main door to see Keith's twiglet body flying down the stairs.

"Before you say anything, I've got somewhere to be straight after work, and since I won't have enough time to get changed, I'm dressed for the occasion now."

"I hope this isn't for Mani," Keith said knowingly, while looking his colleague up and down.

"Oh my God, is that what you think? Hell no, don't flatter him. It's Lauren's surprise birthday party, which I've organised. I need to get to the venue after work, so I'll just add a little lippy and head straight there."

She spoke with absolute conviction and was pleased with how convincing she sounded.

"Hmmm, a surprise birthday party on a Wednesday night? I'm not sold, Briony Greene."

Bollocks! She had to think quickly.

"Well, Keith," she began, just to give her some thinking time. "It's Lauren's birthday today and she sets sail again tomorrow, so the party can't wait." She stamped her foot to emphasise her point.

"Yes, yes, I get that, but wouldn't you have celebrated over the weekend and not on a school night?"

Rage began to bubble up inside Briony. Keith was so bloody nosy. She took a deep breath to compose herself. None of this was part of the plan, and she wasn't willing to fall at the first hurdle.

"Lauren went home to her mum's for the weekend, and she came back to the flat late last night to pack ready to leave for her next ship stint tomorrow."

Ha, in your face! she thought to herself, confident he wouldn't have a comeback to that.

Like a toddler being refused his own way, he muttered under his breath just loud enough for Briony to hear. "Well, if you say so, but something doesn't add up."

Briony pretended she had an itch and slid her palms down her stockings, encouraging her dress to ride up to reveal the green lace trim. She could feel Keith's eyes burning on her legs and teasingly came back up. He spun on his heel and marched back up the stairs.

"Do you want a coffee?" Briony called after him, trying not to laugh. "I'll go and make one and then come straight to my desk."

There was no reply. Keith had long gone.

This is going to be fun, Briony thought to herself.

She walked down the long corridor towards the kitchen.

The glass of the huge conference room on her left was misted up, which meant there was an official meeting taking place with Mr Schwartzberg and, most probably, Mani. After all, he was over here from the States specifically to learn about the English side of his dad's business. She hurried past both the conference room and the kitchen – where just a day ago she'd had her wicked way with Mani – and headed straight to the green fire exit doors at the bottom of the corridor. As planned, Lauren was waiting on the other side of them, and Briony quickly pulled her inside. Luckily, as so many of the staff used the area behind the doors to smoke, the alarm was turned off during the day, which meant Lauren could get in, quite literally, without raising the alarm.

Briony led her into the kitchen and locked the door behind them. Suddenly, she felt overwhelmed. "I know you don't want to hear this, but please empathise with me if you can. The last time I was in here, I fucked Mani. It started here by the counter and finished with me on top of him in that chair."

"What, you did it on that tatty old thing in the corner?"

Briony looked across at the chair, as if she were seeing it for the first time. How did that old wicker thing survive their thunderous rocking?

"Yeah, that one. Anyway, now that I've got you locked in here, I am experiencing a whole new bunch of feelings. You look stunning by the way."

Lauren had gone for the femme fatale, Miss Scarlett look. She had blood red lips, an enviable cleavage and a red dress with a slit up one side, which almost reached her right hip. She stepped one leg forward, flashing her knee-high boot and the red lace trim of her hold-up stockings. "Thanks, babe," she said, spinning around and teasingly leaning into Briony. "As always, you are breathtaking. Even in work gear, I might add. Let me add the pièce de résistance."

She pushed herself against Briony, who stumbled

25

backwards into the counter, and grabbed the zip of her infamous little black dress. "How far down do you want it?" she asked. She slowly started pulling on the zip, which ran all the way down to the top of Briony's knicker line.

"Just enough for it to look like an accident, but so it's obvious to anyone that it needs to be zipped up."

Lauren spent longer than necessary zipping the zip up and down, giving Briony time to soak up her coconut body lotion and the ever-present Yves Saint *Lauren* perfume. Lauren pulled back but remained close to Briony, so that their noses were almost touching. Briony would have loved to remain there, but she had business to attend to and moved to one side, pointing at the ceiling above the dirty, net-curtained window. "Look, there's the CCTV camera. You're not supposed to be in here, so for our plan to work, we need to cover up the lens."

Lauren nodded and quickly moved underneath the camera so that she was no longer in view. She moved with long strides, showing her leg through the slit in her dress, before turning back to face Briony.

"Did you bring the black tape?" Briony asked her, beginning to panic. Lauren nodded. "But where is it, you haven't got a bag?"

Lauren leaned forward, revealing a clear view of her cleavage, stuck her hand into her bra and pulled out a small roll of black tape. "If the original *Mary Poppins* was filmed today, she wouldn't have a carpet bag, she'd keep everything in her bra."

She flung her hair back and the girls laughed. Briony agreed that she had a good point.

"I don't want to touch your sexy chair," Lauren said, screwing up her nose, "but that seems to be the only thing in here that I can stand on to reach the camera."

Briony scanned the room. Lauren was right, she'd have to touch the chair where Mani's naked bum had sat just hours earlier. Lauren pretended to shield her eyes with one hand and held onto Briony's shoulder with the other, as she clambered onto the wicker seat.

Rip!

Lauren's heel tore through the centre of the chair, sending her foot thundering through it. "Shit!" she said, as she began to pull her boot from the ripped weave. "It's a stupid bloody chair anyway!"

Briony tried hard not to laugh. "Actually, this could work to our advantage," she said. "Funny how things happen for a reason, huh?"

Briony stopped smiling when she realised Lauren wasn't sharing her merriment. She really was still pissed with Mani, and the chair was still the enemy.

Chapter Five

B riony had been working at her desk for over an hour when people began to emerge from the conference room downstairs. Working was a loose term, as really she was just sitting at her desk with the computer on.

Soon enough, she could hear the familiar sound of Mr Schwartzberg stomping across the office floor. His steps became closer and closer until they stopped right behind her. Her heart raced. It was just like in *Jurassic Park*, with the altercation with the T-Rex pending.

"Good morning, Miss Greene. How are you feeling today?"

Briony froze, remembering how the night before she had been ushered out of her boss's house following Mani's indecent proposal. She spun around to face him, and was relieved to see genuine concern on his face.

"Ah, hi, Mr S, yes, I'm feeling much better this morning. It must have been one of those twenty-four hour things." She chose not to throw Mani under the bus and apologised to her boss for abruptly leaving his house.

"Not a problem," Mr Schwartzberg replied. "And might I

add that you look really nice today. Your standards never seem to drop, Miss Greene."

Briony blushed and he walked off to his office. As he reached it, she could hear him shouting his son's name. Her stomach hit the floor and she shuddered. Looking up, she saw Mani strolling confidently through the main office. His muscles rippled underneath his shiny shirt, and his legs, toned by hours of squats and deadlifts, looked amazing in his signature tight trousers. And then there was his chiselled jaw and his smouldering smile. But no, Briony wasn't interested this time. To her, that smile now hid a dirty secret. When Mani's eyes reached Briony's, his smile dimmed a little, as if sensing her disdain. Meanwhile, Briony felt a flood of power surge through her body, as if she were Adora after yelling, "For the honour of Grayskull!" and transforming into She-Ra.

"Morning, Briony," Mani said. "I agree with Pops, you are looking enticing, as always. But I see you're out to tease me, by yet again not getting fully dressed." He moved over to her desk, and she felt his warm hand against the back of her neck as he zipped her up. She was the temptress, and Miss Scarlett was waiting in the wings.

"Oh no, not again. Silly me," she said sweetly, intending to leave Mani wondering whether Lauren had even shown her the recording of him suggesting the threesome.

* * *

It took a few minutes for Briony to calm down and return to her 'work' before Keith came over again. "What now? I'm quite busy, you know."

"I saw the interaction between you and Mani. What have you done?"

"Nothing, I have done nothing! There was no interaction. I

29

think you must be seeing things." She rolled her eyes at her inquisitive colleague.

"Something isn't adding up, Briony, and you know me, I will get to the bottom of this."

Briony knew that he would, but by then she'd be out of Schwartzberg Finance Ltd for good. "OK, Keith, it really is surprising how intuitive you are, but today, I am afraid your radar has been spun off target. You're not missing anything and there certainly wasn't any kind of interaction between Mani and me."

She could see from his face how frustrated he was becoming, and it really didn't cease to amaze her how well her line manager read people and situations.

"We'll see!" said Keith, ensuring he had the last word before following his nose into Mr Schwartzberg's office. It was obvious to Briony that he was going to see if he could get anything out of Mani.

She opened her iPhone with her thumbprint and went into WhatsApp.

Meet me in the kitchen at 10:00, she typed, and then pressed send.

She looked over the top of her computer screen and could see Mani in his dad's office reaching into his trouser pocket. Just as planned, he looked straight over to her desk. Briony could see two blue ticks by her message, meaning that he'd seen her request. Her heart beat an army march against her ribcage as he briefly appeared to question her motives. Then he flashed a sexy grin in her direction, making it obvious he thought he was in the clear and in for a repeat performance.

See you there :) he replied a moment later.

Yuck, there was no need for a smiley face. She immediately messaged Lauren.

I hope you're OK, Miss Scarlett. I'm sorry the dwelling you

have found yourself in is much below par, but green lights from up here. Mani will be down in half an hour. See you in a bit. I've just got to be careful because Keith is on our trail. xxxxxx

* * *

Downstairs, Lauren was fidgeting on the cistern in a cubicle in the ladies' toilets. She smiled as she read the message from Briony. It really hadn't been part of the plan for her to sit in the toilets, but they'd realised it was the only place she could hide unnoticed. Just in case someone looked under the door, she'd locked it and sat on the cistern with her boots on the toilet lid. She figured that if there were no visible shoes then it would look like the toilet was out of order. In the last half hour, though, only one other woman had been in to use the facilities.

She looked at Briony's message again and felt flushed with excitement. Soon enough, she heard the familiar clip-clop of her friend's heels as they hit the marble floor.

"Laur, babe?"

Like a jack-in-the-box, Lauren sprung out of her cubicle. Briony could see that she was buzzing. On the other hand, she was now feeling a little apprehensive.

Lauren could see the fear in Briony's eyes, and she threw her arms around her. "Don't worry, I've got this," she reassured her. "Mani will only get what is coming to him. Did you remember to print off your resignation letter?"

Briony tensed, remembering her two jobs: to get Mani downstairs alone and print out the letter. At least she'd done one of them.

"You forgot, didn't you?"

Lauren pulled Briony in front of her and she nodded.

"OK, that's fine, don't panic, you can email it anyway." She pushed some loose strands of Briony's hair behind her ears. "I know you're feeling uncomfortable about all of this, so just get it into your head that it's just a show.

"Now, I know you can act. In fact, acting was what brought us together in the first place, when we used to mess around in drama class together, and then out of school at am-dram. I know how good you are. Step away from the real Briony for this scene. It's not emotional, there are no feelings involved, and it will be blockbusting."

Lauren actively felt Briony's muscles relax as the smile returned to her lovely face. "Good pep talk, babe. I'm ready," she said.

The women weaved their fingers together as they left the toilets and, after checking the coast was clear, headed for the kitchen, where the finale was set to take place.

Chapter Six

Mani tried to open the door to the kitchen, but Briony had locked it from the inside. He pushed the handle down even harder. "Bri, are you in there? It's ten," he excitedly called.

The women gave each other a quick squeeze and the show began. Lauren sat elegantly in the wicker chair with her legs crossed, revealing her leather boot and stocking trim, while Briony pulled the bolt and opened the door.

Mani almost knocked Briony over as he bounced into the room. His energy deflated as soon as he saw Lauren in the corner.

"Morning," Lauren cooed in her sexiest voice.

"What's happening here?" Mani ran his hands through his hair while Briony slipped behind him and snapped the bolt back across the door. She appeared from underneath his arm. "But isn't this what you wanted, Mani?" She could see a flicker of interest in his eyes as he looked from Lauren and back to Briony in front of him. His forehead started to shine, and he reached for his handkerchief and wiped his brow. Both women had to stifle their laughter and avoid looking at each other. They shared the opinion that men with handkerchiefs looked utterly ridiculous, and here in front of them was a prime example. The worst thing was that he was young, too.

"I'm not sure what you mean. Did you show her the recording, Lauren?"

Lauren bit her lip to prevent her laughter from bursting out. After licking her lips and pretending to consider her answer, she replied, "I sure did, Mani, but do you know what?"

He raised his shoulders in response and Lauren stood up. Right on cue, she and Briony sauntered over to the window. Lauren noted how Mani ran his eyes up her leg and to her waist, before bringing them to rest on her chest. She put her arm around Briony's waist and pulled her in close. "We talked about it last night, and we actually think you were onto something."

The women locked bodies and pressed their cheeks together, facing Mani head on. Mani opened his top button and fanned his shirt, showing the girls that he was most definitely having a response to their show. "Really? You're joking, right?"

"No, Mani, we're really not," said Lauren.

Briony pulled Lauren round to face her, leaned in and whispered softly, so that Mani didn't hear, "Best show ever, Miss Scarlett." Then she very gently kissed Lauren as Mani looked on. Briony loved kissing Lauren. There was no urgency like she often felt when kissing men. It was just lovely and slow and affectionate.

The girls broke away from each other and looked at Mani, whose caramel eyes were popping out of his head, just like Jim Carrey's in *The Mask*. "I'm not gonna lie, that was very hot and most unexpected. Does it mean I can get in on the action?"

Lauren smiled at Briony and slowly walked across the room to Mani. She pushed her chest against his, whilst trying not to throw up. Getting intimate with a man was not in her soul, but she was doing it for Briony. She kissed his neck, immediately wanting to spit out the aftershave taste and detesting the feel of his stubble on her lips. She put her arm out to pull Briony in. Briony kissed Mani on the lips, while Lauren moved away from him and began gently kissing Briony's face and neck. Then she unzipped her dress and carried onto her shoulders.

Lauren watched Briony's hand slide down Mani's shirt and over his belt. She unzipped his trousers and started rubbing his growing erection. From the look on Mani's face, she could see that her friend was an expert at what she was doing. She pulled Briony away from him. "Surprise!" she announced.

Mani caught his breath and had a sudden moment of clarity. He turned to the door and was relieved to see the bolt already in place. "You got this?"

Briony nodded. "I learned from last time and couldn't risk Keith coming in again."

Mani looked all around the kitchen, suddenly fearful. "Wait, wait, hold on a minute. Where's the camera? Are you filming me again?"

"No, Mani," said Lauren. "Like I said, Briony and I had a chat, and we think you're right."

In his relief, Mani didn't question how convincing the girls sounded. It took him no time at all to unbutton his shirt down to his belt, revealing his tight, bulging pecks and the top of his six pack.

Lauren moved behind Briony, teasing Mani by slowly lifting her zip up and down, revealing glimpses of her black and emerald lace bra, before covering her back up again. "So, you know this dress, Mani?" she asked.

"I most certainly do," he replied, winking at Briony. Lauren rolled her eyes and pulled the zip all the way down to the top of Briony's matching lace knickers. She shimmied the dress

35

down to her strappy heels. Briony slowly stepped out of the dress, exposing her petite, toned body and large, pert breasts.

Lauren watched Mani peel his tongue off the floor. She upped the game by cupping Briony's breasts and kissing her.

This wasn't something Briony had experienced before, and Lauren's sweet caresses made her tingle all over.

Lauren pulled away, leaving Briony wanting more, though she quickly snapped back into the seductress character she was playing in the scene. "Mani, there's our chair," she said, pointing to the wicker seat they'd had sex in, and the one Lauren had been draped over when he'd come into the kitchen just now. Mani nodded expectantly. "Why don't you take your clothes off and take a seat, and Lauren and I will join you and fulfil your every fantasy."

Lauren put her arm over Briony's shoulder and seductively slipped her bra strap off her shoulder. Mani didn't need to be asked twice. He slipped his arms out of his shirt and removed his trousers. As he pulled down his Ralph Lauren boxer shorts, his erection sprung out of them. Without question, he did as instructed and went to sit down.

Earlier, Lauren had found a long-sleeved top with the Schwartzberg Finance Ltd logo printed on it. She'd tied the arms around the broken chair, covering the hole she'd made with her boot. While she'd made sure the makeshift repair was strong enough to hold her weight, she wasn't sure it would work for Mani, who was obviously significantly heavier.

Now wearing only his socks, Mani was sat in all his glory ready for what he thought was going to be the greatest day of his life, and it appeared the chair was holding up. Lauren squeezed Briony from behind and then shimmied out of her own dress, revealing her matching red, lace underwear. She took Briony by the hand and together they knelt in front of Mani. They could tell he was so aroused that he might explode if one of them touched him. It was evident from his expression that he thought all his Christmases had come at once. After all, two gorgeous women, wearing only their underwear and heels, were kneeling in front of him and giving the clear impression they were ready to perform all sorts of things for him.

Lauren leaned into Briony and whispered, "Here we go. One, two, three." She pulled on the make-do knot she'd made in the shirt and released the arms. The girls then took a thigh each and pushed down on Mani's hips.

The force and the weight on the weakened wicker seat caused it to tear right open, and Mani fell through the centre, so that his small hips were encased in the rim of the chair, which was holding his weight from the crease of his knees. His butt skimmed the floor. He was well and truly stuck.

"What the actual fuck?" he said as he squirmed. The girls threw their dresses back on and Lauren zipped up Briony's. Now fully dressed, they towered over their victim.

"Mani, Mani, Mani, nothing good comes from insulting a woman's intelligence and assuming she is just a piece of meat that you can fulfil your sexual needs with. Would you ask your mum's friends for a threesome?"

Mani quickly realised that this was a rhetorical question, and they weren't expecting an answer.

"No, you wouldn't, because you respect them. Yet you clearly don't respect Briony and me. And for that, this is what happens."

Tall in her boots, Lauren circled the nearly naked man below her, before coming to a stop in front of him.

"Look, I don't even know my mum – she left when I was a kid. I guess she'd be in her sixties, so it's not the same."

He tried to pull himself out of the chair, but with his movement limited he remained stuck.

Lauren took a second to think. She wasn't aware of Mani's missing mum and felt a little empathy for him. She softened her tone like a teacher talking to primary school children. "I'm sorry about your mum, Mani, really I am. I didn't know, but besides, I think you're missing the point. The fact is, you went behind your date's back, got me in a room on my own and laid it out that you wanted a threesome with Briony and me. This was clearly without any consideration for our feelings, and I think you arrogantly assumed we were going to be flattered and jump straight in. Well, news flash!"

"This is all so fucked up. I mean, what is going on here? You two were making out and we all got undressed."

Just as they had planned, Briony stepped forward and took the baton. "I don't want to work with you, Mani, because, like Lauren said, it's clear you don't respect me; us. And now I don't have much respect for you, so my work will most definitely suffer. It'll be awkward and uncomfortable, and I will resent coming to work, which sucks, because up until now, I quite enjoyed my job. You made all this happen, not me and not Lauren.

"So, I am going to email your dad today and give him my four weeks' notice. He's going to ask why. And what do you think I'm going to tell him? Don't forget that the CCTV camera is filming over there, too."

Mani gulped and looked like he was going to throw-up. "You two are witches, you know that. But we can sort this out. You don't have to be so drastic, Bri. I can deal with the CCTV like I did before, that's not a problem. Can you at least help me out of this chair, please? What do you want me to do?"

Lauren bent down to Mani's level and looked straight into his deep, caramel eyes . . . the same ones that Briony had dissolved into after meeting him a couple of Saturdays ago.

"You may be able to remove the CCTV recording, but someone might actually be watching it right now," Briony teased, knowing full well that the lens was covered with black tape and couldn't have recorded anything.

She returned the baton to Lauren.

"Briony could say to your dad that she has come into some money, some inheritance maybe?" She maintained eye contact, lifted her left eyebrow and waited for the penny to drop.

"Oh, so you want money? Fuck me, really? No way!" As he spoke, Mani fought like a caged animal to get out of the chair.

Briony and Lauren decided it was time to help him out of his predicament. Briony encouraged him to drop forward and lie on his tummy while she held him, and Lauren pulled the chair along his legs and over his feet. He scrambled to get his clothes back on and ran his hands through his hair.

Briony was the next to speak, softly this time. "Mani, I really did have fun the first time we were in here, and admittedly, I hoped we might have become a bit more serious. However, you made it clear in the video that you wanted Lauren, and you went in to kiss her behind my back. I was, like, only in the next room."

"Yes, I did behave like a complete dick," Mani admitted. "He flicked his eyes between the two women, searching for some sympathy. "And you're both right, I didn't consider your feelings, Bri, but then again, we weren't exclusive or anything."

Briony looked to Lauren for help. After all, it was true, they hadn't had *the* conversation.

"OK, look, we could bitch about who's to blame all day," Lauren jumped in, "but here's the thing, Mani. Briony doesn't want to work with you because of what you did and, therefore, she won't have a job or an income. I'll be back on the ships soon, too, so she won't have me to help her out with the bills.

"Personally, I don't think any of this is her fault, and I reckon the decent thing would be for you to give her a year's salary to cover her whilst she finds a new job."

"A year's salary?!" Mani squealed. He sounded like a pubescent boy whose voice was breaking.

"Come on, it's not like you aren't good for it, and if you consider the emotional impact, the stress of finding a new job and other contributing factors, it's a perfectly fair gesture."

Briony stepped in again for the finishing touch. She put her arm around Lauren's shoulder. "Mani, you didn't see me last night. I was crying my eyes out. It wasn't pretty, and suffice to say, if I hadn't seen your actions on the video I most definitely wouldn't have been in tears."

She picked up her phone and showed Mani an email addressed to Mr Schwartzberg. "This is my resignation."

They all watched as she pressed the send arrow, which was closely followed by the sound of the email swooping to its recipient.

"My last day will be four weeks this Friday. That'll give you enough time to come up with the money, or else we'll just expose your true colours. Imagine what that will do to your dad's business. His customer service reputation is a massive credit to him, beyond what any competitors can deliver, and that's why the company continues to grow. You know this, and I'm sure you wouldn't want to be the reason for him losing everything he has built up over the years."

In his temper, Mani kicked the broken chair and again reached his hands up to run them through his hair. He was disintegrating in despair in front of them.

Briony felt a little uncomfortable. She couldn't help empathising with her victim. The show had definitely come to an end, and she didn't want to be Briony the seductress anymore. "I'm sorry it's come to this," she said. "But you must agree that it'll be better for us both when I no longer work here."

"Our date at Sauce can't be the most expensive of my life," Mani replied. "I *really* don't want to have to pay you to keep quiet."

Lauren sucked her breath in ready to talk, but Briony had had enough and put her hand over her mouth to prevent her from speaking. "It's really up to you, Mani. We've laid out what we think is a fair end to all of this, and is it really all that bad? After all, you didn't start your day thinking you'd have two chicks in lacy underwear performing for you in the work kitchen."

He looked at them both, and Briony realised she'd triggered the visuals of them in their underwear, which softened him slightly. "I agree with you on that, Bri, you two are very sexy women, and it's every straight man's dream when you're together, but I refuse to pay for that memory."

With that, Mani walked out of the kitchen.

There was silence as the two women reflected on their performance.

"Laur, do you think we've gone a bit too far?" Briony asked.

"No, babe. You were stunning. I was so proud of you."

Briony quivered. How did Lauren do this to her? She re-ran the kitchen episode in her head, but this time through her eyes and seeing all the good bits. "OK, maybe you're right. We were amazing, weren't we, and we followed the plan to a tee. In fact, we totally smashed it. Thank you, it really was a good plan. I did feel sorry for Mani, though."

"Yeah, I know, babe, but in four weeks' time you'll never have to see him again and this'll be just another of those things that happens in life. It'll be the same for Mani. And don't worry about the money, he'll come through. Like I said, he's good for it. I'm pretty sure thirty-two grand isn't going to make a significant dent in his wealth."

Briony checked her watch. "Shit, it's eleven. How on earth were we down here for over an hour? I'd better get back upstairs, or Keith will be sticking his nose in again. He's already questioned me this morning over why I look fancier than normal. I had to think on the spot, so I told him that it's your surprise birthday party after work tonight."

"A surprise birthday party for me? Oh, you shouldn't have," Lauren teased, though really she was flattered.

"Look, I need to get you out of here, like, right now," Briony said, pushing Lauren towards the door.

"OK, I've had my fun. I'm sorry you've got to stay and work, though."

Genuinely, Lauren was concerned over how Briony would survive for the next six and a half hours. The adrenaline was sure to stop pumping soon, and then her hangover and tiredness would really kick in.

"I'll be OK," Briony insisted, though Lauren wasn't convinced. "Shit, what's that? There's someone coming down the corridor."

The door flew open, and the girls held their breaths, as if that would prevent the intruder from seeing them.

"I knew it!" said Keith, bursting into the kitchen. "Come on, Briony Jane Greene, spill! I just saw Mani march up the stairs, grab his car keys and storm out of the office. He looked extremely stressed, and I knew something, or someone, must have upset him down here. It wasn't a client because the conference finished ages ago. And now here you are, and with the birthday girl, too. Lauren, you're looking very nice. Might I ask what you're doing here, though?"

Briony rolled her eyes and sighed. She berated herself for not having seen this coming.

"Hey, Keith. I haven't seen you for a while," said Lauren. "You're looking well."

Briony noticed that Lauren's voice didn't carry quite the same interest as it had during their first performance.

Keith beamed, obviously pleased with himself. "If you don't tell me what went on down here, I'll go and check the CCTV. I know it's working because I checked it after I caught you down here with Mani yesterday and he said it was out of order. In actual fact, it was fine. However, that morning's recording had mysteriously been removed."

The atmosphere in the kitchen was tense and Briony was coming to the end of wanting to hide from her line manager. How much longer was this going to go on for? "Keith, I would ask you to take a seat but as you can see, there's been an accident," she said

He looked most intrigued as he assessed the upside down, split wicker chair.

Briony put it back in position and looked at her friend. "Can you hold this for me, Laur?"

As requested, Lauren held onto the chair whilst Briony took her heels off. Balancing her weight on either side of the chair's rim, she reached up to the CCTV camera and removed the black tape.

Before Keith could say a word, she stepped down, pulled Lauren behind the camera and kissed her, hoping this would distract Keith from his quest for answers. Her tactic worked and, mesmerised by the sight in front of him, he fell silent, his expression mirroring Mani's just a few minutes earlier.

"There'll be no recordings in here from about quarter to nine this morning up to now," Briony said, while waving the strip of black tape that she'd peeled off the camera lens at her colleague. "Since I have just handed in my notice, I have nothing to lose, and yes, I will tell you everything that has just happened, but not here. And certainly not while being filmed." She looked up at the now unblocked CCTV camera. "Laur, we really need to get you out of here."

Lauren nodded and escaped into the corridor with the Schwartzberg Finance Ltd top she'd used to temporarily patch up the wicker chair draped over her head. She then swiftly slid through the smokers' fire exit.

Keith looked hurt. He hadn't been privy to the kitchen

party or Briony's resignation. Without saying a word, he followed Briony outside. She could tell he was trying to pre-empt what he was about to be told, but he didn't have a cat in hell's chance of being able to figure it out. *Nobody* could have guessed what had just gone down in the work kitchen at Schwartzberg Finance Ltd.

When he finally looked up, he saw the girls waiting for him with their arms linked. His mood lifted. "I'm loving this," he said, pointing his finger from Briony to Lauren and back again. "You know, there's always been something between you two."

Briony rolled her eyes and Lauren smiled at her.

Chapter Seven

"Mummy, it's nice to see that Daddy's nose is getting better now," said Bethany, through a mouthful of Rice Krispies and milk. "He must have stopped snoring because he's not sleeping down here anymore."

Natalie was conscious of her seven-year-old daughter's acute powers of observation.

"Are you going to see that man from the taxi again?" she continued. "I don't like him."

Upon hearing those words, Natalie was convinced that her heart actually stopped beating, and it took her some time to regain her composure and process what she'd heard. Not only had she betrayed her husband in the worst possible way by cheating on him with Jason, but when Bethany had seen her kissing him from her bedroom window, she'd obviously been damaged, too. She pulled up a stool next to her daughter at the breakfast counter, kissed her cheek and put an arm around her shoulder. "I'm not going to see him again, darling. I don't like him, either."

"But Mummy, you kissed him goodbye, just how you said

you always do after spin class."

Natalie underestimated the force of the blow she felt to her stomach and had to take a big gulp of air before replying. "I know, I know, but sometimes people fall out and make mistakes. I'm not going to see Jason again because you don't want me to, and that is a good enough reason for me."

Bethany flashed her pleased-with-herself smile and didn't question her mum any further. Instead, she drank the remaining milk from the bottom of her cereal bowl.

Natalie turned her attention to Milo. Yet again, he hadn't eaten his Marmite on toast, but she didn't have the energy to fight with her three-year-old for what seemed like the millionth morning on the trot. He'd have to learn for himself that without breakfast he would soon start feeling hungry at preschool. She'd told him often enough.

She piled the kids into the car and dropped them off at their respective schools. Fortunately, they were on the same grounds, so it was only one drop off. Bethany soon shot off to join her friends in the playground, and Natalie escorted Milo to his classroom. Her usual routine was then to venture into town to do some food shopping and maybe grab a coffee.

She drove around the roundabout, passed the junction she needed and continued until she got to the one that took her to the leisure centre. She resisted the temptation to follow the familiar route and drove on. It was weird how she felt about the place; she couldn't understand why she suddenly felt as if she was missing out on something by not going. Only yesterday she'd hated it and had vowed never to return. But it was as if the gym was an ex that still had a hold over her. The relationship had finished far too suddenly and there'd been no proper closure.

She drove around the roundabout for a second time, slowing down as she approached the junction for the gym. Once again, she managed to resist the urge to turn into it and carried on to the supermarket, where she parked up. She rolled her eyes as she put coins into the ticket machine and waited as it whirred and processed her two-hour pass. She tossed the ticket onto the dashboard and hastily walked towards the supermarket entrance. Was this her life now – washing, cleaning and food shopping? Her frustration was visible to all as she lobbed items into the trolley without even looking at them. The other shoppers quickly moved out of her way, seeing the tension on her pretty face as a warning sign to keep their distance.

Natalie so wanted to be a role model for her kids, but being a stay-at-home mum wasn't even inspiring to her. She knew she needed something else. She had found an outlet through the gym and spinning, until her fling with Jason had ruined everything. She still craved the buzz she felt when all her endorphins were coursing through her body. While her relationship with Jason was well and truly over, the one she had with exercise was still burning, and it was a passion she desperately wanted to keep alive.

After paying for her selection of random goods, she moved her shopping bags from the trolley into her Audi Q8, a recent gift from Martin to reward her for making such progress at the gym, and presented to her well before her affair with Jason had come to light. Around the same time as getting her new car, she suddenly remembered seeing a poster on one of the gym noticeboards offering an intensive course to become a personal trainer in just six weeks. Wanting to investigate further and without really thinking about it, she locked the car and began walking in the direction of the leisure centre.

No, turn around, the voice inside her head suddenly screamed. *You don't want to go back to that place. There are plenty of other gyms. What if you see Jason? You only cancelled your membership less than twenty-four hours ago.*

But the convenience of the gym's location won, and soon

she was stepping into the centre's reception area, where she was immediately clocked.

"Hold on, there, didn't you cancel your membership yesterday?" the receptionist asked from behind the counter.

Natalie's head spoke to her heart. *You should have listened to me*, it said.

"Yes, you're right, I did cancel my membership," she explained, "but as you quite clearly stated to me, I couldn't cancel my contract until the year is up, so I am still paying monthly and entitled to use the facilities until September."

Point made, Natalie swiped her membership card through the security turnstile and pushed through into the gym itself. She was filled with conflicting emotions. On the one hand, she was nervous about the prospect of seeing Jason; she really didn't want to bump into him, but she welcomed the familiar, cool air-conditioning, the music, the sound of weights clinking and crashing to the floor and the cardio equipment whirring. She walked quickly past the free-weights section and towards the noticeboard by the gym office and consultation room. The relevant poster was next to the group exercise timetable. She immediately spotted Jason's name by the spin classes she used to attend, and she cringed at the memory of their last encounter. He had met her as usual after class, in the storeroom near the indoor bowling green. Even more fired up than usual, and without her consent, he'd used a spare TRX suspension strap to tie her wrists together. In a heightened state of arousal, he had then pushed her up against the wall with her hands above her head, catching her leg on the corner of the table in the process and burning her wrists with the strap. She shook the memory away and turned her attention to the course poster and the only reason she had returned to the gym.

Like a rabbit in the headlights, she was suddenly caught in the beaming smile of the hottie featured on the poster. It was a face she knew so well . . . the Mediterranean skin, the blue eyes under long eyelashes and the dark, curly hair. Of all the people, Jason was going to be running the course. She couldn't believe her bad luck and she certainly didn't remember seeing his face on the poster before. Different thoughts crowded her mind. She reasoned that she didn't have to like her teacher or have any sort of relationship with him. She could just do the course, get her qualification and walk away. In just six weeks, she'd be able to start working again and making her own money.

Despite all of these practical thoughts, another voice was screaming at the top of its voice, *Get out! Get out! Get out!*

She was still considering her options when the door to the office gym opened, and out stepped Jason with a TRX suspension band in his hand. He doubled up the strap and pulled it hard from each end so that it snapped loudly. Natalie swallowed hard and found herself frozen to the spot.

Jason's smile instantly disappeared. He looked at the TRX strap and made the quick decision to step back and throw it into the office.

"Nat?"

"Jason."

It was as if Queen Elsa from *Frozen* had splayed the gym with ice and time had stood still. They continued to stare at each other, waiting and hoping that the other would speak first. On the positive side, Natalie quickly realised that all her feelings for Jason had evaporated, like a patch of melted ice in the sun. His recent behaviour had changed her attitude towards him forever.

"Jase, I want to train as a PT, and it says on the board that you're the teacher," she said, fidgeting nervously as she spoke.

"Yep, that's right, and what a great idea. You have one sexy body, which many women will aspire to emulate."

Natalie's cheeks flushed with rage. "What's my body got to

do with it? Is that what you say to all your students?"

Jason moved quickly and opened the door to the consultation room, ushering Natalie inside. She stormed in, and for the first time looked around the room, taking in the computer on the desk, the collection of colourful ring binders stuffed with papers, the motivational posters on the wall and the two fancy machines to measure clients' weight and body fat. She hadn't noticed any of these things before, and she also clocked how the coats that had been strategically hung up to cover the windows when she and Jason had a quick smooch before spin class were still in place.

"Are you fucking kidding?" she snapped. Jason's strong shoulders immediately shrunk. "We have nothing. Nothing! I just want to study to be a personal trainer, and annoyingly, it's you that I have to train under."

Jason sniggered at the reference to Natalie being under him, which didn't sit well with her. "Forget it! I'll find someone else. This simply can't happen."

She made for the door but was prevented from leaving by Jason, who stepped in front of her. As if he had the lurgy, she immediately backed away from him.

"OK, OK, I'm sorry. It's just that you make me so nervous, and when I'm around you I can't help but say and do the wrong things."

Natalie looked like she was going to scream.

"Before you say that I'm blaming you for my behaviour, I think you're right, I am a bit. I just can't help the way you make me feel. That's all. When I see you, I lose control. And I know I've got to learn how to behave normally around you. I'm just not sure how."

Natalie's anger subsided. He was just a man who had feelings for her that, for whatever reason, he couldn't control. She empathised greatly, because when she was deep in it with him, she couldn't control herself around him, either. She wanted to be needed and desired. "Thank you, Jase, that really means a lot." She paused for a minute, considering whether it was the time to tell him about her miscarriage, but she quickly decided against it. "Can we put our fling behind us, please? I really want to learn to be a PT, and I think I'll be good at it. You are great at your job, and it'll probably be beneficial for me to learn from you."

"I'm not going to lie, I'm happy you've come back, and if this is the only way I will get to see you from now on, then I'd be happy to coach you."

Natalie wasn't about to fall for Jason's charms again, but she had to admit that he was getting to her. She didn't fancy him, she didn't want him, but she did almost feel sorry for him. "I'm married and I have two beautiful children," she softly explained. "What we did was a mistake, and I am sorry if it was me that led you on, but we can only have a strictly professional relationship."

It became clear to her that she had more to get off her chest. "You physically hurt me, Jase. I know now that it wasn't your intention, but you still did it. You burnt my wrists until they bled, and you hammered me into the corner of the table, which pierced and bruised my leg. Not long after, I miscarried your baby."

She watched as the strong man in front of her weakened, and tears filled his eyes. "Shit, Natalie. I am really sorry."

A single tear spilled over and ran down his cheek. Natalie was in unknown territory. She needed the invisible forcefield around him to stay in place so that she wouldn't touch him, but the poor guy was crying. She opened her arms and enveloped him. He sobbed onto her shoulder. "My baby," he cried.

Natalie's heart went out to him. There were so many unsaid words, and it was clear there was much more to Jason than she realised. With him in her arms, she worried the old urge to rip his clothes off might kick in, but she was overwhelmingly grateful to feel none of that desire for him return. He stepped aside and wiped his face with a gym-branded towel.

"It's weird, isn't it," she began, as he looked at her with red-rimmed eyes. "I still need you, just not in the way I did before. This time I need you to train me to be a PT."

Natalie's blatant selfishness shone through as she strived to get exactly what she wanted. "I didn't expect this from you, and it does make me sad to see you cry, but I need you to grieve for the old us so that we can move into the new us. I'm going to pay you for that privilege, too." Natalie couldn't help finishing off her plea with a flirtatious wink. This made Jason smile, and she knew she was the one with all the power now. She was no longer controlled by her obsession.

Jason reached his hand out for her to shake. "My name is Jason Perez; English mum, Spanish dad," he said, as if they were meeting for the first time. And there it was . . . the elusive surname she'd been unaware of when Briony had questioned her about him, and the reason behind his gorgeous Mediterranean features. Despite the many sexual encounters they'd shared, until this point, she hadn't even known his full name. "I'm going to be your instructor on this course, and in just six weeks, you will be a fully qualified personal trainer. It's such good timing because the next course starts in a couple of weeks. I'll get your theory books ordered, and they'll arrive in three to four days. That'll enable you to get a head start."

The idea of studying and spending her evenings reading books wasn't something Natalie had considered, and despite the end goal, it wasn't something she relished. Briony was the one who loved to learn, and if Natalie was studying with someone else, she knew it would give her the motivation she needed. "Could Briony get on the course as well?" she asked.

Natalie saw the glimmer of recognition in Jason's red-rimmed, post-crying eyes, as his forehead creased up. Briony and Jason had met unexpectedly at the restaurant Sauce, on the night Natalie was planning to tell her lover she was pregnant with his baby. She ended up keeping her secret, while Briony had been understandably hostile towards Jason. She hoped Jason could get past that and reserve a space on the course for her plus one. She could see that he wasn't keen on the idea of being on the receiving end of Briony's wrath again, but she also knew that once her friend found out who was running the course, she wouldn't want her doing it on her own.

"Oh, your friend who's dating the American fella?" Jason said, clearly trying to play down his memory of Briony. "I don't think she liked me, but if she wants to sign up, I'll make sure there's room."

Natalie's Cheshire Cat smile widened. "Thanks, Jase, I'll confirm with Briony and let you know. Do we need to pay upfront?"

Jason opened the door and invited Natalie to exit ahead of him. "Yeah, please pay at reception and we'll get you onto the course. Nat, it's been good seeing you and I'm looking forward to getting you fully qualified as a PT. You know, I could probably get you a job here at the gym."

"Ah, cheers, Jason, but I want to do this on my own, outside of the gym, and work around the kids."

Jason nodded his head of curls and watched her head down the stairs towards reception. Natalie could feel his eyes burning into her and smiled, resisting the urge to turn around. She was looking forward to the next chapter in her relationship with Jason and was pleased she had followed her heart's advice.

"Nat, what the fuck are you doing here?"

The familiar voice pulled her from her trance. She looked

up to see Lauren in a long red dress with a slit up the side and sexy knee-high boots.

"You're not with that guy, are you?"

Natalie took a second before replying. "Bloody hell, Lauren, you look gorgeous! Never mind what I'm doing, what the fuck are you doing here? More importantly, why are you so dressy for this place?"

Lauren shook her head. "Nah, you first. You're not seeing that guy again, are you?"

Natalie knew she had nothing to hide but felt guilty all the same. "I haven't *been* with Jason, but I have been with him. Come and have a coffee and I'll tell you everything."

Lauren wasn't convinced but hooked her arm through Natalie's as they headed to the gym café. Natalie went to fetch them both a cappuccino, while Lauren sat drumming her fingers on the table.

"I'm gagging to know what you've been up to," said Natalie, when she returned with the coffees, "but you've made it clear you won't unlock that information until I have traded mine."

She saw a playful smile appear on Lauren's glossy red lips; it was obvious there was a good story in store. "So, yes, I was upstairs with Jason," she admitted once again.

Lauren's face was turning as red as her dress, and Natalie had to act quickly to stop the burning lava of accusation flowing from her mouth. "Look," she started, "you and Briony are both amazing. You are living the dream singing on the ships and Briony seems to enjoy her job, but what do I have?"

"Oh, poor you, Natalie, with your big house, lovely husband and beautiful children," Lauren replied.

Natalie took it on the chin; she knew she deserved it. "I want Bethany and Milo to be proud of what Mummy does, and I think I know how I can do that. I want to make my own money again."

Lauren calmed down slightly and started really listening to her friend.

"I've mentioned it to Martin, so none of this is a secret. Well, not all of it – he might take a little more convincing now – but I'm going to train to be a PT. I don't want to be in a gym, I want to be independent and work around the kids. There's this school mum who has a fab body, lovely highlights and the best workout gear. She drives a new BMW to pick up her kids, and it turns out she's a PT. I can do that."

Lauren nodded, but Natalie could see she wasn't entirely happy with her explanation. "OK, OK, so the personal trainer instructor is Jason, but before you say anything, let me finish. It turns out I have no feelings for him left at all, but I do need him to help me change my life. He said he was sorry for what he did, and that he needs to learn how to behave around me. Apparently, I make him lose control."

Natalie looked ashamed but at the same time smug. Lauren knew how much her friend loved control, and for people to do exactly what she wanted, but she and Briony had been friends with her for so long now that power or control issues didn't feature in their relationship. The love and respect they had for each other was on another level, and that was one of the reasons they worked so well together. It also meant Lauren wasn't afraid to challenge her friend's behaviour. "I know you, Nat, and I know how you always try to do the right thing. I guess in theory you are doing that here, but are you doing the right thing by your family, especially by Martin?"

Natalie was prepared for the question. "I am, and that is why I have signed Briony up, too."

Lauren rolled her eyes. "Well done, Nat, well played, and might I add clever, too."

Natalie smiled the same smile that Bethany had flashed over breakfast that morning.

"I can see why it's a good plan," Lauren continued. "If

Briony's with you, she'll be able to watch your every move. And knowing that you're not alone with Jason will help Martin, too. Plus, our Briony is a massive boffin who loves to learn."

For the first time since Natalie had put the coffees down, Lauren picked up her mug and took a sip. She licked the chocolate powder from her top lip and smiled. "Back to me, then. Briony and I set the stickiest honey trap this morning."

Natalie saw the look of love shine from Lauren as she mentioned Briony and felt all fuzzy inside for her friends.

"So, Briony resigned today, which is good because now it looks like she has a new career lined up as a personal trainer. Clever, Nat."

Lauren winked at Natalie, who was ready with the popcorn to hear what else her friend had to say. Her life was so glamorous, and her tales often sounded like they'd come from a movie. Lauren leaned forward, as if she were about to share classified information.

Natalie grew impatient. "Look, I first just need to know why you're here. Why are you dressed like that, and how on earth did you end up in the gym?"

"I was going to go for a swim. Look, I've got my wristband on. I'm not a member because I'm never here for long enough, but I do like a dip from time to time. This pool is no comparison to the one on the top deck of the ship, but it does the job."

Lauren lifted her wrist up to Natalie's face to show her the wristband. "I wanted to wash that man off me, and I figured the chlorine would do the best job of removing all trace of him."

"Friggin' hell, Lauren, you never cease to amaze me. What on earth have you been up to?"

Lauren laughed. "Have you finished with the questions now?" Natalie nodded. "OK, then I shall begin."

Chapter Eight

Back in the offices of Schwartzberg Finance Ltd, Briony's hangover was really starting to kick in when she was summoned to her boss's office. She figured he must have opened her resignation email. Admittedly, she'd felt much more confident about her future when she was alongside her sidekick, Lauren. Now, all on her own and with a pounding head, she was full of apprehension. She considered saying it had all been a big mistake, but then she'd have to continue working alongside Mani and disappoint Lauren.

Taking a deep breath, she put on her 'Best Actress' Oscar-winning smile and made her way to Mr S's open office door.

"Can we have a chat?" he bellowed. "Meet me in the kitchen in twenty minutes."

Briony instantly began to sweat. Why on earth would he want to see her in the kitchen? Did he know what had been going on in there? What had he seen? Had the black tape failed to work? Oh God, had Mani told him he was being blackmailed, and why?

"In the kitchen? But there's nowhere to sit," Briony reasoned.

"That's not an issue. The kitchen it is, Miss Greene."

And with that, he spun back round on his chair, facing away from her so that all she could see was the back of his big head and his wet-look, gelled hair. The conversation was clearly over. Briony spun round, too, searching for Keith. Of all the people in the world, how could it be that she now actually needed him? She couldn't believe how much the tables had turned in such a short space of time. She reached for her phone but there were no messages from either Lauren or Keith. She realised she was on her own. She spent the next twenty minutes distracting herself by looking at Facebook and Instagram on her phone and uploading selfies of her with Lauren and Natalie from the night before. They all looked slightly inebriated, but it was nothing a filter couldn't fix. She took a big swig of water from the bottle on her desk and looked around again for Mr Schwartzberg or Keith, but there was no sign of either of them.

Slowly, she crept down the stairs and dragged her heels along the corridor and past the conference room to the kitchen. Loud as ever, she could hear Mr Schwartzberg talking to someone inside. Cautiously, she knocked on the door, took a deep breath and prepared her smile.

Mr Schwartzberg pulled the door open with a force that nearly sucked her slight figure into the kitchen. "Thanks so much for coming down here, Miss Greene," he said.

So terrified of her fate, Briony was sure her eyeballs were pulsating with the beat of her heart.

"Don't look so worried," said her boss, beckoning her inside and ending the conversation he was having on his mobile. She was relieved to see that someone had removed the broken wicker chair. "I just wanted to talk to you down here to say how sorry I am that you are leaving."

Briony gulped. Was Mr Schwartzberg winding things up

ready to deliver the ultimate blow? She couldn't be sure. His face didn't change. She looked at the floor.

"My office is my space, so I knew that seeing you in there would immediately put you on the back foot and take you out of your comfort zone."

Briony nodded, still anticipating the blow.

"After receiving the sad news that you've chosen to move on, I wanted to talk to you in a more neutral setting. I thought this old kitchen would be ideal because I rarely come down here and it swings both ways."

Briony immediately burst into uncontrollable laughter. "It swings both ways," she kept repeating, thinking of how it was here where she'd had sex with Mani and made out with Lauren.

Mr Schwartzberg waited until Briony had regained control.

"I'm so, so sorry, Mr S," she giggled, "it's just that you're talking about this kitchen as if it were a human. Do you really reckon you know its sexuality?"

She raised her hands, palms facing up, as if she were juggling the weight of the question. But it was clear that her soon-to-be ex-boss didn't find the swinging kitchen quite so funny. The irony was lost on him. He cleared his throat and Briony held her breath.

"I wasn't referring to the kitchen's sexuality, Miss Greene, rather the fact that it's neither more me nor more you. However, after being in here, I've realised I do need to decorate; it's very out of date. I can't imagine why anyone would want to hang out down here."

Briony was on the brink of losing her shit again, and her whole body shook. "Sorry, excuse me, Mr S," she said.

"My gran's old wicker chair, all the way from Texas, used to be in here, but it seems to have gone missing. Do you have any idea where it might have got to?"

Again, Briony wondered what he knew. Was the arachnid

spinning his web ready to catch her, or was he genuinely just asking her about the missing furniture? She thought about the action his dear old gran's chair had taken part in over the last couple of days. She knew she needed to find it, and get the rip repaired so that it could be returned as good as new.

"I don't know where it's gone, but I'm sure it'll turn up," she said. "You know what the staff are like, they borrow things and then don't put them back."

She bit her lip and counted down from three, bracing herself for the worst.

"Oh, I'm sure you're right, Miss Greene. Anyway, I am going to be very sorry to see you go. Mani says you've come into some inheritance money?"

Briony looked up at her boss. Was he for real? Was that all Mani had told him, and was he really considering giving her the money? She waited for him to continue before realising he'd said all he wanted to say. "Yeah, I've been very fortunate, Mr S. I don't really know what I want to do, so I'm going to take some time off – with Lauren, I think – and figure it out."

Mr Schwartzberg winked knowingly at Briony. She could see that he had spotted there was something between her and Lauren, too. How on earth did everyone else see it but them?

"That's a great idea, Miss Greene. I support having time out to focus on what you really want out of life." He looked around to make sure no one else was in earshot. "There'll always be a job here for you, Miss Greene. If you decide after six months you want to come back, then just let me know. Hell, you can do that even if that happens after two years."

Briony couldn't help tearing up. She blew her nose with a tissue and wiped her eyes, smearing mascara into the corners. "Gosh, that is the nicest thing anybody has ever done for me," she said.

She remembered saying a similar thing to Lauren that

morning, for taking her make up off whilst she slept. That was lovely in an affectionate way, but this was something else.

Mr Schwartzberg looked uncomfortable at the sight of the small woman crying in front of him. Briony's emotions had obviously been intensified by the morning's performance and the previous night. Mid sob, she wondered if Mani would ever be out of her life. What if she did have to return to the job one day?

"Mr S, please may I take the afternoon off as leave or in lieu or something? I'm a little overwhelmed after handing in my resignation and your kind, kind offer just now."

"You know what, Miss Greene, I have an even better idea. Why don't you take the rest of the week off. Go and make some plans, hang out with Miss Newland, and then start your four weeks' notice from Monday. Between you and me—" he leaned in even closer to Briony "—Barbie enjoyed the company of you girls last night, and she's going back to America next week. So, if you keep in contact with Mani, it'll be lovely to have you both back for dinner. Say, Saturday night?"

Briony's heart warmed even more at the mention of Barbie, but she froze when Mani's name came up. "Thanks so much, Mr S, we'd love to come, and thank you, for everything."

Her reply came out of her mouth before she'd even had a chance to think about it. Her kind and generous employer clearly had a heart of gold, and she couldn't face declining his offer. She'd break the news to Lauren later. Awkwardly, she extended her tiny hand for her boss to shake, and he nearly shook her off the spot. Normally, she would have gone in for a hug, but she deemed it a bit inappropriate. Plus, she'd only end up getting mascara on his shirt.

She was the first to exit the kitchen, with Mr Schwartzberg following her close behind down the corridor and then up the stairs to the main office. She was aware that he must be able to see the top of her stockings as she swayed in front of him up the steps, and she could only hope he was more of a gentleman than his son.

* * *

After gathering her things together, Briony left the office and walked across the car park towards her empty space, before remembering that Lauren had driven Gina home with the plan to pick her up at the end of the day. After everything she had already done for her that morning, she was reluctant to ask for a lift, so she strolled in the direction of town, figuring she would take the bus home.

She reached the town centre and walked aimlessly down the main shopping street. It looked so different to how it had when she was younger, and the highlight of her week had been a Saturday trip into town to buy some Rimmel Heather Shimmer lipstick from Boots or a CD from HMV. These days, she ordered everything online, even her Marks & Spencer grocery shop. Her nana had set the bar high when it came to food shopping, and no other supermarket would do.

She remembered how the town used to be buzzing with an active market, happy people and lots of shops, restaurants and cafés. Now there were three pound shops, lots of boarded-up windows, a few charity shops, a bookies and a fast food venue. She was disappointed by how the world was changing and decided to head to the warm and familiar surroundings of the Red Lion. As she stepped onto the creaky, wooden floorboards, she felt instantly soothed and made her way to the bottom bar. She looked over at her usual booth and, seeing it empty, suddenly missed her friends. Again, the question of what Lauren was to her niggled. She realised that perhaps the butterflies she felt when she thought of her had always been present, only now there were far more of them.

"Briony Greene, it's always a pleasure."

She turned her face towards the familiar voice from behind the bar. Flo wasn't any taller than Briony, so for once she didn't have to look up as well.

Flo gave Briony the once over and then winked at her knowingly. "You are looking most dressed up for this time of day, and maybe lost in a daydream without a destination?"

Briony blushed. How on earth did Flo seem to know *everything*?

"Ah, yeah, I forgot I was wearing this," Briony replied, pressing her hands down the front of her dress to ensure it was covering the lace of her stockings. "And you're right, my head is all over the place."

"Thinking about Lauren?"

Briony was taken aback yet again. Was this woman inside her head? If she was, she wasn't an unwelcome visitor.

"How do you do it, Flo? How do you know everything I'm doing and thinking?"

"Briony, sweetheart, I have worked behind this bar for a long time, and I have seen many things. I recognise that glow and the sparkle in your eyes—"

"Oh, yuck, Flo. But really, is it that obvious?" She sat down on the nearest bar stool, interested in what the landlady had to say.

"It is to me, and I love that you have found each other. I had my heart broken by a girl a hundred years ago now, and I will never find love like that again."

Briony looked deep into Flo's blue eyes. She could see the hurt the memory was causing her. Fabulous laughter lines feathered her face, and they obviously held many stories and secrets.

Flo turned to the young boy who was busy stocking the fridges with beers. "Alex, can you go and get us a couple of bowls of ice cream, please? Strawberry with chocolate sauce for Briony and just plain chocolate for me."

Alex scrambled to his feet and ran out back.

Briony smiled. This woman was one of a kind. "Flo, how do you remember things like my favourite ice cream flavour?"

Flo ignored the question. "Do you want a drink, Briony. I'm going to have a coffee."

"Yeah, a coffee would be great. Thanks, Flo. White with one heaped sugar, please, and may I have a glass of water, too? I'm hanging a bit from last night."

Flo nodded, bringing the drinks to the bar at the same time as Alex arrived with the two bowls of ice cream. The landlady then perched on the tall stool next to Briony on the customers' side of the bar.

"So, we have the ice cream," Briony began, "and Flo, you've listened to me weep over my latest failed love affair many times over. Now, may I switch position? Would you like to talk about yours?"

At first, Flo didn't react, and Briony wondered whether she'd crossed a line.

"Oh, Briony, like I said, it was a hundred years ago now."

"But it still hurts, doesn't it?" Briony said the words before she'd even thought about how they would sound. She watched Flo put her spoon back into her bowl and bring her full attention back to her.

"You're like one of those little terriers; you keep biting at my ankle."

Briony wasn't sure whether to take that as an insult or not. "I'm really sorry, Flo, I didn't mean to pry. It's good to talk, though. You know what I mean."

"Bloody hell, don't mind me," replied Flo, patting Briony on the shoulder. "And yeah, you're right, it *is* good to talk."

Briony watched Flo take a deep breath. "I haven't spoken about Michelle now for years," she said, "but I do still think about her."

Hearing the name of Flo's past love made Briony feel even more empathetic.

"It's funny really, because you youngsters talk about having a connection with someone as if it's a new thing, when really it isn't. It's as old as time, and personally, I think it's also a private thing. Why can't it *just* be an emotion that is felt and shared between a couple? When people post about 'their rock' on Facebook it makes me cringe, because it's nobody else's business, and if you have to shout about it then what are you trying to prove? You lot need to learn to be present and in the moment."

Briony didn't answer Flo's rhetorical question. She could sense she was on a roll and desperately needed to talk.

"It was back in the '80s, the days of mad perms, shoulder pads and the best music, ever. When I met Michelle, we immediately clicked and totally got one another. We loved being in each other's company and spent every day together; it was never forced. We hadn't been friends for long when we got drunk one night and everything between us changed. It was a secret thing between us, but it wasn't an intentional secret. I mean, we didn't even discuss our relationship, we just carried on with our lives. Other people got suspicious about what was going on, but, quite innocently, we had no label for it. We just bloody loved each other."

Flo stopped speaking and Briony could see that she was recalling old memories. She could tell that her story of experiencing the truest form of love was about to take a turn for the worst.

"Because of the suspicions, her parents didn't like me. They thought I was sabotaging their daughter's chance of happiness and taking her away from meeting her future husband and the father of her children. Blah, blah, blah. First, they banned me from the house, and it got worse from thereon. Her dad was a brigadier in the army, and he didn't want the rumour spreading around the officers' mess that his daughter was gay, or whatever. This was despite the fact we weren't – aren't – gay as such, we were just being human.

"He started organising dates for Michelle with the new Second Lieutenants, who were fresh out of Sandhurst. We tried to make time for each other, but he was a very manipulative man and a stand-out leader; people tended to do what he asked of them without question. In the end, Michelle felt like she had no choice but to get married. Obviously, I wasn't invited to the wedding, and conveniently, her husband was posted abroad shortly afterwards. I have no idea where she went, as she didn't leave an address or a phone number, and we didn't have mobile phones back then."

"Fuck, Flo, that's awful. I'm so, so sorry."

Again, Flo batted away Briony's concerns. "Don't feel sorry for me," she said. "I have loved and I have felt real love. I know so many men and women who have just settled and will never feel about their spouse the way Michelle and I felt about each other. My heart is undoubtedly broken, but I feel so blessed to have experienced love like that, and that is enough for me."

Flo had been staring into the distance as she told her sad story, and only now returned her gaze to Briony. "Oh, bloody hell, girl, get a grip," she said and pulled a tissue from her sleeve. She couldn't help chuckling at Briony, who was a quivering mess, with tears and snot rolling down her face.

The landlady's tough love response had the required effect, and Briony pulled herself out of the emotional puddle that she had become.

"Look, I don't hate men," Flo explained. "In fact, I rather like them, and they can be useful. Now, what did Cher say?" She pondered for a minute before nodding and carrying on. "In a Parkinson interview from way back, she said that men are a luxury and not a necessity. She compared them to a dessert; you don't need them but it's nice to have them sometimes."

Flo delivered the line perfectly, with the emphasis in all the right places, and both women laughed.

"All I can say, Briony, love, is that as long as you and Lauren are happy, nothing else matters."

Somehow, the afternoon had slipped away from the two women. They had gotten lost chatting about anything and everything. After learning about her tragic love story, Briony felt a deeper love for her landlady.

"I really enjoyed our chat this afternoon," Flo said, as she walked her favourite customer to the door. "And you were right, it's good to talk. Now, you get home to your girl."

"I had the best afternoon, Flo, thank you so much. Maybe you could help with one more thing before I go. How do I refer to Lauren now? I don't like the word girlfriend." She scrunched up her face. "No offence, but I didn't even like you saying, 'Home to *your girl*.'"

"We live in a world where society needs to label people and put them in a box," replied Flo. "I completely understand how you feel, but I can't answer your question – you need to talk to Lauren. I'm classed as a spinster because I never married, but does anyone stop to consider whether I might be happy on my own?"

Briony nodded ferociously.

"I loved and I lost and that is enough heartache for me," Flo continued. "So, like you, I am me and I am happy."

Briony's eyes brimmed with tears once again. "Oh, Flo, I do love you," she said.

"Ah, be gone with you. You'll set me off."

Briony smiled and – still fully focused on Flo – went to leave without paying any attention to where she was placing her foot. She misjudged the height of the step, causing her ankle to buckle. She went down like a ton of bricks.

Flo immediately reached her hand down, trying her hardest not to laugh out loud as she helped her up. "You are one clumsy girl, but you're not hurt, are you?"

Briony wiped down her dress, while her eyes were far away. Flo could see she wasn't listening.

"Lauren isn't my girlfriend," she announced. "We've realised there is something different between us, which apparently everyone else knew about but us—" she rolled her eyes and Flo smiled "—but I don't want us labelled. She's Laur and I'm Bri, and anything else is nobody else's business."

"Exactly, Briony! Now, you look where you're going and get home safe to Lauren."

Flo waved Briony out of the pub and watched her walk down the road, while thinking again about what a lovely lass she was.

Chapter Nine

Briony checked her watch and couldn't believe it was four-thirty already. Luckily, she still had enough time to make it home before Lauren left to pick her up from work. As she got off the bus, the warm spring breeze blew through her hair, and she suddenly felt alive and hangover free. She wondered whether work exacerbated her hangover symptoms and was still considering this possibility when she noticed a flash of purple on the pavement.

She bent down and picked up two twenty-pound notes, folded into four quarters. Given their shape, it appeared they had fallen out of someone's back pocket. She looked around a couple of times but there was no one about, which gave her a dilemma. Should she take the money? If she didn't and left it there, then someone else would definitely grab it. But what if the person who lost it came back, and they really needed the money? She reasoned that the chances of this happening were slim. She'd once asked for forty quid cashback out of the Morrisons self-checkout till, only to foolishly forget to take it as she picked up her shopping bags. She remembered just minutes later and rushed back, but the cash was already gone.

She reasoned this was the universe returning her money, and with one last check over her shoulder, she slipped the notes into her bra.

Arriving home, she could hear Madonna coming from the flat as she climbed the stairs to her front door. She assumed Lauren had asked Alexa to play the singer's *Immaculate Collection*, as she couldn't remember *Cherish* being on any other album. She opened the door and was hit by the sweet scent of bleach, floor cleaner, clean washing and lavender. It was clear that Lauren was in the midst of one of her cleaning missions. Natalie reckoned she behaved like a nesting pregnant woman, only the chances of Lauren being up the duff were a big fat zero. Her behaviour certainly wasn't related to her hormones, but it normally happened within the first week of her returning home from the ships. As if an alarm had gone off inside her, here she was now in the middle of a deep clean. Briony wasn't about to complain – housework wasn't one of her favourite pastimes.

She walked into the lounge to find Lauren in full '90s get up. She was wearing combat trousers and a tight crop top, which showed off her petite shape. Her hair was tied up in a messy ponytail, and she looked like Billie Piper from her *Because We Want To* video. Briony watched her gently swaying her hips as she reached her feather duster to the ceiling, to remove the big cobweb that had hung there for God only knew how long. She was transfixed by her teeny-tiny waist and flat tummy, and she decided to sneak up behind her.

Lauren was singing along to Madonna and was completely oblivious to the fact that Briony had come into the flat, let alone was right behind her. Briony grabbed Lauren's bare skin, flattening her palms around her waist and enjoying how soft and warm she felt. It was the first time she'd instigated such a move and she secretly congratulated herself for taking this big step forward. Meanwhile, utterly spooked, Lauren jumped up and promptly started hitting Briony with the feather duster. Briony immediately let go of Lauren's waist and grabbed her head to protect it from the brutal beating. When the penny dropped, Lauren threw her 'weapon' on the floor and wrapped her arms around her cowering 'attacker'.

Briony pushed her away. "What was that? Who on earth did you think I was?"

"Oh, babe," smiled Lauren. "I don't know who I thought you were, and I'm really sorry for beating you with a feather duster, but you made me jump out of my skin." She looked at the floor, trying hard to keep a straight face and meeting Briony's gaze only when she was sure she could be serious. "I also must apologise for covering your hair in old cobwebs. You look like a dinner lady wearing a hairnet." She dissolved into fits of giggles.

"Gee, thanks."

As she ran her hand over the top of her head and removed the sticky webs from her hair, Briony didn't find the moment quite so amusing.

Lauren finally pulled herself together. "How was the rest of your day?" she asked, this time with empathy. "Oh, and what are you doing home so early? I was supposed to pick you up, remember?"

Lauren's navy blue eyes pulled Briony back in. All was forgiven. Meanwhile, Lauren watched Briony's expression change. The frown that she secretly loved to see on her friend's face had transformed into a much gentler look, which penetrated her soul. She reached forward, took hold of Briony's hands and placed them on her bare sides, where Briony had originally put them prior to the feather duster attack. The women were now hip-to-hip, chest-to-chest and near enough nose-to-nose. They remained this way for a good two minutes before Lauren pulled away. "I was thinking about getting a McDonald's in for dinner," she announced.

"You totally read my mind," Briony gushed. "I was thinking how a Maccy D's would be just the thing. No washing up, no cooking, just pure, unadulterated stodge."

Both girls reflected for a moment on how they often shared the same thoughts. It had happened a lot in their friendship, but somehow it meant something different now.

Briony proceeded to scrabble around in her bra. She pulled out the cash she'd found earlier. "Well, how perfect is this," she said. "I found this on the floor on the way home; it'll pay for our dinner."

Lauren was impressed that Briony had taken the money – she knew her conscience was far more present than her own. If she was given an opportunity, she barely had to think twice about taking it. On the other hand, Briony was far more indecisive and had to deliberate over her options. It was pretty much cut and dry with Lauren.

"That's bloody awesome," she said. "What are the chances? And what are the chances of you actually putting the money in your pocket, or, in this instance, your bra?" She waited for a reaction from Briony, who just raised her shoulders. "I bet you looked around for the person who had lost the cash so that you could return it, while secretly hoping no one would turn up."

Briony playfully pushed Lauren away. "I love it when you think you know everything. It was nothing like that."

"Oh, really? Well, tell me what did happen, then?" Lauren teased.

"Would you like a drink?" Briony asked, quickly changing the subject.

Lauren threw her head back and decided not to pursue the subject anymore. Briony's silence was enough to tell her she was right on the money about the cash.

"A squash, please, babe, with ice."

Lauren picked up the keys for Gina and put them in her pocket ready to head out. She knew Briony would need an early night, so before collecting the takeaway she decided to set the table. Formal dining was rare for them and not something they usually did with a takeaway, but it would prevent Briony from getting comfy on the sofa and falling asleep after filling her belly. Lauren had said in the cellar they had a lot to talk about, and for that to happen Briony obviously needed to be conscious.

When Briony had cleared out her nana and papa's bungalow, the only things she'd kept were the dining table and chairs. This wasn't because the rest of the furniture wasn't nice or nostalgic, it was more that she didn't really need it and wanted to help others who would benefit more. So, she sold it all off and gave the money to the British Heart Foundation. Now, Lauren laid out the Christmas placemats – the only ones they had – and fancily fan-folded them each a napkin. She didn't bother with any cutlery. After all, they'd be eating burgers.

"Wow, you did that fast," said Briony, as she trotted back into the lounge with two glasses of squash, the ice clinking against the sides of the glasses. She placed them on coasters and turned to Lauren. "This is certainly different for a McDonald's."

Lauren rolled her eyes. "I thought it'd be nice," she said.

"You're right, babe," Briony replied, after thinking things over for a moment. "We can talk, and I *won't* fall asleep."

"Yes, well, that's the plan. I know it won't be a late night tonight, but instead of wasting it on the sofa watching some crap, why don't we sit at the table and eat, talk and play Uno or Snakes and Ladders or something? I can just be me and you can just be you."

A tingle fluttered all the way through Briony's body, as she looked deep into the eyes she knew so well. She realised there was a whole new depth to them, and she longed to go deeper. "I spoke to Flo today," she said.

"When on earth did you do that?" Lauren still assumed that Briony had been at work all day.

"Oh, I've got so much to tell you. So—"

Lauren stopped Briony mid-sentence by placing her index finger over her lips. "Shhh. Tell me in a minute. I'm gonna go to the drive-thru and then we can talk over our tea. What do you fancy?"

"Same as usual, please. A couple of double cheeseburgers and a box of nine nuggets for us to share with some sweet curry sauce."

Lauren leaned in and pecked Briony on the lips. "I didn't need to ask, did I." Briony fluttered her long lashes. "I'll be back in a bit. Meanwhile, whatever you do, don't fall asleep. Well, not in the Freddy Kruger sense, just please don't nod off."

* * *

Luckily for the girls, the McDonald's drive-thru was only a five-minute car journey from the flat, giving Briony just enough time to get out of her stockings, shake her hair out and put on her rainbow unicorn onesie before Lauren's return.

As they sat down to tuck into their takeaway, Briony told Lauren about how Mr Schwartzberg had given her the rest of the week off and also offered her a forever job. Then she recounted Flo's past; how she'd fallen deeply in love with Michelle back in the '80s, and the heartache that had followed.

When the story ended, the girls realised they had no music on.

"Bloody hell, Briony, we haven't listened to anything since Madge," said Lauren.

"I didn't even notice," replied Briony. "You know me, I

usually need a constant sound in the background, but today I didn't even miss it." She raised her shoulders, bewildered but comforted. "There's a reason for that, though." She smiled at Lauren, who nodded and smiled back. They both knew.

Lauren then sprang into action and divulged her entertaining morning at the leisure centre, where she hadn't even managed her planned swim to wash away Mani.

Briony giggled. "I can't believe you did that whole performance. You were good, though." She rubbed her unicorn paw against Lauren's combats under the table.

"I know," said Lauren, raising her right eyebrow. She then got onto the meaty part of her story. Briony didn't have the energy to fully respond to the news she was going to be training as a PT. "Nothing is ever easy for us three," she sighed, "but then I guess that only makes us stronger. I'll assess how I feel about everything tomorrow, because I'm really starting to fade now. I most definitely won't message Nat until the morning."

"I think that's a good idea," Lauren replied. Even though it was still light outside, she could see that Briony's still perfectly made-up eyes were tired. She went to the bathroom to fetch her Body Shop skincare set, before pulling up her chair next to Briony. Ever since the '90s, when her signature scent was White Musk, she'd bought all of her make up and toiletries from The Body Shop. They always smelt delicious and were a hundred per cent cruelty free. "Turn round and look at me," she instructed, and Briony did as she was told. Lauren wet Briony's face with a sponge and then washed her make up off with some face wash, which bubbled over her skin. She then rinsed that off and dried her cheeks with a warm towel taken from the heated towel rail. Gently, she circled some serum into her face, followed by a blob of moisturising cream, ensuring she covered her neck, too. "There you go, babe, all ready for bed."

Briony's face glowed with happiness and health both inside and out. She watched as Lauren followed the same skincare routine, only this time on her own face.

"I forgot to tell you," she began, as Lauren patted her face dry. "I was talking to Flo about us and the labels that come with relationships." She stopped and waited for Lauren to finish her routine and give her full attention. "She called you 'my girl', and I didn't like it."

Briony looked uncomfortable about saying something potentially upsetting. But Lauren remained calm and maintained eye contact with Briony, willing her to continue.

"I love us, and I love what we have, but I don't want to put a label on it. I don't want to have to explain myself to anyone."

Briony's shoulders tensed, fearing the worst from Lauren, who leaned in and gently tucked her hair behind her ears. She cupped her face and said, "I don't care what people think, and you know that about me. I've had to grow a protective forcefield around me over the years. But I don't really care what you call me, either. You can call me an asshole for all I care, because as two people, as two women, as two fuzzy balls of energy on this crazy planet floating in the middle of space, I know that the connection we have is something very special. And Briony, that is all that matters to me."

Briony felt warm tears fill up behind her eyes and then spill down her cheeks. Lauren leaned in and kissed them before they reached her chin. "I'd hazard a guess that if there is a category we fit into, then it's the soulmates one."

Briony allowed her face to rest in Lauren's palms, and she gazed into her eyes, hanging on her words. Her uneasiness about not wanting a label to please society faded. "You're so right," she said. "Fuck people and their need to put everyone in boxes. What we have needs no definition, and it's bigger than us. We've been brought together on purpose, and I love that there is no explanation needed for that, other than how we feel about each other."

Lauren pulled Briony's face to hers and they kissed. All her life, Lauren had wanted to kiss a girl with the passion she was sharing with Briony, and to mutually feel a connection both emotionally and physically. She couldn't be happier. "Let me run you a bath," she said.

Once again, Briony was left with her eyes closed and her mouth open as Lauren pulled away. "Do you want to come in with me?" she said, the words leaving her mouth before she'd even thought them through, which was most unlike her. But she wasn't worried, as it all felt so right. Lauren flashed her dazzling smile and Briony recognised how gorgeous she was, even with a bare face. "You know, you don't need to wear make up," she said. "You're so pretty."

Lauren blushed and winked at Briony. "Neither do you, babe. You're stunning with it and beautiful without it."

Now it was Briony's turn to blush, as Lauren skipped towards the bathroom.

As the water poured into the bath, Lauren added some coconut bubble bath and threw in a Lush bath bomb. The steam rising from the hot water fogged up the mirror, and she drew a heart with a cupid's arrow through the middle, adding their names to either side of the puncture. Then Briony joined her in the bathroom, closing the door behind her.

Chapter Ten

The calmness and sexual heat coming from Briony's flat wasn't replicated at Natalie's house. She'd picked up Bethany and Milo from school and preschool, but now the dreaded 'can't be bothered' feeling was taking over, as her hangover really began to kick in. She was supposed to be helping Bethany with her homework, but instead she was allowing her to watch YouTube on her iPad. Meanwhile, Milo was stuffing his face with crisps because he couldn't wait until dinner. She understood that by allowing him to fill up on junk now she was breaking one of the golden rules of parenting, but she'd also learned that he was a bottomless pit and always so busy that he needed the constant fuel. She looked in the freezer for some inspiration and then the dry food cupboard, but deep down she knew it was a waste of time, as she had no real intention of cooking tonight.

"How about McDonald's?" she called to the kids.

* * *

After devouring their treats, the kids were for once happy to do exactly as they were told. Although Milo was in the middle of learning to sleep without a nappy, Natalie was aware the salty meal had made him drink more than usual, and she couldn't face getting up in the night to a wet bed and child. So, for purely selfish reasons, she decided it was definitely a pull-ups night for him.

She was watching telly on the sofa, wrapped up in her zebra patterned throw, when Martin arrived home from work. In truth, she wasn't paying much attention to the programme, as Facebook, Instagram and Twitter were far more compelling.

"Were you at the leisure centre today?" Martin asked in a louder than usual voice.

Natalie rolled her eyes. How had he found out? She was sure Lauren wouldn't have told him. She sat up and looked over at her husband standing in the doorway. She saw a bedraggled man with messy hair, red-rimmed eyes and a loosened, skew-whiff tie.

"Oh, Mart—" she began.

"Don't 'oh, Mart me'! What the fuck were you paying the leisure centre two grand for? That fella's services can't be worth that much."

Natalie had to catch her breath before responding. "I don't like what you're implying," she said. "Are you accusing me of paying to sleep with Jason? That's a bit low, huh, Martin." She crossed her arms and legs, highlighting with her body language that she really wasn't impressed.

Martin quickly reflected on the unintentional allegation made in the heat of the moment. "No, no, I didn't mean that."

"Well, what did you mean?" Natalie said, before deciding to tease Martin a little. "Funnily enough, I *did* pay for his services."

She watched Martin's head and shoulders drop. He threw himself into the armchair, so he was the same level as Natalie, and she saw his eyes begin to sparkle with fresh tears. But she wasn't about to give in and provide sympathy. She was tired, hungover and sick of Martin constantly bringing up what she'd got up to with Jason.

She waited a moment, leaving her husband on tenterhooks, before deigning to reply. "Jason, the PT, the spin instructor, the man who fathered the baby I miscarried, is going to teach me to become a personal trainer."

The blood drained from Martin's face, as Natalie's words sucked it from him like a hungry vampire.

"For exactly how long are you intending to punish me?" Natalie continued. "I can't live the rest of my life like this. I know what I did was wrong, and that I hurt you, but I am trying my hardest. Yes, it's unfortunate that Jason will be the one training me, but I have also signed Briony up – that's why it was so expensive. She can report back to you, and she'll pay you back, too. After six weeks, I'll be a PT and will hopefully be able to start my own business around the kids."

She watched Martin's expression change as he processed her words. "Don't do that!" he yelled. "You're not the victim in this. The manipulation is so off the scale, I just don't know what's true anymore."

Natalie was on the brunt of rage she'd never witnessed before. Martin was usually so soft. "Keep your voice down," she whispered. "Don't wake the kids up."

She matched the pitch of his anger, just with less volume. And then, as if an invisible switch had been turned on, Martin got to his feet and stormed over to where Natalie was sitting. He leaned over her in a threatening manner that sent a wave of fear through her, even though she knew he would never hurt her. "'Don't wake the kids?'" he said, his pointed finger just millimetres from Natalie's nose. "Are you fucking kidding me? You vacuumed the face off that guy outside our house, letting our seven-year-old daughter watch you do it. Then you gave her a load of total bullshit by way of explanation, instead of being the role model grown-up she needs and taking responsibility for your actions."

His breath was hot and fierce as it made contact with Natalie's face. She could smell coffee and, unusually, whiskey, too, but right at that moment, she wasn't about to question his drinking. She could see that he was waiting for an apology, but she couldn't say that word sorry again; it was obvious it didn't mean anything anymore. The seconds passed and the elongated silence seemed to push the gas pedal to her husband's rage. He reached down and picked up her phone, lobbing it with force at the wall behind her. They both heard the screen crack before it fell behind the sofa with a thud.

"He won't be able to talk to you without a phone."

"Fuck, Mart. What are you doing?" Natalie said. She was beginning to really sweat now.

He still didn't move away from her. "This is all you," he said. "You've done this to me."

Natalie fell to her side, rolled out from underneath Martin and got to her feet. She took a step back, creating distance between them. "What is it with you men, blaming me for your actions?"

She realised her mistake as soon as she said it.

"Whaaat? Are you saying I'm similar to what's-his-name? I guess he made you sleep with him, huh? What else did he make you do?"

Natalie considered telling him about the involuntary wounds she'd sustained from the TRX suspension strap and the corner of the table, but she decided it wasn't the best time to bring that up. "You're right," she began. Martin looked perturbed, and she could see the confusion on his face as he waited for her to go on. "He did make me sleep with him, because he told me how much he wanted me. He made *me* feel sexy and exciting."

Martin rested his arm on the wooden bookshelf, which wobbled slightly in response. Natalie watched him shake the shelf a bit more, and then really hard. In a flash, he had pulled it clean off the wall and thrown it at the floor. All the books, CDs and DVDs ended up strewn across the carpet. He looked blankly at the damage he had caused and didn't seem at all phased.

"So, what's this? Are you having a tantrum now?"

The flame of his anger rose with her every dig.

"Well, you've done me a favour, actually, because we never listen to these CDs anymore or watch the DVDs, so they can all go to *MusicMagpie*."

"It's all a joke to you, isn't it. All the years we've been together, yet I feel like I don't know who you are anymore."

That hurt. Natalie had already explained how she'd lost herself after having the children, which had led to her falling for Jason's charms. "Who are you, though?" she shot back. "Where has all this anger come from? I've never seen you like this before."

"Well, you've only got yourself to blame."

Natalie knew how to hit Martin where it really hurt. "Since you clearly can't control your rage," she said, "I'm going to take Bethany and Milo to Mum and Dad's for a few days."

Martin began furiously stamping all over the mess on the floor, pushing pieces of broken wood and plastic deeper into the carpet. He followed that up by punching the wall, leaving a hefty dent in the plasterboard.

Natalie grabbed her phone; even though the screen was cracked, she was relieved to see it still had power. "I think we need some space, Mart," she said. "And you need to calm down. This anger and violence is no good for anyone. I've told you I'm sorry, but I don't know what else I can do."

He didn't reply. Instead, he crumbled to the floor in tears. His shoulders heaved and big, loud sobs echoed around the entire ground floor. Natalie could see his knuckles were red and bleeding, but she couldn't go to him. Instead, she went up the stairs to the bathroom and then took herself to bed. She felt unbelievably guilty, but Martin's behaviour was so new to her that she didn't know how to respond to it. Her defence was always to throw everything back at her opponent, because more often than not she would win the fight, but not tonight. She knew the kids would be happy to have a sleepover with their grandparents for a couple of nights, and she figured she'd stay with Briony and Lauren until things had calmed down. She didn't anticipate Martin joining her upstairs; he'd probably stay on the sofa bed in the lounge again. She sent a quick message to Briony and eventually drifted off to the sound of her husband hoovering up the mess downstairs.

* * *

Across town in Briony's bedroom, Yankee Candles were dotted around the room, giving off a sweet, floral aroma. Her phone was on silent, and she didn't notice it vibrating on her bedside table. The cluster climax that Lauren had just given her had rendered her breathless. As the biggest orgasm rippled through her body, she started to jerk and shake. She couldn't take anymore.

"Babe, I . . . I . . ."

Lauren could tell Briony was at the place of no return, where the female body feels at its most fragile, as if it's ready to break into a million pieces and fly away into the wind. She rolled out of bed and pulled on her pyjamas, which had earlier been discarded on the floor. She handed Briony hers and then slowly slipped back under the covers. "You OK, babe?" she asked.

"Flipping heck, am I OK? I think even my hair had an orgasm!"

Lauren smiled knowingly at the response to her performance. Briony pulled her pyjamas on under the covers and then sat up straight, gathering the duvet around her chest and holding it in place under her armpits. "I have never experienced or imagined such pleasure."

This time, Lauren blushed.

"I have been giving blokes BJs for what, must be fifteen years now, and yeah, I'm fucking good at them, but when I hand the baton over to them, they have no idea what they're doing down there, even the ones who've had loads of practice."

Lauren screwed her face up and tried to shake away the thought of oral sex with a man and the memory of Mani's erection springing out of his pants earlier. "Yeah, we're so differ—"

"There's got to be a better word for it, Lauren. We're not just different, that was stunning – literally breathtaking."

Lauren could tell that Briony had a lot to say and decided to remain silent.

"I know you won't want to hear some of what I am about to tell you, but the connection I felt – feel – for you is incomparable to anyone else. When I snog a fella, it's so rapid, and they mostly just plunge their tongue into my mouth and throw it around without any thought. Then there's the dick." Lauren rolled her eyes. "It'll get all aroused and then, even if I don't want to, I'll feel obliged to touch it. I guess what I'm saying is that because he has a boner, I feel I need to finish it, with either my hand, my mouth or, well, you know. But with you, there's no rush. I feel that you kiss me because you want to kiss me." She pointed to her chest. "You touched me as if you wanted to touch me, and not for what you'll get in return." She paused for a moment. "Oh, God, but I *do* want to make you shake like I did, because when I reached the pinnacle, I couldn't even speak!"

Lauren laughed gently. "Listen to your own words, Bri, there's no rush, no rush at all. I really enjoyed myself, too, and like you say, there's something spiritual, something deeper than just our physical connection."

Briony's lustful gaze returned, and she slipped her hand up Lauren's pyjama top, reaching for her bare breast and nipple. She then kissed her on the lips and pulled the top all the way over her head, ready to work her way down her body. "I really love you, Laur," she said.

"You too, babe," Lauren replied. She closed her eyes in response to the feel of Briony's mouth and touch and then squeezed her glutes and lifted her hips, already dissolving into pre-orgasmic pleasure.

Chapter Eleven

Briony was the first to wake the next morning, her limbs entwined with Lauren's. She recalled them snuggling up together before going to sleep, and it appeared that neither of them had moved a muscle during the night. She smiled to herself before slipping out from under the covers, careful not to wake her bedfellow, and grabbing her phone from her bedside table.

In the kitchen, she switched on *Good Morning Britain*. Typically, it was the same old misery, with no good news, so she turned it straight off. She looked out of her kitchen window and watched the hustle and bustle of everyday life on the street below, enjoying that she had no plans and didn't have to go into work. Then she remembered that she had agreed to go to Mr Schwartzberg's on Saturday night, and she wondered how on earth she was going to persuade Lauren to join her. She was still lost in this thought when she picked up Natalie's panicked message from the night before. She immediately called her, but frustratingly, it went straight to voicemail. She knew exactly why and how she had managed to miss the message and was disappointed with herself for not being there when her friend needed her. She rang again, and when Natalie failed to answer a second time, she ran into the bedroom to talk to Lauren, who was now wide awake and on the phone herself.

"Is that Nat?" she asked.

Lauren shook her head and carried on with her phone call, ushering Briony away.

"We need to get hold of Nat, I think she's in trouble," Briony said, pressing Lauren to get off the phone.

"Thanks so much, we'll see you later." Lauren hung up. "What?"

"She messaged me last night, but I've only just picked it up. We didn't hear it. She said that Martin went mad when she told him she was going to be training with that Jason fella. She's going to take the kids to Paula and Ted's and wants to spend a couple of days here."

Lauren was clearly worried about her friend, but Briony could also see from her expression that she wasn't exactly enamoured with the idea of Natalie coming to stay. "What? You can't expect her to stay at home if she doesn't feel safe!" she said.

"No, no, of course I want her here, too, but I've just booked us a night at that swanky hotel you wanted to stay at in London. Demi, my roommate on the ships, stayed there and says it's fab. Plus, apparently, back in the day, the Spice Girls stayed there."

Lauren knew the famous girl band formed in the '90s would get Briony's attention. "Since you've got some time off, I thought why not. It's right in the West End, not far from the Savoy, and I thought we could see a show, or maybe just go for dinner and then to a cocktail bar or something."

"Well, we can still do all that but with Nat." Briony was thinking out loud. "She'll probably need it more than us, and I bet the rooms are big enough to stick in an extra single.

Failing that, there'll be plenty of room for the three of us in a five-star bed."

Lauren nodded. Briony was right.

"The only problem is she's not answering her phone."

"OK, don't panic, she'll call you back. I'm sure she's just got her hands full trying to get the kids off to school."

Briony agreed, but there was also a flicker of worry that Martin might have hurt her friend. Over the years, she'd watched plenty of murder documentaries and seen how seemingly caring husbands could reveal themselves as raging psychopaths capable of finishing off their families. She tried to put those disturbing thoughts to the back of her mind as she had a coffee with Lauren before heading for the shower. She was still in the bathroom when the song *Maneater* by Daryl Hall and John Oates began playing from her phone. Lauren picked it up and could see Natalie's face smiling from the screen. Briony had chosen the song as Natalie's personal ringtone, and Lauren laughed at how appropriate it was. Despite being a married woman, men always sidled up to her when they were out, and she loved the attention.

"Hey, Nat, you OK? It's Lauren. Bri's in the shower."

"Please don't panic, I'm OK," Natalie replied. "I think Mart and I just need a bit of space. Do you mind if I stay for a couple of nights?"

"Martin didn't take the PT news well?"

"You could say that. By the way, why isn't Briony at work?"

Lauren filled Natalie in on Briony's employment situation and the plan for the three of them to hit the capital later.

"I'd love to join you," Natalie confirmed. "I've just taken the kids to school and I'm on my way to my parents' with their overnight bags. Wish me luck."

* * *

"No, I'm fine. We're fine," Natalie said to her mum, as she dropped Bethany and Milo's overnight bags at the bottom of the stairs. There was no need to upset her just yet, she hadn't even worked out what was going on herself.

"Why can't they stay at home with Martin? What have you done this time?" asked Paula, her eyes burning like laser beams into Natalie's. "I thought everything was OK between the two of you now?"

The questions came thick and fast, and Natalie did her best to avoid them, but her mum was persistent. She accepted that Paula had every right to ask, but the trouble was she hadn't actually figured out a reason for why the children couldn't stay put.

"Mum, it's cool," she eventually said. "It's just that Mart is away on some team bonding trip. He's on a narrow boat on the Norfolk Broads."

Pleased with the lie that had slipped so effortlessly from her lips, Natalie smiled her Cheshire Cat smile at her mum, who didn't fully believe her daughter. However, without the means to investigate further, she reluctantly gave Natalie the benefit of the doubt and agreed to look after her grandchildren. "Remind me again why you can't look after your own kids?" she asked, with more than a hint of sarcasm.

Natalie spun round on her way out. "I'm going to London with Briony and Lauren. Thanks, Mum."

And with that, she was out the door. As well as packing for the kids, she'd also sorted out an overnight bag for herself. On reflection, she realised she'd only thrown in comfy clothes and pyjamas, so she popped home for a dressy dress, heels and perfume. After all, a night in London deserved the effort.

When she got to Briony's, she found the door unlocked and strolled right in. The flat felt different somehow, but she couldn't put her finger on why.

"Bri, Lauren?" she called.

"In the lounge, babe," Lauren replied.

When Natalie walked into the room, she realised exactly what was different and felt a warm, fuzzy feeling inside. Her two friends were sitting next to each other on the sofa, watching a repeat of *The Hills*, which in itself wasn't unusual, only now they were nestled much closer together. It was clearly love that had changed the atmosphere in the flat, and Natalie was happy to have left the tense situation at home to be with her friends, who accepted her exactly the way she was.

Briony got up first and enveloped her friend in a tight hug, which immediately made Natalie start to cry.

"Coffee?" Lauren asked. There was something about her mischievous grin that told Briony she was planning to perk them up with more than just caffeine.

While she busied herself in the kitchen, Lauren could hear Natalie telling Briony everything. She poured the coffee and then opened the cupboard where they kept the alcohol, pulling out a bottle of Baileys and sloshing a generous helping into each cup, turning the dark liquid white. To the unsuspecting eye, it looked like a regular coffee with milk. When she entered the living room with the drinks on a tray and a plate of Jammie Dodgers, Natalie and Briony were discussing the logistics of training with Jason. It seemed that Natalie had somehow convinced Briony it was a good idea.

Briony sipped her coffee first, immediately appreciating the velvety texture that the Baileys added. "Laur, babe, you are naughty. It's, like, only ten-thirty."

"What's going on?" said Natalie, who was yet to try her coffee.

"Drink up, girls," Lauren said. "Let's start as we mean to go on." She raised her mug while Briony and Natalie tapped the top and the bottom of theirs together.

"Tits and arse!" they all cried in unison.

Despite all their worries – Natalie's for her marriage and

Briony's for the impending social at her boss's house – the best friends were intent on partying like it was 1999. After all, that was the year they had all turned seventeen and had started frequenting Yates and Bar Med up town. Those were the days before people had to give their IDs on the door, and they could easily get away with drinking underage.

Chapter Twelve

The girls travelled into London off-peak and managed to sit down on every train they took. Finding three, blue-checked seats next to each other on the Tube was a rarity and, like all the other passengers, they sat in silence listening to the clang of metal as the train moved along the rails and the screech of brakes as it arrived at each station.

Lauren had claimed the role of their tour guide for the day. "We'll be getting off at Leicester Square, and then changing for the Piccadilly Line, where it's one stop to the fabulous Covent Garden," she explained. As someone who could easily be a city girl, she was buzzing. On the other hand, Briony wasn't a fan of the Underground. She found it too hot and didn't like being crammed together with complete strangers. At least today it wasn't too busy. She remembered once witnessing two Portuguese sisters become separated on the platform, when only one of them managed to cram into the carriage before the doors closed. The look of fear and panic on the girls' faces as the train pulled away was heartrending, and Briony hated that she couldn't communicate with the sister on the train in her own language. All she could do was nod and smile and say,

"Esta bien," hoping that she would understand Spanish. It was worth a try. The sister got off the train at the next station and Briony hoped that sibling telepathy would kick in and allow the girls to be quickly reunited.

As their journey ended, and they stepped off the train at Covent Garden, Briony ruffled her hair and pulled her sunglasses down. She took Lauren's hand as they reached the exit and with her free one grabbed Natalie's.

"Don't you just love the colour of the station?" Natalie said. Her eyes were sparkling, and she was clearly relaxed. "That rich, red brickwork is stunning."

"I know," Lauren enthused. "Look at the writing on the sign. It's so cool and old-fashioned."

"It's like we've just skipped across the Monopoly board. I'm the boot!" Briony joined in.

The girls laughed, thinking about the other stations they'd passed through and debating the best Monopoly playing pieces.

They walked round the corner and up the street towards their hotel. At the entrance, they were greeted by two doormen wearing top hats and tails. Lauren flirted outrageously with them, while refusing any help in carrying their overnight cases.

After check-in, they went to get the lift to their room on the fourth floor. Lauren pressed the number four button, but nothing happened, so Briony had a go. Again, the lift stayed put. As they waited, a cleaner came in pushing a trolley. She pressed her card to the sensor pad, which shut the door and allowed her to direct the lift.

"Oh!" the girls said in unison, and then Briony noticed the clear instructions on how to use the lift printed above the buttons. She rolled her eyes, remembering a scene from the 1990 film *Pretty Woman*, when Richard Gere's Edward Lewis struggles with his keycard as he tries to get into the penthouse suite of the Beverly Wiltshire Hotel. "Oh, I miss keys," he says. She wondered how he'd cope now, having to use a keycard to get the lift working as well as to access his room.

The cleaner promptly got out on the second floor and in stepped an extremely glamorous woman. She was around the same age as Briony, Lauren and Natalie and had stunning, tiger-like eyes. She was wearing a tight gold dress and heels, which worked together to accentuate her slender body and feminine curves. The girls couldn't help but notice that she was also dripping with diamonds. Her earrings, necklaces and rings all matched. As the lift door closed behind her, she looked her travelling companions up and down. The air was thick with the cloying scent of her perfume, and Briony didn't much like how she came to rest her gaze on Lauren.

"Hi, girls, where are you from and what are you doing tonight?" she asked, her voice clear and confident.

Briony pushed across Natalie and slid in next to Lauren, intertwining their fingers. "Hey, girl, you're very abrupt," she said.

Lauren smirked at Briony's unsubtle attempt to mark her territory. There followed an awkward silence as the lift whirred into motion.

"I'm sorry, I didn't mean to be so rude. I'm Grace." She put her hand forward in the direction of Lauren. Despite being outnumbered in the lift, her confidence clearly hadn't wavered in the slightest.

Lauren momentarily shook Grace's hand and then pulled away to point to Briony and Natalie, whom she introduced by name. "I'm Lauren," she added. "We've come from Hampshire and we're here to let our hair down and have a girls' night."

"And there's no better place to do it," Grace beamed. "I'm going to be downstairs in the bar this evening, if you'd like to join me?" She winked in the direction of Briony.

Before Briony had the chance to politely decline the

invitation, they reached the fourth floor, and she was relieved to be able to escape the woman's company. However, Grace stepped out of the lift with them.

"Hold on, why are you getting off here?" Briony asked. "You only got in the lift on the second floor."

Lauren whipped round to look at Briony, who realised she had spoken without thinking.

"I must apologise for Briony, Grace," Lauren said, "it's none of our business what floor you get off at."

Briony dipped her head, embarrassed over letting her emotions get the better of her.

"We haven't got any plans set in stone," said Lauren. "So, we might see you later."

Grace smirked and fluttered her long, dark eyelashes. "I look forward to it," she said.

As she headed right to her room and they turned left down the corridor, Natalie voiced her opinion that the glamorous stranger was most certainly interested in Lauren. Briony was clearly still in a mood.

"Did you really think I was interested back?" Lauren asked Briony, linking arms with her as she spoke softly into her ear.

Briony pulled her arm away and Lauren enjoyed the troubled toddler expression on her face.

"She was totally hitting on you," Briony said.

"Maybe, but I wasn't in the slightest bit interested. I've got you."

The comment softened Briony slightly. "It's just that you're so flirty."

"I only told her that we're from Hampshire. That's hardly flirty," said Lauren.

"It's the way you said it, and the way you were looking at her."

"Oh, you're jealous, it's so cute!" Lauren teased, squeezing Briony's cheeks.

Natalie sniggered, but Briony wasn't at all amused and looked away. "You two think you're so funny," she moaned.

"But honey, we are," Lauren teased, as she tapped their bedroom door with the keycard. She hadn't got round to requesting an extra bed, so they'd all have to share the king size one. Briony was the first to jump onto the mattress, followed by Natalie and Lauren, who flopped either side of her. They were all surprised by how much room they had.

The old-worldly Edwardian room had high ceilings with decorative coving and floor-to-ceiling curtains. The classy look had been completed with shimmery wallpaper and a huge mirror above the mahogany desk opposite the bed. The door to the en suite bathroom was open, giving them a view inside.

"Well, ladies," said Lauren. "I think I'll take a bath in that fabulous marble tub, if you don't mind?"

Before Briony could say anything, Natalie jumped in. "In that case, I'm going to check out the gym," she said. "It'll be good to burn away some calories and make room for dinner and booze tonight."

"I think I'll join you," said Briony, figuring that maybe Natalie was more serious about a career in fitness than she'd thought. "I could do with a quick 5k on the tredders, just to get the jealousy out of my system." Before either Lauren or Natalie had a chance to take the piss, she reached for their hands. "Yes, you were both right," she said. "From now on, I'll try to keep myself in check."

Lauren turned to her and kissed her briefly on the lips. "It's actually quite adorable. Anyway, I've got a hot and bubbly bath to run with posh hotel products. If you two are going to be gone for a while, I've got a good book to finish on my Kindle, or maybe I'll watch a little telly in the bathroom." She winked at the girls, truly happy that she was living it up in such luxurious surroundings.

* * *

It took Briony and Natalie a few rides up and down in the lift to work out what level the gym was on.

"It's always so disorientating when you arrive at a hotel and don't know where anything is," said Natalie. "Maybe we should stay for two nights, because tomorrow finding our way around will be a breeze."

Briony smiled at her friend; she wasn't convinced she wanted to stay away for two nights. "Let's see how tonight goes," she said.

They'd finally reached the gym and Natalie flung open the door. They were both surprised at how spacious and well equipped it was.

Briony scanned the room for the cardio section and started making her way over to the treadmill. Meanwhile, Natalie was drawn to the free weights area.

"Nat, come on," Briony said, rolling her eyes and tugging at her friend's hand.

"That dark-haired man in the blue vest over there is stunning," said Natalie. "Look at the sweat shining from his body, and you can see the definition of his abs through his top."

Natalie's eyes were practically popping out of her head, but Briony couldn't help but agree with her. She also noticed that the man had an attractive mate. He looked a little like Nick Carter from the *Backstreet Boys*, with blue eyes and messy blond hair. In her opinion, he had an even sexier body.

"Yes, Nat, they're very good looking boys, but I'm sure they know it. And anyway, we're not interested, are we?"

"No, no, you're right, though it would be interesting to find out about their training regime. For purely educational reasons, of course."

"Nah, that's not cool, and you know it. Even though things are pretty shit at home, you are still a married woman."

Briony could see the dangerous intent in Natalie's eyes and knew her words were unlikely to make any difference. It seemed her friend had been bewitched by an athletic body, just as she had been by Jason.

Briony clicked her fingers in front of her friend's eyes. "Uh, hello! No, we don't need any extra training info, thank you, so let's stick to Plan A. We work out for half an hour then it's back upstairs to get ready for our night out."

Natalie looked disappointed, but deep down she was grateful for her friend standing up to her. "I know, I know, you're right," she said, before turning her attention away from the free weights and following Briony to the cardio section. "Whilst you do your 5k, I'll do a program on the cross trainer."

Briony squinted at her friend, silently scrutinising her honesty, and then waited until she was on the trainer and pressing the buttons. With her friend safely pumping her arms and legs to the rhythm of the machine, she slowly got herself ready for the 5k. She put in her wireless earphones and pressed play on an exercise playlist on her phone, which she tucked safely inside her sports bra. She was reluctant to take her eyes off Natalie, but finally gave into the fact that running whilst looking over her shoulder was probably going to result in an injury. She turned to face forwards and started following her distance, speed and time.

* * *

Meanwhile, Natalie could feel a pair of eyes burning into her back. Or was it her butt? She couldn't be sure. She waited until Briony was in full running mode before slowly looking over her shoulder. To her utter disappointment, the dark-haired guy wasn't actually looking at her at all. It had all been in her head. But now she couldn't take her eyes off him.

In one slick motion, he lifted his heavy barbell until he was standing tall. Then he hinged at the hips and lowered it again. Natalie felt herself tingle and realised she couldn't help herself. These fit men, with their defined, strong muscles really excited her, and it wasn't a feeling she ever experienced when looking at her husband's bod. It wasn't just his physique that Martin neglected. She even had to book his hair appointments for him, because if she didn't, he would just let his locks grow wild. These men's dedication to self-care and their desire to look good was such a turn-on for Natalie, and it made her realise she no longer wanted to mother her husband. Martin was a good guy, and he did provide for her and the children, but the sexual fire she'd experienced recently wasn't something that came naturally to him. And yes, he had been trying, and yes, their sex life had improved since he'd found out about Jason, but again, Natalie could tell it wasn't something he was entirely comfortable with. They both knew he was trying to be something he wasn't. His own realisation of this must have contributed to his behaviour the previous night. It wasn't her fault, and it certainly wasn't his, but Natalie had gone through an awakening of sorts and had a better understanding of what she wanted in the bedroom.

She shook her head, trying to remove the dangerous thoughts of what she wanted to do with the guy in the blue vest. Checking that Briony was still busy running, she stepped off the cross trainer and bent down to pick up her towel and water bottle. Then she felt it again – the eyes burning into her behind. Without straightening up, she looked around, and there he was. He stepped to the side, raised his eyebrows and nodded, showing Natalie his approval of her butt. The tingle accelerated from deep between her hips and travelled through her whole body. It was a feeling she couldn't control, and she loved it.

She watched him take a step forward. Was he coming towards her? Yes, it appeared so. Briony was slowing down, but while her heart rate was dropping, Natalie's was speeding up. This time, it was through fear of how her friend would react if she saw her talking to this beautiful man, rather than because of how he was making her feel.

"Hi, how are you doing? I'm Jake." His heavy London accent matched the weight he had just dead-lifted, and his deep brown eyes on her body made her feel like she was standing before him naked. She glanced towards the treadmills, and it was as if Briony's disapproving eyes were on stems.

"Hi, I'm Natalie, an . . . and this is my best friend, Briony."

Right on cue, Briony stepped off her machine and extended her hand. "Hi, did you say your name was Jake? Yeah, we're away for a girls' night. Nat's husband is looking after the kids."

Briony's warning cymbal crashed in both Natalie and Jake's ears. Natalie nodded, pointing to her ring finger before realising there was nothing on it. She'd clean forgotten about leaving her wedding and engagement rings at home. Everyone noticed, and Briony rolled her eyes at her friend.

"Well, I just wanted to say hi," said Jake. "Danny and I are members of the gym here."

They all looked over at Danny, who put both his thumbs up in acknowledgement.

Briony grabbed hold of Natalie's hand. "Well, it's been really nice to meet you guys, but we've got dinner plans," she said.

"Yeah, it's been sweet. Maybe after you've eaten, we could meet for a drink in the bar this evening?" suggested Jake.

Natalie looked hopefully at Briony, who mouthed, "Are you fucking kidding me?"

"I don't know, Jake, maybe. We'll see." Natalie had the final word, before she was pulled out of the gym.

Once the door had closed behind them, Briony let go of Natalie's hand. "What on earth do you think you are doing?" she asked.

Without speaking, Natalie slid down the wall, thumped to the floor and started to cry. Briony was surprised to see this kind of reaction from her friend, as she was always so in control. "I just don't know," she sobbed.

Briony cradled Natalie as her shoulders heaved. Despite her friend's questionable behaviour just now, she couldn't fail to empathise with the obvious pain she was feeling.

As Natalie's tears began to subside, Briony sat cross-legged opposite her, wiped her tears away and held onto her hands.

"Oh, Bri, I've made such a mess of things, and I don't know what to do."

Briony let her friend talk.

"It's Martin. I don't think I want to spend the rest of my life with him anymore. Actually, I know I don't."

Briony took a deep breath. "This is huge, what has changed?" she asked.

"Oh Bri, please be gentle, it's only just hit me. I think I settled down too early."

"Oh, come on, is this to do with *that* Jake? The grass isn't always greener, you know. You've got an amazing man who loves you very much. Plus, you've made a good life together."

Natalie's frustration was seeping out of her. "Look, just listen to me, please. You've got no idea how hard this is for me to admit to myself. I haven't got all the answers, but please just let me talk."

Briony remained silent and reasoned that maybe she *didn't* understand what Natalie was dealing with. After all, it was only a few days ago that she'd been able to admit to herself that she was sexually attracted to Lauren. Life and love were nothing if not complicated. She squeezed Natalie's hands to show her that she'd been heard.

"It's true that Jake has really helped me," said Natalie.

Briony tried her hardest not to scrunch up her face in response.

"Jason, and now Jake, light something inside of me. And before you say anything, this isn't just about lust. It's about this absolute burning of want and need, which I have never really felt with Martin."

She took a deep breath, giving Briony a second to think about what she'd just heard. What Natalie had described was exactly how Lauren made her feel.

"Don't I have a right to feel this turned on when I see my husband?" Natalie continued. "It's a feeling that I can't just conjure up. And it's got me thinking that maybe I just followed what Mum and Dad expected of me. Maybe there's a whole other life that I should be leading.

"I don't want to spend the rest of my days missing that feeling, but at the same time, what about Bethany and Milo? When you found out I was pregnant with Jason's baby, you asked me whether I wanted to split their Christmases. The answer is no, of course I don't. So, I'm asking you, what is the right thing to do?"

The women sat in silence, deep in thought, until finally Briony spoke up. "I don't know, babe. I'm sorry I don't have the answer, but I've got you. I guess I'm just concerned that what you want isn't real life. Look at what happened with Jason."

Natalie reluctantly acknowledged that her friend was right about the spin instructor.

"Come on, let's get showered and then get drunk," Briony

said, pulling Natalie to her feet and hugging her tightly. "It'll all work out in the end," she reassured her.

Natalie didn't have much confidence in Briony's words, and in truth, nor did Briony, but they both needed to hear them. They were still embracing when the gym door opened, and Danny and Jake stepped out.

"Easy now, girls, time to get a room," Danny teased. "Or maybe we should all have a sauna together?"

"Ignore him," said Jake. "He's so charged from the weights that all he can think about is his date with Pamela Handerson."

Briony sniggered, but Natalie was confused. Was Danny going for a date with the real Pammie? After all, it was a posh hotel. The men squeezed past the embracing women and Jake made sure he locked eyes with Natalie. "Maybe catch you later, huh?" he said.

Once they were out of earshot, Natalie asked, "Do you reckon Danny will bring Pamela to the bar tonight?"

"Oh, man," said Briony, throwing her head back and laughing.

* * *

Back in the room, Lauren was enjoying her time in the tub. They only had showers on the ships, so a bath was always a treat. She loved lying back, with the water covering her ears so that she could listen to her heartbeat echoing through it. Right now, it made her feel alive, grateful and so in love. Whitney Houston's *The Greatest Love of All*, her favourite song, was playing softly through her phone and she sang along to it. The hit always made her cry, but they were happy tears that made her feel strong.

Another of her favourites was Whitney and Mariah Carey duetting with *When You Believe*. As with *The Greatest Love of All*, she found the words transformative. Her favourite lyric was on the subject of prayers and miracles, and how they don't necessarily come to be as soon as you voice them. Lauren's silent prayer for someone to love and to love her back had been answered in the most spectacular and unexpected way. She was truly grateful for what she had with Briony, and she wondered if they should even change their preferred karaoke song. She knew Briony could hit Mariah's high notes.

Suddenly, what sounded like a knock at the door brought her out of her musical meditation. A little shook up, she rose to the surface of the water.

"Bloody hell, Bri, have you forgotten your keycard?"

There was another knock, but she couldn't hear Briony's voice. Throwing on her white hotel dressing gown, she opened the door with a big smile on her face. "Oh, it's you," she said, the grin disappearing.

Chapter Thirteen

Lauren was confused. She had expected to see her sorry and sweaty friends pleading to be let in, but to her utter surprise, it was Grace at their bedroom door. Lauren couldn't speak. The glamorous woman from the lift, who had made Briony crazy jealous, was in tatters in front of her. In floods of tears, her mascara had smudged around her eyes and had started to run down her face.

Lauren wondered how this woman knew which room she was in, and why was she crying? Briony would do her nut if she saw her there, even more so because Lauren had just gotten out of the bath and was obviously completely naked beneath her dressing gown.

"What are you doing here?" Lauren asked, crossing her arms to secure the opening of her gown, ensuring she didn't accidentally reveal herself.

"Can I come in?" Grace asked.

"No, you can't, and anyway, how did you know which room we're in?"

Lauren wasn't the type to suffer fools gladly.

"My boyfriend has robbed me," Grace sobbed. "He's taken

everything. I have nothing left in our room. He packed the lot up and fled, taking all my clothes, jewellery, cash and bank cards. Randomly, he did leave my toiletries and pyjamas."

In the silence that followed this major revelation, Lauren quietly questioned the woman's honesty, before deciding she may have been a tad harsh in her initial judgement, which was influenced by Briony's jealousy. She stepped forward and embraced her unexpected visitor.

As if Grace had timed her ambush on Lauren to the second, just at that moment, Briony and Natalie turned into the corridor towards their room. Briony was walking backwards as she chatted to Natalie, so it was Natalie who was first to notice the women hugging. Seeing the perplexed expression on her friend's face, Briony quickly spun round, clouting Lauren and Grace as she crashed into them. Lauren lost hold of her dressing gown, revealing her hairless, glowing body. All three women got an eyeful of her pert breasts, defined stomach and seemingly limitless legs, as well as her electric purple toenails.

"Lauren, cover yourself up!" Briony huffed, waltzing right past her and straight into the bedroom. Natalie clenched her teeth and grimaced at Lauren, asking without words what was going on.

"OK everyone, I hope you enjoyed the show," said Lauren. "Grace, I'm really sorry your partner has shit on you, which is something that probably wouldn't happen if you dated women, but never mind that, I have Briony to deal with now. Nat, would you take over here for me?"

"OK, sure," said Natalie, though she felt like she'd been thrown under the bus, as Lauren just disappeared without explaining anything and went off in search of Briony, who was waiting for her with her hands firmly planted on her hips.

"I told you she wanted you," she said. "But what the fuck

is she doing here? Why were you hugging her and, most importantly, why aren't you wearing any clothes?"

Lauren told herself that when you expect the worst then anything better is a bonus, but this was an outcome she had wanted to avoid, and she completely understood what it looked like. "Nothing happened," she began to explain. "Grace knocked on the door when I was in the bath. I thought it was you, and that you'd lost or forgotten your keycard. She was blubbing and feeling extremely sorry for herself, because apparently her fella has robbed her. Honestly, though, I have no idea why she turned up at our door."

"Did you by any chance tell her our room number in the lift?"

Lauren rolled her eyes at Detective Greene. "No, I didn't. You would have heard me if I had. I've got no idea how she knew our room number. Maybe she saw us going in or something." Lauren raised her hands, palms facing the ceiling. As she did so, the tie on her dressing gown came loose again, this time revealing only the top half of her body. Briony looked at her breasts and felt the tingle from between her legs circulate through her body. She could never stay mad at Lauren for long, yet she wasn't about to let this go. "What were you hugging her for?" she asked.

Lauren tightened the tie again and stepped towards Briony, sensing she was almost forgiven. "I felt sorry for her, that's all. Apparently, her boyfriend has completely cleaned out their room. She seemed pretty genuine. I guess she just needed some female company."

"I still don't trust her," said Briony, as Lauren put her arms around her neck.

"That's fine, but if you were in her position, surely you'd want to see a friendly face."

Briony couldn't resist Lauren now; she'd passed the test. She slipped her hands inside her dressing gown, her fingers cold on Lauren's warm waist. This time, it was Lauren who felt the tingle. She leaned in and kissed Briony long and hard.

"OK, OK, maybe," Briony said, when they finally came up for air. "But it's not something I need to worry about. You would never do that to me."

"Exactly!"

There was a tap at the door.

"I still don't want her in here, though," Briony reiterated.

"It's only me, and don't worry, Grace has gone."

Natalie had heard Briony through the door. She'd certainly voiced her feelings loud enough for Grace to have heard, had she still been present.

The door opened. "Are we all made up now?" Natalie asked. "It went quiet, so I assumed everything was OK."

Natalie realised that she was really quite enjoying the drama, especially as she knew Briony and Lauren so well. Plus, it took her mind off her own problems. "So, it seems that when Grace went back to her room after seeing us in the lift, she found that it had been totally vacuumed," Natalie explained. "And that was just in the ten to fifteen minutes she'd been away doing a recce of the hotel. She has no clothes or money, as her purse with all her cards in it and her Fendi handbag have both been taken. Apparently, Lauren, she'd seen our room number on the receipt you were holding in the lift." She switched her focus to Briony. "It wasn't planned or anything," she reassured her, "she just noticed it, that's all."

All in all, Natalie was pleased with her delivery of the key facts of the case. "I've got her mobile number, as luckily she had her phone on her when she left the room," she continued. She's going to report the incident to the police, and I was thinking that afterwards she might like to join us for a drink at the bar. Of course, Briony, I wanted to check that it's OK with you first."

Briony shrugged. "Why wouldn't it be OK with me?" she asked, all innocent.

They all laughed.

Lauren waved the room service menu. "How about we get a pizza in here and then just go downstairs to the bar?" she suggested.

They all nodded in agreement, simultaneously thinking how ten years ago they would have been out on the town, but these days, now that they were in their early to mid-thirties, the more responsible, subdued and low-maintenance option was far more appealing.

"OK, cool. While you two have showers, I'll finally get to put some clothes on and then I'll order the food," said Lauren.

"Do you have to get dressed?" Natalie teased. "Your body is so damn sexy."

Lauren blushed at her friend's purely platonic words.

Whilst Briony showered, the pizza appeared, and Natalie filled Lauren in on the epiphany she'd had in the hotel gym, and how sexually attracted she was to men who worked out and took care of themselves. It was maybe a little narcissistic of them, but it turned Natalie on, and it wasn't something Martin ever bothered with.

"I experienced the same kind of feelings, but at a much younger age," Lauren recalled. "Do you remember watching *Home and Away* back in the day? Well, I loved, loved, loved the character Angel, who was played by Melissa George. You guys were all buzzing about Dieter Brummer, who played Shane, Angel's girlfriend, but not me. I'm lucky I had such an early awakening, because when everyone was starting to get off with boys, I really wasn't interested. Even Briony was part of the in crowd and with that, oh, what was his name?"

"I remember, it was Lewis Day," said Natalie. "She was with him in Year Nine I think." She smiled at the memory of their schooldays.

"Yeah, that's him. I wonder what he'd say now?" The girls laughed, considering how Briony's ex would feel about her now being with a woman, and not just any woman, but Lauren, who was in the same year group at school.

"I've got mixed feelings about what's going on with me," said Natalie. "In a way, I've come to accept who I am, which I guess has been healing and feels good, but shit, there is so much destruction ahead. And I've got Martin's feelings to think about."

"Maybe I was lucky in that I knew who I was much earlier," said Lauren. "My mum may have been a pothead who liked a drink – still does – but she was also a free spirit and never once judged me. Maybe because of the freedom I had at home, I was able to see myself more clearly. I don't know, but it doesn't matter where we came from, what matters now is that we've got each other, and we all accept and love each other for who we are. None of us is perfect."

Natalie nodded in agreement.

"What's this about us not being perfect?" Briony opened the bathroom door and caught the tail end of the conversation. "I think that together we have a perfect friendship. I'm not me without you two, and you both know that, but enough of all this lovey-dovey business—" she put her fingers in her mouth and pretended to be sick "—let's get drinking and have some fun. And by the way, that last piece of pizza is mine."

Chapter Fourteen

Down in the bar, the girls sat in big armchairs around a circular white table. As they started on their second bottle of Malbec, their familiarity and ease with each other was clear to see.

Briony had her back to the bar and was facing the entrance, meaning she was the first to notice Grace walk in. To her delight, she'd seemingly lost her arrogant air from earlier. She was still wearing the same dress, her hair was limp and her face was bare of make up. Admitting to herself that her nemesis actually looked much prettier without the face paint, Briony gave in to her jealousy. "Your friend's here, babe," she said, winking in the direction of Lauren and then flicking her eyes towards Grace.

Lauren followed her gaze before turning her attention back to Briony. "Be nice, please," she said. In full view of Grace and to ensure Briony got the upper hand from the get-go, she leaned across the table and kissed her full on the lips. When she pulled away, she rolled her eyes at Briony's extremely smug expression.

As Grace approached their table, Lauren said to her, "Grab

a glass and pull up a chair. We've got wine and you can tell us how it went with the police."

"Aw, thanks so much, Lauren, but I'm going to need something a bit stronger. Luckily, I got to the bank before it closed, so I was able to withdraw some cash."

Lauren wasn't completely sure about Grace's state of mind and vowed to keep an eye on her. She had the feeling she might hit the self-destruct button and get absolutely wasted. She knew and had experienced the signs.

Grace returned from the bar with what looked like a whiskey on ice. Lauren realised her instincts were bang on. What with Grace on a drinking mission, Briony's jealousy and the possibility of the gym boys turning up, they were in for a rollercoaster of an evening.

As if on cue, in walked Jake and Danny. "Oh shit, here we go!" Lauren said, pulling up her chair next to Briony. She felt the prickles from her friend's cactus needles and decided that she too needed a spot of Dutch courage. She downed two big mouthfuls of wine and added, "Babe, can you chill the fuck out, please? I can literally feel your spikes. Let's just enjoy the night."

Briony looked deep into Lauren's navy blues and agreed wholeheartedly with her. She didn't want to cause upset, but they both knew that her jealousy was an unknown entity and could strike at any time.

"Thanks so much for letting me join you," said Grace. "I didn't fancy going home and having to face up to the fact that the fella I've been dating for, like, six weeks robbed me blind."

Grace's voice was soft and vulnerable and Briony saw a flicker of sincerity, but she wasn't willing to discount her gut feelings just yet. "Six weeks. What a shit, eh? Didn't you ever get a bad feeling about him?" she asked.

"No, Briony, I didn't. He seemed like a nice guy from a nice family. He had a good job and car, and he was extremely good in bed."

The three friends simultaneously screwed up their faces.

"Ah, man, that really sucks," said Briony. "I'm so lucky I have Lauren. She's awesome in bed, too."

Lauren blushed. "Well, that's the feedback I've had," she said, winking at Briony, who was glad to have made her point.

"I know that sex with a woman is hot," admitted Grace. "But it can be just as good with a man. To me, it's not about what gender people are, but how we connect. I obviously just didn't read George very well."

There followed an awkward silence. Natalie looked at Lauren. "Oh shit!" she mouthed. Lauren looked towards Briony, whose cactus needles were firmly stuck in the sides of everyone at the table.

"I told you!" Briony said to Lauren.

It was an instinct that Natalie and Lauren knew so well. Briony was an expert at reading people.

Lauren wondered whether Grace was actually interested in her, or were her words just a coincidence?

"Look, I don't want to cause any trouble," Grace eventually piped up. "Let me get some shots in and we'll soon break the ice. You'll see."

No one resisted Grace's offer and they all watched her walk to the bar, slip in between Jake and Danny and start flirting with them.

"Oh my word, she is a one!" said Briony. "She's a proper black widow. First you, Lauren, and now the guys from the gym. How many others do you think she's got her sights on?"

Lauren and Natalie recognised that Briony had a point. Grace clearly wasn't as innocent as she was trying to make out.

Lauren stroked Briony's face. "OK, you're right," she said.

"With that in mind, though, did you ever think I'd want a piece of her?"

Clearly embarrassed, Briony slowly shook her head. "Of course I didn't," she replied.

"So, with that cleared up, can we all now just get on with the evening?" Lauren said. "And Nat, if Grace's flirtatiousness gets her with one of the boys from the gym it won't matter, because they're not yours."

Feeling like the comment was a little unjustified, all Natalie could muster in response was a "yep".

* * *

Grace's shot suggestion seemed to have had the desired effect, and the evening quickly turned into a fun-filled piss up. They played the revealing *Never Have I Ever* drinking game and took it in turns to get the rounds in, which increasingly loosened their inhibitions. Jake and Danny had joined the party pretty early on and everyone was at ease with one another.

Briony's lips were stained Marilyn Manson blue from the wine, and the bottom half of Natalie's dress had ridden up her legs. She was talking to Grace but paying more attention to Jake, as he unashamedly trailed his eyes up and down her thighs while bantering with his buddy. The alcohol was making her feel so, so sexy, and right then she knew she was going to sleep with this man. Home and Martin felt a million miles away.

Briony stumbled to the ladies' and plonked herself on the toilet. She'd reached the point in the evening when this was her safe space, and she'd take a few moments to get her head together before returning to the chaos.

The main door to the ladies' opened and she hoped it was Lauren. Alas, it wasn't. Sylphlike, she lowered herself to the floor and looked under the door, which wasn't something she'd ever consider doing whilst sober. She saw the faux snakeskin boots of Grace at the basin. As slinkily as she had eased herself to the floor, she reverted back to the toilet seat and hugged her knees into her chest. Again, this contortion act was only something she was able to do after a skinful.

Just then, Grace's phone rang. Briony remained as quiet as a mouse.

"Yo, yeah, what's up?" Briony was instantly alarmed. This wasn't Grace's usual voice. Just who was she?

"OK, so I've got matey's MacBook, his proper nice watch, his phone and the keys to the Lambo. He's still sleeping. The Benadryl I put in his whisky won't wear off for a good while, and by that point we'll be long gone. I tried another room, but there wasn't anything worth taking. Still, we've had a good day. Pick me up in twenty."

The silence that followed Grace's call was deafening, and it increased Briony's awareness that she needed to keep quiet. She couldn't wait to tell Lauren that this time, Detective Greene was right. Grace might not have been the black widow she'd first suspected her to be, but she was most certainly a wolf in sheep's clothing.

The door opened again, followed by the familiar click of Lauren's heels. Briony knew she had to bide her time. Due to the alcohol, though, all her actions were exaggerated, and she was shaking from holding her muscles so still on the toilet.

"Thank you so much for tonight, Lauren. I really needed it." Grace's pretty, feminine voice had returned.

"Ah, you're welcome," Lauren replied. "I hope everything gets sorted."

Briony heard her walk towards the cubicle next to hers. She opened the door a fraction to try and get her attention.

Just then, she saw Grace take hold of Lauren's hand and spin her around. "I was wondering if I could make it up to you?" she said. Lauren, tall in her heels, looked down at Grace, who was a good two inches shorter.

Inside her cubicle, Briony's heart was pumping in her ears.

"You're good, thanks," Lauren replied, and Briony was pleased to hear her disinterest. She wondered if there was a low that Grace wouldn't sink to.

Undeterred, Grace held onto Lauren's hand and pulled her in so that their waists were touching.

Lauren flinched like she'd been burnt with a hot poker and swatted Grace away like a fly. "What don't you understand? I'm not interested."

"But Lauren, you've been giving me signals all night," Grace persisted.

"What? No, I haven't!"

Confined to her cubicle, and as if she were in a *I'm a Celebrity* Bushtucker Trial, Briony felt jealousy crawling all over her body like a swarm of ants. Exactly what signs had Lauren been giving her?

"Oh, come on, I haven't given you any signals," said Lauren, struggling to believe the ludicrous things coming from Grace's mouth.

"But you've been buying me drinks all night, *and* you said I could stay in your room."

Lauren threw her head back and laughed out loud. "I felt sorry for you, and besides, you wouldn't just be with me. I'm sharing a room with Briony and Natalie, remember? I think we need to part company now, though, it's all got a bit weird."

"But where will I go?" said Grace.

"Are you kidding me, Scarlett O'Hara? Frankly, my dear, I don't give a damn. I should have listened to Briony. She had a feeling about you."

Inside the cubicle, Briony beamed from ear to ear. It was as if a golden light was shining from her.

Outside, Lauren was beginning to worry. Her new 'friend's'

sweet, innocent, hard-done-by face had frozen into hard stone. "Briony was right," Grace confirmed. "I just hope my 'boyfriend' hasn't robbed your room, too."

Lauren gulped. No longer stealth-like, Briony fell through the cubicle door like Bambi learning to walk.

"Bloody hell, Briony, you always know how to make an entrance! How long have you been in there, babe?" Lauren looked ever so relieved.

Before Briony could reply, Grace was gone, quite literally, like a thief in the night.

Lauren opened her arms to Briony. "That was all a bit fucked up," she said. "I should have listened to you."

Briony rested her head on Lauren's chest and pulled her closer. "Yeah, you should have, but that's not all. I reckon Grace – if that is her name – is a bit of a con-artist. Before you came in, I heard her on the phone talking in a weird voice to someone about how she'd slipped some drugs into a fella's whiskey and taken a bunch of his stuff. Even the keys to his Lamborghini."

Lauren looked shocked. "What? Really? Oh my God, what a weirdo. I wonder why she hooked onto us?"

Briony's drunkenness had eased slightly, allowing her to fully consider the question. "I don't know, but maybe she'd set her sights on you, and you were supposed to be her trophy for the night?"

"Detective Greene, please don't fraternise with me under these incriminating circumstances. It's more than your job is worth," Lauren shot back.

"What a crazy woman, though. I also heard her say she'd tried another room but didn't find anything. You don't think that was our one, do you?"

"Did she really say that?" said Lauren. "Fuck me, that girl has some issues. Oh, yeah, you're right." Briony smiled coyly. "She said she hoped her *boyfriend* hadn't robbed my room as well, didn't she! Coming out to play with us with no make up on, just to get sympathy. And maybe she did think she could have me, too. It must take a deluded type of self-confidence to assume you can get someone who's clearly already taken."

Briony squirmed; the jealousy hadn't quite left her system. "You read about these crazy people, but you never think you're going to meet one, huh?" she said. "And did she actually pay for that first round, or was the barman in on it, too? We'd better go and check our room, in case she's ransacked it."

Briony led Lauren out of the toilets by the hand. She was surprised to find the bar empty. "Where's Nat?" she said.

"And where are the guys from the gym?" added Lauren.

"Perhaps Nat's gone to bed," Briony said, moving with a little more urgency, as she prayed her friend was being sensible.

When they got up to their room, Lauren couldn't find her keycard. "I specifically put it in my phone cover so I wouldn't lose it," she said. "I don't know where it's gone."

"Maybe Grace took it?" said Briony. The girls laughed, but on reflection it wasn't an impossible suggestion.

Briony rummaged around in her bra trying to find her own keycard.

Lauren stepped closer. "Do you need some help?" she teased, reaching her cold hand into Briony's left cup and running her finger over her nipple, which immediately stood to attention.

"Bloody hell, your hand's freezing."

"Hmmm, but you're lovely and warm."

Briony shook her head affectionately and pulled out the keycard. She gently pushed Lauren away, giving her room to rest the card against the reader. The light turned green, and she pushed the door open and put the key into the slot on the wall to turn on the lights. Both girls gasped.

"Nat? Are you in here?" Briony called, rushing through the

door. The wardrobe and drawers had been flung open, clothes were strewn all over the floor and all their make up had been emptied out onto the vanity unit.

"Lucky we're only booked for one night," said Lauren. "The only things in here are today's dirty undies and clothes, tomorrow's outfits and our toiletries, pyjamas and make up." She looked around the room and couldn't see anything missing. "What a strange girl. What on earth did she expect to find?"

"Maybe she thought we had tons of drug money stashed in here, ready to transport to the States?" Briony mused.

"Ha, ha, we could be like Alex and Piper from Netflix's *Orange Is the New Black*," Lauren enthusiastically replied.

"Oh my gosh, you know how much I love that show. We could be just like them before they're nicked for trafficking drug money. I'd be naïve Piper Chapman and you'd be the sexy temptress, Alex Vause."

Briony thought for a second and then fluttered her eyelashes. "Alex's weakness is Piper, so does that make me yours?"

Lauren fidgeted before replying, and Briony noticed the uncomfortable pause. "What is it?" she asked.

"I've never thought about it like that before, but just then something really pulled hard, deep down in the pit of my tummy." She paused, before adding, "Maybe you are."

Lauren's vulnerability surprised Briony, because she was usually so confident. Somehow, the deep pull of love that Lauren was feeling transferred into her own stomach. "I've never felt like this before," she said, "but fuck me, love does actually hurt."

After hearing her feelings were reciprocated, Lauren opened her arms and the girls held each other tight. "Unfortunately for Grace, we don't work for an international drug cartel and have a suitcase stuffed with cash in our hotel room," she said. "I'm unemployed and you're soon to be without a job, too."

"What?" replied Briony. "What about the ships? Aren't you going back?"

Lauren flashed her gorgeous smile, which Briony could never resist. "I quit, babe." She stopped talking and looked deep into Briony's bright blues for a moment, before adding, "Long distance relationships don't work. I've seen them and tried them, and to be honest, I'm over living out of a suitcase, and I really don't want to be away from you."

When she wasn't prepared for a situation, Briony could only see the cons. "But what about money?"

Lauren knew Briony's panicked reaction all too well. "Look, I told you in the pub that I have saved up from working away, and you helped me to save more by letting me stay with you between contracts. For now, we don't need to worry about money, and Mani's payment will come through soon, too. I can sing anywhere. Besides, I really don't want to spend the best part of our lives apart. We're lucky we have this opportunity, let's not waste it."

Briony felt backed into a corner, but it was a comfortable one. She guessed that Lauren had probably wanted her for a lot longer than they'd both realised. After all, this type of planning didn't just happen overnight. She liked that thought. "Lauren Newland, you certainly are something else, and I bloody love you." Lauren smiled, but before she could reply, Briony threw in, "By the way, we're going to Mr Schwartzberg's on Saturday night." She took the shot, knowing they'd be even.

Lauren licked her lips and smiled. "Just how long were you going to keep that from me, then?"

"For just as long as you kept quiet about quitting your job."

Lauren took Briony's hand in hers and suggestively said,

"I'm not sure about you, but I feel really dirty knowing that someone has rifled through all our stuff. I need to take a shower."

Briony agreed that right at that moment, she felt incredibly dirty, too, so she *definitely* needed a wash. Lauren pulled her into the bathroom, turned on the shower and shut the door behind them.

Chapter Fifteen

E arlier, in the bar, Natalie couldn't believe her luck when she found herself alone with Jake. His buddy Danny had disappeared, and she had no idea where Briony, Lauren and Grace had gotten to.

Maybe it's fate, she said to herself. Her inhibitions had fled, while her confidence had hit a sudden high. "It looks like we've been dumped," she commented.

Jake smiled, and Natalie felt as if he was undressing her with his eyes. "It does look that way. Maybe we should go and look for everyone."

Natalie was a little confused by Jake's response, and she considered that possibly he wasn't too good at sexy bants. "Oh, well, we could do that," she said, "but I was hoping we could go for a walk. Just the two of us." She hadn't just laid her cards on the table, she had thrown them down.

"Yeah, we might bump into them," Jake replied enthusiastically. Natalie couldn't help rolling her eyes. Yes, he was delightful to look at, but maybe role-play and improv weren't his strongest subjects. Abandoning any hint of subtlety, she grabbed hold of his hand and led him gently out of the bar, across the foyer and into the lift. As soon as the doors shut, he bundled her into the corner, keeping his finger on the button to keep them closed. Then he pressed his big, soft lips against hers and started padding around her mouth with his tongue, as if he were playing hand drums.

It was all so fast, with no tenderness, which was new to Natalie. Jason had liked it quick, yet he had never smothered her face with his lips. The one similarity between the two men was that they were both strong and moved with intent. She ran her hands down Jake's shirt, feeling the ripple of his defined abs before moving down to his hips and then to his glutes, which were as hard as steel. She could grab his entire butt without it moving. Just the thought of how much he'd worked out to get a backside so perfect drove her wild. She didn't even notice when the lift started to move. They broke away from each other when the recorded female voice informed them they'd reached the ground floor and the doors started sliding open. Luckily, there wasn't anyone waiting to come in.

Natalie could sense Jake's eagerness as he stood back to look at her, and she enjoyed the anticipation of what was to come – quite literally. Seconds later, he pulled her out of the lift, down a corridor, past some bedrooms and into an empty hallway. Against the left-hand wall was a trolley, its top half filled with complimentary toiletries, cleaning products and cloths, and the bottom with fresh towels and bedding. Natalie reasoned the rooms leading off from the corridor were for housekeeping. As she thought this, Jake turned her around to face him before pushing her against the trolley and aggressively entering her mouth once again. Like the lacquer of a clown's smile, she could feel saliva around her lips and up to her nose, but she still revelled in how much he clearly wanted her. She resumed touching his body – to distract herself from the assault on her mouth more than anything –

and ran her fingers over his studded belt before placing her hand over his protruding erection. She rubbed up and down its length and the thing encompassed most of her hand. Once it was loose, she didn't think she'd be able to touch her thumb to her finger around its circumference. She'd never felt anything so big, or so hard. She could tell it wouldn't be long before she got to meet the beast.

Encouraged by Natalie's touch, Jake moved his slobber down her neck and pulled her dress down low enough to reveal her breasts. The rapid movement of his tongue was much more appreciated on her nipples, and she momentarily forgot about the size of his forbidding manhood. She could hear his belt buckle being opened and the sound of his jeans hitting the floor. He was bent over, still with one of her nipples in his mouth. She looked down and watched him tugging at his boxers. His penis sprang out like a coiled spring. He moved away from her breasts to pull a wrapped condom from his jeans pocket, which he expertly slid onto his engorged member. Natalie felt grateful for his thoughtfulness, as admittedly, in the heat of the moment, she hadn't even thought about contraception.

Gently, he cupped her face. "You OK?" he asked.

Once again, she was touched by his attentiveness and consented by nodding her head in his palms. The simple question lit something in her, and she couldn't wait to feel him inside her. He didn't need telling twice and pulled down her knickers. He was tall, but his strong thighs meant he could hold himself underneath her. As she tensed from the reality of just how big he was, she clenched hold of the towels on the trolley behind her. As he thrust into her, things didn't seem quite so fun anymore. The rocking trolley kept hitting the wall, sending little bottles of shampoo and conditioner cascading to the carpet. Oblivious, Jake was in full flow now and started to speed up. Natalie hoped he would finish soon.

She realised she was just a fuck to him and that this didn't mean anything. Despite her initial arousal, she felt just the same as when Jason had tied her up with the TRX suspension strap.

Suddenly, they both heard a sound coming from behind one of the doors. As a handle was pushed down, Jake slipped out of her and in one swift movement pulled up his boxers and jeans. Then he was gone.

Natalie turned to the door as a woman dressed in a sleek pencil skirt and matching jacket stepped into the corridor, her glasses resting on top of her neat black chignon. Her smartness contrasted sharply with Natalie's dishevelled state. Her knickers were around her ankles and her dress was more like a belt, hitched up over her hips and pulled down to her belly button, with her breasts on full display. Her alcohol-soaked brain meant her reaction times were slow, and the woman got a full eyeful before she was able to pull up her panties and cover her body with her dress. Mortified, she crumpled to the floor and promptly burst into tears.

"Are you OK?" asked the woman, her gentle Irish accent oozing empathy.

Natalie couldn't reply. She was shaking as well as crying and struggled to catch her breath. The woman bent over and carefully let her paperwork drop to the floor, before pulling her glasses onto her nose.

Through her tears, Natalie noticed how professionally presented she was, which only made her feel worse. "No, I'm not OK," she said. The woman looked worried, and Natalie shook her head. "It's not what you might think. I gave him my full consent. This is my doing. I guess the poor guy just got spooked. Actually, I don't blame him for running."

Snot poured from Natalie's nose. She held onto her knees and found herself rocking back and forth. "I think I'm having a nervous breakdown," she sobbed.

The woman encouraged Natalie to get to her feet. She was probably a few years older, and Natalie could see understanding in her eyes, around which were some lovely smile lines. "Please, can we never speak of this again?" she pleaded. "I'm so sorry to have displayed myself to you like this, in your beautiful hotel." She realised she was clutching at straws, as she considered the possible consequences of her actions.

"Ah, don't worry, hun. We've all had moments of madness."

Natalie couldn't believe the generosity this woman was showing her. If she'd found someone in the same compromising position, she didn't think she'd be quite so kind. "I don't know what to say," she said. "Thank you doesn't seem enough."

"I've worked in the hotel game for years. We see everything, you know." Natalie nodded. "Look, all that matters is that you're not hurt."

"My head is killing me, but that's not because of what just happened."

The woman nodded knowingly and escorted Natalie to the lift. They didn't exchange names, but Natalie knew she would be forever grateful for the kindness shown to her. Upstairs, she hoped to find Briony and Lauren in their room, but initially it appeared empty. Then she heard the shower running and giggles and gasps of pleasure coming from behind the bathroom door.

"Are you kidding me?" she said quietly, before throwing herself onto the bed and putting her head under a pillow to block out the noises she didn't want to hear coming from her best friends.

Fifteen minutes later, the bathroom door opened. Briony walked out first wearing a dressing gown. "Look, Nat's back," she said to Lauren.

They looked over at the bed and were disturbed to see their friend's motionless body, her face under a pillow.

"Oh my God, is she breathing?" said Lauren.

They ran over and grabbed the pillow, relieved to see that Natalie was alive. She was fast asleep on her back, with her head to the side.

"Oh, man, look at her face," said Briony. "She's been crying. We shouldn't have left her alone."

Lauren removed Natalie's shoes and covered her up to her shoulders with a sheet. She stirred but didn't wake up. "Bri, she's a big girl, and it wasn't like we left her alone on purpose. The Grace thing happened, which was weird, and she'd gone by the time we got back to the bar."

"Yes, I know, but what if she'd got herself hurt? She's fragile right now."

"Yeah, OK, you're right. She's not in a good place, is she? But at least she's back here now, safe with us."

Briony pushed the hair from Natalie's face and kissed her forehead.

"I know, I'll take off her make up, like I've done for you," Lauren suggested. "Or else the poor thing will wake up with it dry and crusty all over her face. The salt from her tears will make it even worse."

Lauren fetched her skincare products from the bathroom and sat cross-legged on the floor at Natalie's side of the bed. She gently removed the mess that had not so long ago been her perfectly made-up face and dabbed on some serum and moisturising cream. Then she too kissed her friend on the forehead. She looked up, expecting to see Briony, who had slid into bed, eagerly watching the procedure. But she saw that she was also now fast asleep, while tenderly holding onto Natalie's waist. Turning the lights out, Lauren gently moved in next to Briony and slid her arm across her middle. The three women remained holding onto each other like this all night.

* * *

"Thanks, babe, this is amazing," Briony whispered into Lauren's ear, as they surveyed the sumptuous buffet breakfast in the dining room the following morning. She then gently bit her earlobe, which came as a pleasant surprise to Lauren.

"Very cute, and you're welcome," Lauren said. "I think it cost the best part of twenty quid each, so eat well and stuff your handbag with cakes and doughnuts."

Briony smiled, accepting her challenge, which Lauren knew she wouldn't find difficult. Just like overtaking in the inside lane of a motorway, she was aware of just how much Briony enjoyed breaking the small rules in life.

Natalie didn't seem quite so enthusiastic about the buffet. Almost in a trancelike state, she went straight to the table and sat down. Concerned, Briony followed her. "Let me get your breakfast," she offered. "What do you fancy?"

Natalie's sad, deep brown eyes met Briony's twinkling, happy blues. "Just a croissant will be fine," she replied flatly.

Briony felt the sadness emanating from Natalie like heat. While she had never been so alive and in love, she was also heavy with concern for her friend. Nevertheless, that didn't stop her from filling her plate with the full works when she went to fetch the pastry.

"Babe, I know what I said about eating well, but don't waste it," Lauren said, wondering where she'd put it all. Then she turned her attention to Natalie's plate. "Is that all you're having?" she asked.

Natalie looked up with her eyes sparkling with tears. "I did a bad thing last night," she said.

It was as if the entire dining room had fallen silent. Briony took hold of Natalie's right hand and Lauren grabbed her left.

"I did get it on with *that* Jake." She emphasised his name in the same way Briony had. "We had unabashed, wild sex against a cleaning trolley down a quiet corridor on the ground floor, but he never finished because we were interrupted by a lovely Irish lady who works here at the hotel. He just ran. Meanwhile, I was left there with it all on show; my knickers around my ankles and my dress up over my hips. It was the lowest point of my entire life."

Briony couldn't help visualising the picture Natalie had painted. She sniggered.

"Bri, it's not funny!"

"No, I agree," Briony quickly replied. "But it is a little." She smiled at her friend, knowing she could break her.

Then Lauren added, "Take yourself out of the picture, Nat, and now take a look."

"What a great idea!" said Briony, stroking Natalie's hand. "Forget it was you there, just imagine what this Irish woman must have seen and thought when she opened the door."

Briony could see Natalie considering the scene from a different perspective.

"Annoyingly, although this is completely mortifying for me, you're both right," Natalie eventually agreed. "When I was in despair last night and this lovely woman was showing me immense kindness, I decided that if I'd found someone in the same state, I probably wouldn't have been so sympathetic. Oh, and by the way, you two could have kept it down in the bathroom."

Throughout their friendship, Natalie had always had a habit of trying to project a bit of her guilt onto them.

Briony and Lauren both looked at each other and smiled, remembering their shower together.

"And you can stop all this gazing lovingly at each other," said Natalie. "We're talking about my huge problem here. Speaking of which, don't get me started on the size of his—!"

Briony and Lauren cut Natalie off with their screams of laughter; they were happy to have their friend back.

"I can tell you one thing, I definitely don't want to hear about that," said Lauren, "but you do need a plan."

"Laur, we don't need any more of your plans," Briony interjected.

"No, not a plan-plan, but a plan."

The women nodded knowingly and began to eat, with Natalie now ploughing into Briony's feast along with her pastry.

Chapter Sixteen

Pulling into the driveway she shared with her husband, Natalie felt a growing sense of unease. Why was his silver Audi A8 parked there? Why wasn't he at work? With trepidation, she crept up to the front door and pushed the handle; it didn't budge. Her key in the lock wouldn't turn.

All kinds of things ran through her head. What was he doing inside? Had he changed the locks? She banged on the door. "Mart, are you in there? Mart? Let me in, please?" She knocked even harder but there was no answer. She worried that after the state she'd left him in on Wednesday, he could have done something stupid. Over the years, she'd watched his moods fluctuate wildly; he could be up one day and then down another. He was always worse after alcohol, but he was aware of that, so he barely drank and left Natalie to the hangovers after her nights out with Briony and Lauren. Every now and again he shared a joint with his best mate from school, Dylan, who was now manager at the town's fishing supplies store. He embodied the chilled out, bachelor lifestyle and Natalie liked that Martin had an outlet with him, as he didn't seem to have any other close mates.

In the grand scheme of things, Natalie realised that she could have been more considerate of Martin's feelings. Jason was the worst person in the world to be learning the PT trade from, but she reasoned that it wasn't all her fault. After all, it was just a coincidence that her former lover was going to be her teacher, and it seemed that Briony was up for joining her with the training. While her self-righteousness overruled her guilt, she couldn't deny that she was worried about Martin. She remembered noticing the whisky on his breath, which was unusual and a reason to be concerned.

She started to heat up and rolled up her sleeves, shaking her hands to fan under her chin. Her mind was whirring, her bad thoughts escalating. What had she done? Not only with Jason, but now with Jake. She was pretty sure Martin would never find out about her most recent indiscretion, and she sure wasn't going to tell him, but even so, had she pushed her husband too far?

She walked to the end of the driveway towards the 10ft wooden gate that her dad had installed a few years ago to give them privacy and keep the kids safe. Instantly, she recognised the sound of her husband's heavy breathing. What on earth was he up to?

Then she heard a woman say, "That's it, try a little deeper." She didn't recognise the voice and her mind spun as she thought of what could be causing her husband's quickening of breath.

Barging through the gate, she called out accusingly, "Just what is going on here?"

Martin looked up from his press-up position, his skin shining with sweat. He was wearing his West Ham shorts and what looked like a new Adidas workout vest. It was bright yellow, which Natalie thought looked ridiculous against his pasty white skin. Next to him was a petite blonde kitted out in a matching Nike baseball cap, workout vest, leggings and trainers. Her legs were solid and defined, and she had a dinky waist and a gorgeous, tight butt. Her hair was pulled back into a ponytail, which fitted sleekly through the opening at the back of her cap.

No one spoke, so only the birds singing and Martin's heavy breathing could be heard. Natalie scrutinised the young woman's face. Her skin was glowing and the only make up she had on was a touch of mascara. She had bright blue eyes, which were quite similar to Briony's.

"Hi, it's Natalie, isn't it? I'm Jade," the woman said confidently. She extended her hand, but Natalie didn't shake it.

"Yes, I am, but how do you know my name?" she said. Her eyes flicked to Martin, who during the interruption had been desperately holding his body in the plank position. Exhausted now, he fell flat onto his stomach.

"Martin called me, I'm a personal trainer," said Jade. Hearing that pulled Natalie's insides apart. That was her thing. Why was Martin trying to muscle in on her interest? Couldn't he find something of his own? "He feels he's let himself go over the years and wants to get into better shape for you."

Jade spoke softly, bigging up her client. The rims of Natalie's eyes reddened – not because she was about to cry, but from the sense of injustice and anger she felt.

"He said you wouldn't be home until later, and we figured your garden is the perfect size for some bodyweight exercises and a bit of cardio," Jade continued.

Natalie understood the PT vocabulary much more than her husband. "Well, it's really lovely to meet you, Jade," she said, finally taking her hand and matching her strength of handshake. "Now, do me a favour and beast the shit out of him!"

Jade smiled awkwardly, sensing something was amiss

between the married couple. "With pleasure, Natalie," she said. She moved over to Martin and squatted to his level. "You heard the woman. So, we're going to go military style today, on your wife's orders!"

Natalie smirked. She decided she actually quite liked Jade.

"So, you can stay where you are, and we'll start on the floor; thirty seconds on and ten off, alternating between mountain climbers and burpees. We'll do five sets, and that's only five minutes of work. It'll be over before you know it, and you'll reap the benefits from the short recovery increasing your fitness levels faster."

Martin turned his attention to Natalie, who was looking extremely pleased with herself. "Are you going to watch?" he asked. Natalie understood that it was more of a don't watch request and stepped towards the back door. "Is this open?" she said. "The front door was locked, and I couldn't open it with my key."

"Oh, yeah, it is," Martin replied. "But I don't know why you couldn't get in through the front." He looked almost convincing, but Natalie was sure he was hiding something.

"Right, let's stop procrastinating. Martin, we've got work to do," interjected Jade.

In the kitchen, the bright spring sunshine shone through the windows, and Natalie made herself an instant coffee straight from her boiling water tap. She watched Martin doing mountain climbers on the floor. To help him correct his technique, engage the intended muscle group and avoid injury, Jade pushed down on his bum. Despite the intimacy of the movement, Natalie could tell she had zero sexual interest in her client. Then, remembering the front door, she spun round and saw Martin's key in the lock. Just like his dad, he was vigilant about safety and would check all the doors were locked every night before bed. Natalie wasn't such a worrier and often took the mick out of her husband for his habit. She couldn't remember him ever leaving his key in the front door, though. Had he done it on purpose?

She pulled his key from the lock and inspected it, as if it would give her an answer. The hangover clouds were starting to settle, the caffeine was barely improving matters and constant irritability wasn't far away. Even so, she had a sudden moment of clarity. "He thought he was going to get laid, didn't he?" she said out loud. "What a total knobhead!" She laughed. It wasn't the thought of her husband having sex with another woman that she found funny, but the idea that Martin reckoned he was in with a chance with Jade.

Martin came in just after half twelve to find Natalie reading a magazine at the breakfast bar while the radio played in the background. In front of her were two mugs of coffee and two plates of white bread sandwiches cut into triangles, with a few Doritos on the side. She looked up at the dishevelled mess before her. "Hard work out, dear?" she asked without feeling.

Martin wiped the sweat from his forehead. It had dripped onto his eyebrows and was irritating his eyes. "Well, if you hadn't asked her to beast me then it might not have been so tough. Thanks for that!" His words were tinged with menace.

"I made you lunch," Natalie said, pushing forward his plate.

"Ah, thanks, but I'm not hungry."

The point tallies were beginning to appear.

"What? I've made you lunch and you're not going to eat it? Why? I'm normally starving after a workout. You can't be serious."

Natalie went to stand up.

"Like I said, I'm not hungry. I'm going to have a shower and maybe I'll have it afterwards. I didn't say I wasn't going to eat it."

"Don't split hairs, Martin." Natalie hated it when she sounded like her mother, but when put on the spot, she

135

couldn't think of a better way to voice her irritation than through one of Paula's favourite sayings. "You're not fourteen," she added.

He walked past her towards the stairs before spinning around again. "No, you're right, I'm not fourteen, and neither are you."

"What's that supposed to mean?"

"Oh, look at you, poor victim Natalie, who runs off to London to get drunk rather than dealing with the problem that she brought into the family home."

Without thinking, Natalie pulled a bottle of wine from the cupboard and poured herself a glass.

"Is that such a good idea?" Martin asked. "You look pretty hungover as it is. Was it a late night?"

She sipped the Malbec, playing with it in her mouth as she considered the case that had been brought before her. Martin had a point. Did she need to add another glass of wine to her already hungover body, especially as she still had the school run to do? Then she decided it was his fault for making her want a drink and that she wouldn't be breaking any laws by just having one.

"So, this is all my fault, is it?" she pressed on. "I know I messed up with Jason, and I am sorry, but I can't spend the rest of my life apologising. And don't start telling me when and with whom I can have a drink. Maybe I am a little hungover, but what did you expect? I needed a break from your constant feeling sorry for yourself act." She spread her arms to emphasise how big the problem was. She still had the front door key in her jeans pocket and was ready to pull it out if necessary.

"I do think you're more to blame than I am," said Martin.

Fire blazed in her eyes. She placed the wine glass on the worktop with such force that the stem broke. It didn't bother her, and she let the rest of the glass bounce off the counter and smash into pieces on the floor. Red wine splattered over one of the cupboards and left spots all over the tiles.

Natalie moved closer to Martin. He was only an inch taller than her, so she could look him straight in the eye without having to get up on her tiptoes. Her breasts pushed against his clammy chest. "It's all me, huh?" She nearly laughed in his face, before pulling out the front door key and holding it between them in her open palm. "Did you lock the door because you thought Jade would fuck you?" She spoke to him like he was a child.

He leaned in until their noses almost touched. "Yes. I wanted her. I just love her peachy butt and pert breasts. She's hot."

Martin's words stuck into Natalie like hot pokers. The pert breasts line especially hurt. After having two babies, *he* knew how much she wanted a boob job to lift hers up and make her feel sexier.

Obviously, young Jade hadn't had any kids. Martin was getting personal again, picking at her insecurities. She'd thought he would deny wanting to sleep with Jade, and now she had to deal with the opposite truth. She couldn't move or find the words to respond.

"It hurts, doesn't it." Martin thrust the hot pokers in again.

Natalie didn't know what she was feeling, but she needed to come back and win this. "OK, I get what you're trying to do, but honestly, did you really think a lovely, 25-year-old girl would be attracted to you? Have you seen yourself?"

She attacked his appearance, just like he had hers, but it didn't knock him.

"Yeah, I did. But maybe I've been out of the game for so long now, what with dedicating my life to you, that I no longer know how to pursue a woman and read the signs."

Natalie realised he was serious. "Mart, are you actually looking for someone else?"

When Natalie was in control, which she invariably was, she was confident things would go her way. This was new for her, and she was rattled.

"So, what if you had come home and found Jade and me making love in our bed? Would you be able to just carry on with life as if everything was hunky-dory? Oh, and what if she got pregnant with my baby? Would that be fine, too?" He was on a roll.

The wind had been sucked from Natalie's sails. "I never brought Jason here," she whispered.

Martin laughed. "Oh, that's big of you. I'm really pleased. Thanks, Nat, that makes it all OK."

Maybe it was the alcohol, or the lack of sleep, or the guilt; or maybe it was a combination of everything that caused the curtains to rise ready for Natalie's narration. She crunched shards of glass into the luxury tiles as she walked back and forth practising her lines. She then leaned against the sink and began. "You're right, I have been a bitch, but I refuse to take all the blame. You're a good guy – a really good guy – but you don't make me tingle. You don't excite me, and I'm not sure if that's something I want to spend the rest of my life missing out on. Maybe we got married too young. Maybe we were supposed to get here, because I am eternally thankful for our beautiful children and the life you have given us, but I just don't think I can pretend anymore."

It hurt her to say and accept her words, but it was also a relief to let them out. She saw the tears begin to build behind Martin's eyes, but she had none to shed herself.

"But we've had great sex recently," Martin protested. "Maybe I can be that guy all the time."

Natalie enjoyed that he was starting to retreat. "Yes, you're right, it was amazing, but that's not us. You're trying to be someone else, and that's not right. You're Martin, not Jason, and not Jake."

"Who the fuck is Jake?"

Natalie realised her mistake. "Eh, no one. It was just an example of another bloke's name. The male version of Jade. That's all."

He seemed to accept her explanation.

"We can't carry on a relationship that isn't real," she said. She briefly considered something Briony and Lauren had suggested, about them maybe trying a more modern, open relationship while taking care of the kids together, but it wasn't enough. They had just said some really hurtful things to each other, and she didn't want Bethany and Milo living in such a toxic environment. Her next words left her lips as if she'd been waiting to say them forever. "I think we should get a divorce."

Chapter Seventeen

"I don't like that our London trip is over," Briony said, as she and Lauren walked from the station after bidding Natalie farewell. She slipped her arm into Lauren's, and they connected hands, intertwining their fingers before turning to look into each other's eyes.

"Oh, OK, what were you thinking?"

"Why don't we go on a date, a real bona fide date?"

Lauren smiled. She liked where Briony was heading. She grabbed the top of her jacket with both hands and pulled her in. "I love it! Briony, will you come for a coffee and maybe a sandwich now, and if all goes well, we could meet in the Red Lion tonight for dinner and drinks?"

Even though it had been Briony's idea, Lauren had clearly taken the lead. "Sure, babe, that sounds lovely. Like you say, though, we need to see how the first date goes." She winked. "Why don't you drive Gina home, ditch the suitcase and then meet me in, say, half an hour? It'll be quite perfect, because it'll be midday by then, so not too busy and loud for a first lunch date. I need to pick up some bits anyway, so that'll give me enough time to shop around before we meet."

"But what if I need to pick up some bits, too?"

"I can get them for you," Briony suggested.

Lauren laughed. "I'm only joking. I like this teamwork; us working together." She flashed her dazzling smile at Briony. "We're good."

Briony lit up inside and nodded.

"Why don't we meet at our favourite coffee shop? It's a very chilled, first date kind of place?"

Briony nodded again, enjoying the warm feeling she got whilst looking at Lauren.

"OK, see you in half an hour. But I hope you've got more to say on the actual date?"

"Oh, shut up! Of course I'll have more to say. See you in a bit. I'm not going to kiss you because in this version of the story, I don't have that relationship with you yet. I'm looking forward to getting to know you more, though."

Lauren smiled in agreement. "Me too," she said, turning to walk towards Gina in the train station car park while Briony headed towards the town centre. Before getting into the car, she turned around and watched Briony making her way across the bridge over the main road towards the shopping centre. She climbed into the car feeling full up with affection for the woman she was about to go on a first date with.

While Lauren was making her way home, Briony went straight to The Body Shop, enjoying the delicious scents coming from the cruelty-free products. She caught a glimpse of her make-up free face in the mirror and was shocked by how dull her skin and hair looked, and how bad the dark rims below her eyes appeared. She was a walking hangover and didn't want to go on her first date with Lauren looking so rough. Ticking herself off for letting Lauren leave with all her toiletries in the case, she grabbed a basket and shoved in it some shampoo, conditioner, shower gel, body lotion, foundation, powder, eyeliner, eyeshadow, mascara, blusher, lipstick and gloss. The girl on the check-out couldn't believe the scale of the sale.

"I've got a last-minute date and I don't have time to go home and get ready," Briony explained. "I only came in here to pick up some body lotion."

Next, she went to Boots and bought some Coco Mademoiselle perfume and deodorant, before running to New Look for an outfit. Even though Lauren had seen her dressed up and down countless times, the conundrum of what to wear was real. Was this really a casual date or should she go dressy? Was it going to lead straight onto dinner?

She eventually decided on a denim skirt and a loosely fitting pink and white gingham shirt that tied at the waist and could be unbuttoned just enough at the top to show off her enviable cleavage. She then decided she really needed a shower and texted Lauren.

Babe, please don't rush, I'm going to be a bit longer. Can I meet you at one instead? xx

Lauren immediately messaged back, saying, "Sure, Babe", and adding a bunch of red and pink hearts.

Now Briony just had to decide where she was going to get showered. She trotted through the town on a mission and headed for the leisure centre, where she paid for an adult swim. Her first date was certainly totting up an expensive bill, and it hadn't even started yet.

Once showered, she rough dried her hair using the centre's hairdryer, put some make up on, sprayed herself with perfume and looked in the full-length mirror. Luckily, she had a kink in her hair and rough drying was an easy and presentable option. She felt like she'd embraced her inner Emma Bunton/Baby Spice and smiled at her reflection, excited for her first ever official date with her long-time friend.

Lauren arrived in town in a taxi, as she couldn't face the walk. She opened the door to the coffee shop and glanced around for Briony, who was sitting at a two-person table at the back. When Briony clocked Lauren, she was dazzled by her appearance and stumbled slightly as she stood up to greet her. The sunlight was behind Lauren, and she was the vision of an angel. Her hair was in a messy bun on top of her head, with loose strands falling around her pretty face. She'd paired the blue suede boots that Briony had always coveted with skinny jeans and a tight purple t-shirt that accentuated her tiny waist and big bust. Briony ran her eyes up her long legs and saw the sunlight shining through her sexy thigh gap.

Lauren sniggered at Briony's awkwardness as she stood up. When she had rebalanced herself, she watched her shake her head, allowing her cascade of long blonde hair to trail down her back. Briony had no idea how beautiful Lauren thought she was, both inside and out. She looked so precious in her denim skirt and powder pink shirt, and Lauren couldn't wait for their date to begin. "Would you like a hot chocolate with all the trimmings, babe?" she asked, making a beeline for the counter.

"I've already got you one," Briony replied, pointing to two mugs overloaded with squirty cream and overflowing with marshmallows.

Lauren's face glowed as she elegantly walked over to Briony and took her hand. "You look gorgeous," she said. "Where on earth did you manage to get changed? Ah, now, did you plan all this?" Lauren winked at Briony as she squeezed into the booth next to her.

"There are other seats, you know," Briony teased, though Lauren knew how much she enjoyed their bodies touching.

"I wanted to sit next to you," she said, leaning in and kissing Briony on the cheek. "You smell so good." She kissed her on the other cheek and then settled into her chair.

"No, I didn't plan this. It wasn't until I went to The Body Shop and saw my face in the mirror. I was, like, shit, there's no way I can go on our first date looking like this. That's when I texted you." Lauren nodded, remembering the message.

"So, I bought washing stuff, toiletries, make up, perfume and an outfit and went to the leisure centre for a swim."

She used her fingers in an air quote, to emphasise the irony of not actually going into the pool. "This is already the most expensive date of my life and you've only just arrived."

They both laughed and Lauren looked around to check that nobody was watching. "I really like this new skirt," she said, sliding her hand up Briony's leg and over the denim until she got to the top. "It's so soft." She put one of her fingers inside the waistband and ran it back and forth along the elastic, against Briony's skin. Briony quivered with surprise and delight and then Lauren pushed her whole hand inside her skirt.

Briony took a deep breath as Lauren's hand ventured into the warmth between her legs. A minute hadn't passed before Briony felt things had got too heated and batted Lauren away.

"I now know why you didn't mention buying knickers," Lauren giggled.

"Because I didn't get any," Briony whispered back.

Lauren raised her right eyebrow. "Briony Jane Greene, you're a right little minx. And I like it very much."

They made short work of the hot chocolates. Squirty cream moustaches caused much hilarity between them, and Briony separated all her marshmallows, giving Lauren the pink ones while keeping the white ones for herself.

"I'm not sure if I fancy having lunch here now," Briony said, looking at Lauren for guidance.

"I know, babe. I don't fancy some dry sandwich, either. I'd like something a little fresher. You know what I mean? Something that hasn't been stuck in a fridge for a week or so, something more appetising and moister." Lauren raised her eyebrows in a provocative manner, which sent a tingle through Briony.

"I love this playful thing we have going. It feels so normal, but it's also new and exciting." Briony blushed as she spoke, enclosing Lauren's hands inside her own. "I feel so lucky and grateful that we have found ourselves here. Maybe this was always meant to happen."

In response, Lauren pulled her hands from Briony's and placed them on her thighs, slowly raising her body up against her, like a cobra growing tall. She kissed her neck and Briony fell back against the cushioned wall. Lauren cupped her face and passionately kissed her. A tall, thin man stood up, watching them for a few seconds before clearing his throat to let his presence be known. They carried on, oblivious.

The man cleared his throat again, this time upping his volume, and the girls quickly pulled apart. Briony grabbed hold of the table to pull herself up into a seated position, accidentally sending the two mugs and saucers crashing to the floor. Chips of porcelain scattered far and wide across the room and Briony's new shirt was splashed with the leftovers that had congregated at the bottom of the mugs. Lauren giggled and wiped the smudged lipstick around Briony's lips, quickly grabbing the mirror from her bag so she could clear herself up, too. Briony looked over at the young baristas behind the counter, who, along with the shop's other customers, were looking over to see where the commotion was coming from. Feeling her cheeks on fire, Briony pushed Lauren aside. "You're reapplying your lipstick, really? Come on, we've got to clean this up. Aren't you embarrassed?"

Lauren sat up tall and pushed her shoulders back. "Relax, babe, it was just an accident."

Briony envied Lauren's cool response to situations, but she couldn't just ignore it. "Sorry . . . the table," she called over to the baristas, before realising from the look on their faces that they had seen the whole thing and that she and Lauren were probably going to be their story of the day. Come to think of it, the customers all had something to write home about, too. Her face still scarlet, she went to stand up and instantly spotted a familiar face. "Keith? How long have you been there?"

"I saw the whole thing, Briony," he replied, sounding most pleased with himself.

"Oh, do yourself a favour, we were . . ." She realised there was no point trying to make an excuse for what she and Lauren were doing before the crash. "Look, just help me pick up the broken bits, please."

The three of them crouched down on the floor, which gave Briony time to reflect on Keith's words. "Exactly how long were you standing there for?" she asked, narrowing her eyes, "and why aren't you at work?"

Briony could see from Keith's expression that he had most likely been watching them for longer than necessary.

"There's only one lady for me, Briony," he replied, as if watching them together hadn't had any impact at all. "And I had some holiday time to take. I guess I was inspired by my cushy assistant landing the rest of the week off."

Keith was good at thinking on his feet, and Briony took his pop at her on the chin.

"It's a shame you're only interested in one woman," Lauren said, winking at Keith. "There was just enough room for you to have squeezed in next to me."

He fidgeted uncomfortably and Briony elbowed Lauren in the ribs.

"Ouch!"

"No thanks, Lauren. I saw how your last attempt at a threesome panned out."

He had played his ace and a satisfied grin spread across his face. Meanwhile, a young barista had arrived with a stand-up dustpan and brush, just in time to hear the word "threesome". The boy, who couldn't have been older than seventeen, smirked as he swept up the mess on the floor. Briony smiled at him, but he couldn't meet her eye.

"Why don't we go and see Flo and have a drink and something to eat?" Briony suggested.

"That's a fab idea," said Lauren. "The food is always so hot." She looked Briony up and down and licked her lips. Both women giggled while Keith looked at them expectantly, clearly hoping for an invitation.

"Do you have your car?" Lauren asked, thinking that if he was going to be coming along, they'd at least make use of him.

"If I'd known I was going to be driving you two around, I would have brought my Beamer," Keith boasted, "but as I only needed to pop to Debenhams and pick up some Liz Earl cleanser, I opted for my wife's pink Fiat. It's good for zipping around. So, in answer to your question, yes, I have a car."

"Keith, you never cease to surprise me," Lauren teased. "Liz Earl cleanser and a pink car? People will start to talk."

"Please will you drive us to the Red Lion in your pink ladies' wagon, and if you haven't any other plans, you're more than welcome to join us," said Briony through gritted teeth.

Briony was just as reluctant to share her date with Keith, but she figured it was the right thing to do considering he could give them a lift to the pub.

When they arrived at The Red Lion, they were immediately greeted by its familiar and welcoming smell, a mixture of wood and beer.

Briony breathed in deep. "Oh, I do love this place," she said.

She spun around with her arms wide before stopping and looking for Flo, who didn't appear to be present. She wasn't worried, as she knew she wouldn't be far away. She skipped down the steps to the bottom bar and leaned against the mahogany. "Hi Emma, how's things? Please can we have a bottle of your house rose and three cheese and bacon baguettes with a bowl of chips."

Briony didn't even consider asking what the other two wanted; it was a done deal. She, Lauren and Natalie always had the same when they went to the pub together, and Keith would have to eat what he was given.

"All good, thanks," replied Emma, who had worked at the pub since graduating from uni. "Are you going to be sitting at your usual table?" she asked. She typed their order onto the touchscreen till. "Do you want a tab? Is it going to be an all-dayer?"

Briony squeezed the muscles in her face and looked sweetly at Emma, implying they would probably end up being there for the foreseeable.

"OK, lucky it's karaoke tonight, then!"

"Oh, Emma, you do know how to tease a girl. Lauren and I have just had a boozy night in London. We could have gone home after the baguettes, but now . . . Yeah, I think you'd better set up a tab."

Not everyone was so excited by the news.

"I can't," said Keith. "I've two boys to bath and put to bed *and* a wife to please." He winked and Lauren screwed up her face at the thought of Keith having a boner, but at least they weren't going to have him with them for the entirety of their date.

"Oh, Keith, that image is enough to turn even our Emma here gay," Lauren said.

Emma laughed. "Keith, ignore Lauren, you're gorgeous." She turned to the girls. "He's got two kids, so he's definitely done it twice, hasn't he!"

Lauren loved Emma's bants, which was evidence of the years she'd spent behind the bar gassing to punters.

"I'll have you know we have a very active sex life," Keith carried on, clearly oblivious of when was a good time to call it quits.

Lauren put two fingers in her mouth and pretended to be sick, while Briony placed her hand on Keith's shoulder. "Sure you do, babe."

She picked up the bottle of rose and coaxed Keith over to their booth. Lauren picked up the glasses and followed them across the dance floor and over to the corner.

Briony poured three extra-large glasses and swigged the remaining liquid straight from the bottle. "Laur, babe," she said. "I don't know about you, but I'm going to feel like pure shit at Mr Schwartzberg's tomorrow night."

"Oh, I'd forgotten all about that. You aren't *really* thinking of going, are you?" asked Lauren.

It took just seconds for Briony to realise her mistake. Keith smiled and rubbed his hands together, instantly picking up on the change in atmosphere and pleased that his sex life was no longer under the spotlight.

Briony raised her eyes at him, silently asking him to move out of the booth so that she could switch in next to Lauren. She rubbed Lauren's forearm as she climbed over. "I . . . um . . . . I said yes to Mr S because I was hungover and all a-fluster after what we'd done with Mani. What was I supposed to do?"

"Tell him we couldn't make it. In all honesty, I can't believe you are even considering going. Do you want to see Mani again?"

Briony could see that Lauren was pissed off with her. It was only yesterday that she was wearing the jealous badge, after Grace's flirtatious behaviour, but now it seemed it had been handed over. She kissed Lauren on the cheek, but Lauren made it clear she was waiting for a proper explanation.

"Ellis," she began.

Keith's ears immediately pricked up, and Briony knew it

149

would annoy him, because even he didn't call the boss by his Christian name.

"Ellis invited us round to his mansion after telling me I'd always have a job at Schwartzberg Ltd."

She was speaking to Lauren but looking at Keith. She'd initiated the *He Likes Me Better Than You* game, just like they were brother and sister. Keith shifted uncomfortably and reached for his phone. Briony assumed she'd won and transferred her full attention back to Lauren. "Of course I don't want to see Mani," she said. "I'm feeling a little cornered here, though, and I don't want to snub Mr Schwartzberg's generosity. Barbie's still here, too."

"You know how much I love Barbie, and I would probably consider going just to see her, but Mani? What are we supposed to do? Make small talk and then maybe after a few drinks swap notes about your performance in bed? You've just handed in your resignation; you don't owe them any of your personal time. Just work your notice and get out of there."

"Ouch! Please don't get shitty with me, and on today of all days – our first date." Briony's eyes glistened as she spoke. "As always, though, you're right. I don't owe them anything, and I'll figure out a way to get out of it. I just hadn't thought it over properly."

Lauren purred as if she were a Siamese cat, her tail held high. "You always try to make everyone else happy," she said. "Try and think about yourself more often. I'm looking forward to the next time I can make you happy."

"Laur, look, I'm with you. I don't care about Mani. He made a mistake, but that's what brought us together, so in the end we won."

"Ah, smart move," said Lauren, and Briony released the breath she hadn't realised she'd been holding. "Switching the perspective. Very clever, babe. And yeah, in the grand scheme of things, he has paid the price, but . . ." she paused for

150

dramatic effect ". . . he hasn't *actually* paid the price yet, has he?"

Keith watched on as the ball pinged from one side of the court to the other. He'd learned so much more about Briony's relationship with the Schwartzberg men, and it hurt that he wasn't the top dog he'd pictured himself as.

"Do we have to do this here?" Briony pleaded. She'd forgotten that Keith was listening to every word.

"Yes, yes we do. Let's not leave this conversation unfinished. Do you want to work at Schwartzberg Finance Ltd with Mani or not?"

The question was short and sharp and Briony knew she needed to provide an answer. She leaned forward, and this time it was her who cupped Lauren's face and kissed her gently on the lips. "No, I don't want to work with him. I've resigned, haven't I." Lauren nodded. "I just found it confusing when Mr S said all those nice things after we fly-trapped Mani." Lauren smirked at the memory. "He told me I'll always have a job at the company, and what if I need to take him up on that? The awkwardness with Mani would have faded over time, but now that money's been brought into the equation it's all got a bit messy. Could it look like Mani was paying for our services?"

"Oh, come on," said Lauren, pulling away. "You're giving me whiplash here. You won't ever need to work there again. I've already told you that I have savings. Besides, Mani is good for the money, and it won't even make a dent in his wealth. In my mind, he most certainly hasn't paid for our services, and I can't believe you'd even suggest it."

Briony looked guiltily at Lauren, aware that the words had come out of her mouth without a filter. She hadn't really meant to say them.

"You have no job because you don't want to work with Mani due to what he did. Put simply, he needs to pay both emotionally and physically, with his cash. So far, he's halfway to redemption."

Briony agreed with everything that Lauren was saying in principle, but it still didn't feel right. "I'm sorry," she said. "I didn't mean the paying for our services thing. You know me, I don't think before I speak. I love you and I love how much love you show me, but I can't expect Mani to give me a year's wage just to keep me sweet. Mr Schwartzberg has unknowingly made an even bigger gesture and taken the heat off his son by offering me forever employment with the company."

Lauren was considering Briony's defence just as Emma trotted over from the kitchen with a clay pot filled with knives and forks wrapped in pairs inside napkins. She instantly picked up on the atmosphere. "Is everything OK?" she asked.

Keith took the lead. "Don't worry about it, Emma. The lovers are having a tiff concerning the threesome they had at work."

"Keith!!!" responded Briony and Lauren in unison. He crossed his legs in the feminine fashion he had made his own and looked extremely pleased with himself.

"Tell me about it," said Emma, completely unfazed. "Three is certainly a crowd."

Neither Briony, Lauren nor Keith knew whether Emma was talking from experience or not, but they all watched her saunter back through the kitchen swing doors with open mouths.

"Well, I'll be blowed," Keith laughed. "Who'd have thought it, Emma in a threesome."

He obviously thought he was in the clear, and that his major revelation about Briony and Lauren had been diluted by Emma's equally shocking admission. He couldn't have been more wrong. Lauren pushed herself up and out of the booth, before going over to Keith and towering above him with her hands on her hips. "You will get yourself fucking blown sitting there like that, you tourist straight man. You've sat here and listened to everything Briony and I have said to each other, even when it certainly didn't include you. You are a rude little man." With that, she pushed his chest and he rolled off the back of his stool and into a heap on the floor.

Briony didn't even laugh; she just watched Lauren sashay up the pub towards the ladies'. She hoped she'd turn around and look at her, but she simply pulled open the door and strode in. "You deserved that!" she said to Keith angrily. "Who do you think you are sharing details about our private life, which, might I add, you know nothing about? Lauren might appear all confident and Miss Entertainer, because that's her job, but she's very private, and I don't think she'll forgive you for what you've just said. You are very rude. Why did you sit and watch us fight? You should have walked away."

Keith brushed down his suit and pulled the stool back to the table. His face may have been red, but he didn't seem to be embarrassed. "It was just a joke," he protested. "And why am I the rude one? You two started having pops at each other as soon as we sat down at the table together. Why should I be the one to leave? You should have taken it outside."

"Oh, bugger off," Briony said. She couldn't think how else to respond quickly enough, and maybe Keith was right, maybe they should have gone elsewhere to have their discussion.

"What did Lauren mean when she called me a 'tourist straight man'?" Keith pressed on. "I've got a wife and two kids."

"Oh, change the record, Keith, we've heard it all before. Your personal life and sexual preferences are none of our business, and I apologise for Lauren's accusation, but come on, you did deserve it."

Briony watched Lauren make her way back to their table. She'd reapplied her lipstick and lip gloss, and the way she walked showed she still had fire blazing inside her. As she sidled in next to her, Briony had never felt more attracted to her. Then Emma returned with a big tray carrying the food they'd ordered; three bacon and cheese baguettes and a bowl of chips. She put them down, but still no one spoke.

"Oh, sorry, Emma, thanks so much, it all looks delicious." Briony broke the silence. Lauren repeated the platitude and Briony sighed, thankful to hear her speaking in her normal, less angry voice.

"Would you like any sauces?"

"Yes, please, ketchup and mayo would be fab." Lauren winked at Emma, a silent thank you for being so gracious over Keith's indiscretion.

Briony put her hand on Lauren's knee and turned to face her. "Let me start. Again, I'm really sorry. Like I said a minute ago, I don't think before I speak. I will cancel tomorrow with Mr S. I mean, I fancy Mani about as much as I fancy Keith." Lauren's lips crept upwards and Briony could see she was softening. "And Keith, I'm sorry we didn't move away when we were having a *discussion* that didn't include you."

"It's OK," Keith replied. "And I'm sorry, Lauren. What I said to Emma was below the belt."

"What was that, Keith? Below the belt or blow the belt?" She smirked and he looked all flustered. Briony squeezed her leg just hard enough for her to cry out an "Ow!" She looked at Briony, who shook her head at her. "OK, it's out of my system now, Keith. I'm sorry, too, and I won't mention you getting blown again."

Somehow, that made them all laugh. The food smelled excellent, so they turned their attention to their plates.

Lauren watched Keith tear into his baguette and whispered to Briony, "Look at how wide that man can open his mouth." She didn't need to say anymore; Briony had to hold her laugh in, because she knew just what was being implied. She elbowed Lauren in the ribs.

Despite their recent disagreement, the women looked at peace with one another. They giggled, touched each other and regularly found themselves staring into each other's eyes.

"Miss Briony Jane Greene," Lauren announced, intentionally excluding Keith from the conversation. Briony wasn't sure where Lauren was going but believed there could be a little role-play involved, as she'd used her full name.

Lauren raised her right hand. "Do you swear to tell the truth, the whole truth, and nothing but the truth?"

Briony smiled and raised her matching hand. "I do, your honour."

"You have pleaded not guilty to the charge of *wanting* to work alongside Emmanuel Schwartzberg. Is this correct?" Lauren fluttered her long lashes at Briony, who took the show as her version of an apology.

"I plead not guilty, your honour."

Briony and Keith looked on as Lauren held her audience. "The court finds the defendant . . ."

She looked from Briony to Keith and back again. Briony was ninety-nine per cent sure she was in the clear, but there was still a little niggle of doubt.

"Not guilty."

"Thank fuck for that!" Briony breathed a sigh of relief. "You had me going a bit there, babe."

Lauren put on her innocent face.

"Your honour, I'm here to confess," said Keith, taking the two women by surprise.

"You're what?" Briony asked, concerned that Keith's tone was no longer playful. Instead, he looked rather guilty. "What are you confessing to?"

"That I'm guilty of inviting to the pub the three people who have just walked through the door."

Briony followed his gaze to their large American boss, his son and his petite lady friend. They had clearly never set foot in the place before, as they were making their way to the top bar, which the regulars never used.

"What the fuck, Keith? When did you do that? More to the point, why?"

Keith shrugged. "When you two were mid-tiff. I felt like a spare prick at a wedding, so I thought I'd invite some company. Plus, they were the centre of your discussion anyway. Oh, and poor Mani, who you have completely witch-hunted, already has underlying problems with women, as his mum walked out on him and Mr Schwartzberg when he was just a kid." He looked triumphant.

"You sad little man," said Lauren darkly. "What's your problem with Briony and me?" She rested her elbows on the table and leaned closer to his face.

Briony watched Keith's confidence dissolve and his shoulders droop. "Nothing, Lauren. I . . . I have no problem with the two of you."

No one at the table was convinced by his poor answer. Lauren raised her bum off her chair and leaned even further across the table. "Listen, little man, do not play with me. I am comfortable in my skin, and though I take personal responsibility for letting myself get irritated by your pathetic attempts to make a fool out of me, by tomorrow it won't be bothering me one bit. What you are doing is fuelled by an unhappiness in yourself, and the only person you are hurting is you. Jealousy is a dangerous emotion, so be careful." Lauren held Keith's gaze. Briony rubbed her back, inviting her to retreat.

All the blood had drained from Keith's face. He slowly stood up and pressed the creases out of his trousers. "Right, well, I'm, uh, I'd better go and see Mr Schwartzberg." He spun his body around before his head, leaving Briony wondering whether he had dance experience.

Lauren turned to Briony, stroked her jaw and tucked her loose hair behind her ears. "What a first date, huh?"

Briony relaxed and the two girls laughed.

"That man needs some help," Briony announced. Reading between the lines, she figured that Lauren was onto something regarding his suppressed sexuality. "I think he has a big secret that needs some acceptance therapy. You sure were mad, though."

Lauren nodded. "I know, wasn't I?" She flashed her stunning smile. "I wasn't prepared for getting thrown under the bus with Emma, and now having Mani here." They both looked towards the top bar, but they couldn't see the party. They figured they must have moved to the other side of the room. "I wasn't ready, and you know me, fail to prepare—"

"Prepare to fail!" Briony finished off Lauren's favourite saying. "I can't believe Mani has turned up," she added.

"I guess if his dad said we'd invited him to the pub, he could hardly say no. Or maybe Keith didn't even mention we were here. Don't you worry your pretty little head about him. Let's just roll with it."

"Shall we go to them?" Briony asked cautiously.

"Yes, drink up." She handed Briony her almost-finished glass of rose. "Keith will have gone."

"What? Did you see him leave?"

Lauren shook her head. "No, no, I just have a feeling that he won't want to see me again. He would have made up a last-minute excuse about how he needs to get home." Briony nodded. "Right, are you ready? One dickhead down, one to go."

Briony laughed, and they walked up the pub together hand in hand, as if they'd always done it.

Chapter Eighteen

Natalie bustled through the door after Bethany and Milo carrying coats, bags, lunchboxes, bottles, keys and everything else that had been left in the car. She had a raging headache and felt consumed by lethargy. She hadn't been to a spin class in a week and put it down to a combination of not enough exercise and too much alcohol.

Martin's car wasn't on the drive, and she figured that it was for the best that he was out. She assumed he'd gone to the office and went over their last conversation. Why had she dropped the divorce bomb? Was that really what she wanted?

She knew she was confused and needed time to process what she'd said, but with tea to cook followed by getting two children under eight bathed and ready for bed, she wouldn't have any time to herself for at least the next four hours. She imagined the taste of the strong G&T she was going to pour herself and the sound of the ice cubes rattling against the side of her glass.

"Mummy, can we go outside and play?" asked Bethany, looking as adorable as ever as she skipped into the kitchen in her lilac gingham school dress.

"Yes, the back door key is in the drawer," said Natalie. She smiled as she thought how everyone in the house knew which was 'the drawer'. She watched Bethany spin around, her dress floating around her.

"Oh, look, Daddy's left a mess." Bethany pointed to the kitchen table, which was out of Natalie's sight as she hung the coats on the banister. She assumed that Martin had left out a mass of paperwork, which he knew full well would annoy her as she'd have to tidy it all away before dinner. She walked towards the kitchen, where she was hit by the distinct aroma of cannabis. Instead of paperwork, a heavy, spiky glass ashtray straight from the '80s was overflowing with cigarette butts, ash and what looked like the remnants of a couple of joints. Natalie sighed, figuring that Dylan must have popped by for a smoke. The window next to the table was wide open, causing ash to blow everywhere. Martin had clearly tried to air out the room but had forgotten to clear up after himself. Natalie had only left him alone for two hours. After dropping the D-word, she'd taken herself off to the Starbucks drive-thru and sat with a coffee in the car park until it was time to pick the kids up from school. She reached into the back pocket of her jeans, pulled out her phone and phoned her husband. It rang and rang until an automated female voice told her to leave a message. She wasn't overly concerned. The sight of two smoked joints nearly always meant Dylan was involved.

She noticed a small piece of paper folded up and tucked under the ashtray. Unfurling it, she was slightly puzzled by what she read.

Southampton Central – Waterloo 15:00.

It looked like something Martin had written down whilst on the phone, and she put it back on the table without giving it any further thought.

"Mum, Milo's eating dandelions," Bethany called from the garden, the disgust clear in her voice. Natalie sighed and tried to convince herself that her son would be OK eating flowers, but then she pictured how many cats had pissed on them and went marching to the back door. Bethany was standing at the top of the garden, pointing to a patch of grass behind the garage.

"Milo!" Natalie called.

Her son came running down the garden in his uniform of grey shorts and a white t-shirt, with the preschool's logo printed in purple on the left-hand side. His knees were green from kneeling in the grass. He looked up at his mum with his deep brown Bambi eyes, which got her every time. His lips had what looked like the remnants of Dijon mustard dusted all over them.

"Open your mouth."

In response to the order, Milo managed a cheeky grin while keeping his lips pressed shut.

"Milo, open your mouth, please." Natalie had put on her stern 'mum voice'. This time he shook his head and turned around to face the garden.

Natalie didn't want to, but whenever Milo was behaving like this, in the belief he was being funny, she had to act serious and prompt him to make the right decision. "You know our cats, Ant and Dec?" He nodded, uninterested, still facing the garden rather than his mum. "Well, they like to pee on dandelions. So, if you're eating dandelions, you're also eating your cats' wee. Does it taste nice?"

He spun around, exactly as Natalie had planned. "Do they really pee on dandelions, Mummy?"

"Milo's eaten cat wee, Milo's eaten cat wee," Bethany teased. On cue, the boy started to cry. Natalie closed her eyes and took a deep breath, knowing that the rest of the evening was unlikely to improve. Her tired three-year-old was going to be whiny right up until he fell asleep, and Bethany would no doubt continue to wind him up.

"Right, that's enough!" said Natalie. "Bethany, you're not helping here."

Fully aware of what she was doing, Bethany ran back to the house. Natalie scooped Milo up and took him to the sink, where she washed out his mouth with a piece of wet kitchen roll, gave him his bottle of juice and sat him down in the living room with *Fireman Sam* on the TV. She then turned on the oven, ready to heat up some pizza and chips for tea, and grabbed some Dettol spray, a wet J-cloth and an empty carrier bag to clear up the mess on the table. She tipped the remnants of the ashtray into the bag before scooping the rest of the ash into her hand and shaking it out in the bag, too. She felt an emptiness inside as she worked, accepting that this was the beginning of her new life without her husband. She wished him well and did love him, but she wasn't *in love* anymore. She didn't want him sexually and took the constant point scoring they had recently engaged in as proof they weren't good for each other anymore. As long as they were amicable for the children, she figured that everyone would one day be happy again. She peeled off the wrapper from the Margherita pizza and sprinkled some McCain oven fries onto a baking tray, putting them both in the oven. She then opened a tin of baked beans and poured them into a measuring jug, which she covered with clingfilm before putting them into the microwave ready to heat up. She wasn't hungry enough for a full dinner herself, so she snacked on a couple of breadsticks with hummus.

She presumed Martin didn't want dinner, but there was still a little niggle of worry inside, so she tried to call him again. After a few rings, it went to the automated answer service for a second time. Natalie couldn't help feeling peeved at being ignored. After all, they were still married, and it was

161

only courteous for Martin to tell her where he was. She quickly wiped over the ashtray and, wanting it out of her sight, put it in a top cupboard where they kept their Tupperware. As she wedged it in as far out of sight as she could, she immediately felt a little lighter.

Fortunately for Natalie, the dinner, bath and bed routine went better than expected, and at 7.30 pm sharp, she waltzed into the kitchen to make herself the strong G&T she had been promising herself all evening. She then decamped to the sofa to get lost in a series on Netflix. Without Martin at home, she relished the chance to watch whatever she wanted, although in reality, he usually let her choose anyway.

The sound of the ice popping in the glass against the coolness of the tonic was like music to her ears as she lifted the glass to her lips.

Knock, knock.

"What the fuck?" Natalie said out loud. She moved to the front of the living room and looked out of the window, shocked by the sight of the instantly recognisable blue and yellow stripes that ran down the side of the police car parked outside. Obviously, the cops weren't coming to her house, so she looked across the street, to where two teenage twin boys lived. They were often getting themselves into trouble.

The knock sounded again. This time louder.

They must have the wrong house, Natalie said to herself. She took a big swig of her drink and put it down on the coffee table. She didn't like how the police made her feel guilty, even when she had nothing to be guilty about. On the way to the door, she popped into the downstairs toilet and tidied her hair in the mirror, psyching herself up for the upcoming encounter. She imagined just how much more worrying this would be if her kids were teenagers and weren't tucked up safely in bed.

By the time she finally opened the door, she had pinned a big smile on her face. The officers standing on her doorstep, a man and a woman, looked so smart in their uniforms and hats, but there was something about the look on their faces that sent fear raging through Natalie's body. It looked as if there were serious words brewing behind their closed lips, ones that Natalie really wouldn't want to hear. Her smile quickly faded as the male officer stepped forward, his face full of kindness.

"Mrs Stevenson?"

It took a few seconds for Natalie to recognise her own name.

"Uh, yes, that's me." She wasn't sure why she said those words in the tone of a surly teenager. It was as if she were back at secondary school and being questioned over whether she'd done her homework. It was weird how the sight of a uniform made her react. The policeman cleared his throat and she found herself asking, "Is it Martin?"

"Mrs Stevenson, I'm PC Joseph Bilson and this is PC Penny Appleton."

The only thing that Natalie picked up from the introduction was that the female officer's surname was the same as Nicole Appleton's from the '90s pop band *All Saints*. All she could process in her head were the words to their iconic song, *Never Ever*. She wasn't sure how, but by the time the rendition of the hit going on inside her head had ended, the officers had wiped their feet and were now in her hallway and removing their hats. PC Bilson shut the door behind them. The sound of it closing gave Natalie an overwhelming feeling of finality.

"You might want to sit down," said PC Bilson. "Do you mind if we go through?"

Natalie's lips were as dry as sandpaper as she ushered them into the living room. They waited for her to take a seat and then sat down themselves before starting to speak again.

"I'm afraid we have some awful news," began PC Bilson.

"We believe that your husband, Martin Stevenson, has been killed following an incident with a train. We are so very sorry."

He spoke softly and without taking his eyes off Natalie. She knew she should probably say something, only she couldn't speak. It was as if she were having an out-of-body experience.

"Can I get you a cup of tea?" she asked eventually. She had morphed into her mother. For every disaster, Paula would always make a cuppa, as if trying to dilute the situation. Natalie didn't wait for an answer and promptly headed for the kitchen.

"No, thank you, Mrs Stevenson, we're both fine. Please come and sit down with us."

Natalie was unaware that PC Appleton had followed her out of the living room. She jumped when she felt her warm hand on her elbow. The PC's pretty face was full of sympathy. "We're OK, Natalie. Do you mind if I call you by your first name?"

Natalie looked into PC Appleton's blue eyes and saw a sorrow that seemed to plunge deep into her stomach. It was clear now that Martin hadn't been with Dylan, and that it was all her fault. She'd made her husband take his own life. As the reality sunk in, her balance deserted her, and her legs gave way. As she lay on the floor and sobbed, her nose ran, and saliva stretched like cotton from the top to the bottom of her mouth. She couldn't understand why she was suddenly empathising with Leonardo DiCaprio's portrayal of Jordan Belfort in *The Wolf of Wall Street*, specifically the part in the movie when he's taken too many 'Lemmons' and can't move. She'd only ever watched the movie once and the last person she should be thinking of was the convicted felon, yet he was the only person on her mind. She visualised him making his way down the stairs of a hotel on his stomach, while totally sky high on drugs.

Can I move my head? she wondered, before managing to raise it off the floor. *Can I lift my chest?* She planted her hands shoulder-width apart and pushed her upper torso off the floor. She realised she wasn't Jordan Belfort and had only had a swig or two of G&T. *What was I thinking?* she thought.

She moved to sit cross-legged on the kitchen floor and felt her face, which was wet with tears.

"I know this must have come as a massive shock, and I really can't imagine how hard it is to hear such terrible news."

She recognised the male policeman's voice and looked up to see him standing in the doorway between the kitchen and the living room. He looked so kind and safe. The female PC sat next to her on the floor and put an arm around her. She was comforted by her body heat.

"Do you have anyone you can call?" asked PC Bilson. "Is there someone you can ask to come round this evening and keep you company?"

"Are you sure it's him?" Natalie asked, hoping against hope that they'd got the wrong house and the wrong name.

The officer squeezed his lips together, and although Natalie knew the answer, she prayed her gut was wrong.

"We have good reason to believe that it is Mr Stevenson, but the identity of the deceased has yet to be officially confirmed."

PC Appleton now took over the reins. "A family liaison officer has been assigned to you," she explained, "and they will be in contact with you very soon. You may be asked as the next of kin to formally identify the body, but I must warn you that in some circumstances it might not be in your best interest to do so."

Natalie appreciated the softly spoken message and read between the lines.

"If this is the case," PC Appleton continued, "we can establish the identity of the deceased a number of other ways. If you can recall any unique identifying marks belonging to

Martin, such as scars or tattoos, please inform your family liaison officer."

Natalie had a flashback of her husband's tiger tattoo and tiger pants. It wasn't so funny this time.

"It must be him," Natalie conceded. She grabbed the folded piece of paper from the dining room table. "Look, he left me a train time! I saw it when I came home, along with the ends of a couple of smoked joints."

The tears rolled silently from her eyes as she watched PC Bilson read the note and nod his head. "I would keep hold of that, to show to your appointed family liaison officers. It's their job to keep you updated on the investigation."

Natalie tensed at the word investigation. Is that how they were really describing it? Was she, in fact, the criminal? Martin may have jumped of his own accord, but was she guilty of pushing him? She shook all the darkness away.

"My best friends live close by," she told the officers. "They'll come and stay with me."

Natalie's first thought had been her mum and dad. But she had quickly ruled out calling them. Her mum would be hysterical, and her dad didn't need another excuse to hit the drink. She should call Martin's mum and dad, of course, but how would she break the news to them? Martin's body hadn't been formally identified yet, so she figured there was no reason to tell them right away. Briony and Lauren were her safe space.

The officers looked relieved that Natalie had someone to call. PC Appleton reached into the breast pocket of her jacket and pulled out her card, which she pushed into Natalie's hand. "Here are our contact details," she said. "If you have any questions, just pick up the phone and give us a call. We'll help in any way we can."

Natalie accepted the card but put it on the worktop without even looking at it. The two officers had seen this happen countless times. They knew that eventually, the next of kin would remember receiving the card and end up hunting high and low to find it. They'd heard the story from so many different people.

Natalie followed the officers into the hallway and watched them put their hats back on.

"We really are very sorry that we had to bring this news to you," said PC Appleton. "Call your friends, take care, and if there is anything we can help with, please do call us. Good night."

Natalie waved, unable to speak. The feeling of being in the wilderness consumed her, as she listened to the doors of the police car being opened and closed and the engine being switched on. She watched the reflection from the headlights through the glass panel in the front door, and then the car was gone and there was nothing but silence.

She tiptoed into the living room looking for her phone. It was on the coffee table next to her glass of G&T, which she downed in one go, wiping her mouth with the back of her hand. "What the fuck am I going to do?" she asked out loud.

The living room curtains were open, and she could see her reflection in the glass. She spoke to it as if it were a separate entity. "You don't know, do you? No, why would you? What the fuck am I supposed to tell the kids?"

For the second time in an hour, Natalie collapsed. The gut-wrenching sob that followed was uncontrollable, and she knew she was physically incapable of speaking to anyone. She was literally all on her own, and it was the loneliest she had ever felt. How was she going to survive this?

Chapter Nineteen

"Miss Greene and Miss Newland, what an absolute delight." Mr Schwartzberg's belly wobbled from the projection of his booming voice. Briony felt like her hair had been blown backwards by the force of his words.

Lauren took the lead and stepped forward with her hand out ready to shake. "Hi, Mr S, it's really great to see you, and especially here at our local, too. There's karaoke later." She raised her right eyebrow, planting the seed of the possibility of a singsong.

"Well, how about that?" He laughed and looked towards Barbie, whose smile was as radiant as ever. Lauren wrapped her arms around the petite American, squeezing her tight and breathing in her array of fragrances.

Meanwhile, Briony took her turn to shake her boss's hand. "Like Lauren just said, it's really nice to see you here."

"We have Keith to thank for that," replied Mr Schwartzberg. "He told us this is your regular bar."

Before Briony could reply, Lauren spun out of her embrace with Barbie. "Oh, where is Keith?" she asked. "He was with us one second and gone the next. I thought maybe he'd joined you."

She smiled at Briony, who admired Lauren's boldness.

"Well, here's the thing," said Mani, who until now the girls had completely ignored. "He had to leave. Apparently, there was a family emergency and he had to race home."

Lauren reached for Briony's hand and squeezed it, feeling smug over how her prediction had come true. Briony nodded back and ran her thumb across Lauren's palm. She noticed Mani watching them and the hair on the back of her neck stood on end. It took her right back to him salivating over their performance in the work kitchen. Now he looked her directly in the eye. He seemed softer and even smiled. She took it as a silent signal that things were going to be OK.

"I hope you don't mind Keith messaging us and inviting us over?" he asked.

"We'd love you to join us," Lauren quickly responded, pulling in Briony so that their bodies were tight together. It seemed she wasn't feeling the same level of anxiety regarding Mani, but she did pick up on Briony's unease. "Don't worry, we've got this," she whispered into her ear. "And I've got you."

Briony's nerves settled. Lauren had her back, and they would face whatever was going to happen together. She felt so lucky to have complete trust in the person she loved.

Briony and Lauren took their guests down to the booth at the bottom of the bar and introduced them to the best seats in the house. They watched DJ Steve setting up the karaoke system on the little stage where they had sung *I Know Him So Well* earlier in the week. It already felt like a lifetime ago.

"So, tell us, girls, what's worth eating? I'm famished." Barbie's sweet voice got the conversation going. Briony animatedly described the cheese and bacon baguette while Lauren looked across the table at Mani. Surprisingly, he didn't shift his gaze and kept his deep, caramel eyes locked on her navy blues. He was hard to read.

"Mani, how's things?" she asked, trying to control the situation with small talk.

He smiled and raised his eyebrows, as if silently asking, *Oh, so this is what we're doing?* Lauren despised his arrogance.

"Well, pops has been teaching me about business and it's going well. I'm getting my head around it. Would you like a drink?"

Lauren was confused. Had she read him wrong? He wasn't so arrogant after all. Maybe he'd learned his lesson.

"Yes, can we have a bottle of the house rose? We've already got glasses."

"Pops, Barbie, do you want a drink?" Mani asked, as he stood up to go to the bar.

"Emmanuel, let me come and help you," said Mr Schwartzberg. "I'm going to order some food for Barbie and me."

As the men left, Barbie turned to Briony and Lauren. "Right, girls, gather round. I think we need to talk."

"What's up?" asked Lauren, as she and Briony took a seat either side of her. Why was Barbie suddenly being so serious?

"OK, so Keith has told Ellis that the two of you seduced Mani at work and are holding him to ransom for a year's salary."

She didn't need to wait for an answer; the truth of the matter was written all over the girls' faces.

"What were you doing?" she said. "This is serious, because Ellis sees it as sexual harassment, and he's especially concerned that Keith knows about it. Maybe if you hadn't told him, Ellis could have come to some agreement with you, Briony, but now you're in a bit of a sticky situation."

The silence at the table was palpable, as the three women turned their attention to Mani and Mr Schwartzberg at the bar.

Briony's mouth had dried up and she couldn't speak. She looked to Lauren for help.

"Thanks for the warning, you are fabulous." Barbie blushed. "OK, so did Mani tell you why we did what we did?"

"No, and girls, you have to tell me exactly what happened. I'm so intrigued."

She oozed sexiness and Lauren loved it. Meanwhile, Briony sat with her head in her hands, silently processing what she'd just heard. Lauren gave Barbie a nudge, suggesting that Briony needed some warmth. Barbie immediately picked up on the hint and put her arm around her.

"OK, so watch this video, Barbie, and tell me what you think. Is Mani the innocent party? Oh, and he got me inside that mad *Downton* room by slipping a note into my hand and asking me to meet him there. It was when everyone was singing *Mack the Knife* around the lobby piano. Do you remember?"

"He did *what?*" Barbie appeared shocked by the story. Briony nodded to confirm it was true. Then Lauren pressed play on her phone.

"I just love to go and read in that room," Barbie sighed, as she watched the footage.

"Focus," said Lauren.

Then Briony elbowed Barbie. "They're coming back!" she squealed. Just as Lauren was pushing Mani off her on the screen, she saw the men turning around at the bar.

"It's OK, darlings, I've seen what I need to see. This isn't going to be easy, but don't you worry. Ellis is certainly a fair businessman, and this evidence should, of course, cancel out any nonsense regarding sexual harassment from your end."

Lauren trusted Barbie without question, and although Briony wanted to, her stomach was churning, her head was spinning, and she could only anticipate the worst outcome.

"Now, you didn't get round to telling me what you got up

to in the kitchen," Barbie whispered, as the men approached the booth.

"But why is he being so nice to me?" Briony said under her breath. Was she being led into a trap?

Both Lauren and Barbie were too involved in their whispered conversation to notice her.

"I think you'd have loved it, Barbie." Lauren winked. "I'll tell you more later."

"I look forward to it, darling," she replied, before switching her attention to her long-time friend and his son, who was carrying the drinks. "Oh, thank you so much, Mani," she said. "I've been waiting to enjoy a glass of Pinot Grigio in an English pub my entire life."

"You're welcome, Barbie. Pops got them."

Of course he did, thought Lauren. *Mani doesn't pay for anything, ever.* And because of that, she knew he must have the money for the threesome ransom.

Briony couldn't believe how calm everyone was being. She now knew that the men were sitting on a sexual harassment accusation, but nobody was saying anything. As well as finding that unsettling, she remembered it had been Keith who'd ratted her out. What a bastard! She knew Lauren would be plotting a revenge plan to teach him a lesson. She wondered how she had managed to create so much drama in such a short space of time.

"Bri, let me top you up," said Mani. And suddenly, things were just like they'd been before she'd gotten together with Lauren. When she'd been chasing Mani, he'd called her Bri with that smooth, sexy American accent of his. No one else apart from Lauren and Natalie shortened her name, and his over familiarity had been exciting, but not anymore.

"Yes, please, Mani. Thank you, and thank you, Mr S, for the rose."

"Always a pleasure, Miss Greene," he said, raising his pint

of beer.

Seizing on this, Lauren tapped the top of it with her wine glass. "Tits," she said, before tapping the bottom. "And arse!"

It took a second for Mr Schwartzberg to comprehend what she meant and then he roared with laughter, proceeding to copy Lauren's toast with vigour and pronouncing arse with a British accent.

Considering the seriousness of the accusations against her, it was a confusing situation for Briony.

"Bri, come with me to see DJ Steve," said Lauren. "I want us to sing something different tonight. I just hope he has the song."

Briony was relieved to have an excuse to leave the booth, and she almost jumped out of her seat. Lauren reached for her hand, and they were a united force once again.

"Right, I know this is a totally fucked up situation," Lauren said. "And like you, I don't understand the game yet, but if Barbie says it's going to be OK then it will be. Barbie and I shared that kiss at Schwartzberg manor, remember. There's no way she'll let us down."

Briony's jealousy flickered inside her. She'd forgotten about that kiss, but she talked herself down because it was before she and Lauren had had their talk. "Right, OK, I'll follow your lead. What are we going to sing?"

"Hello, girls, I've already got *I Know Him* – or should I say Her – *So Well* on standby. You don't need to ask." DJ Steve looked extremely pleased at his own efficiency. The girls gazed at each other, having the exact same flashback from when they'd changed the famous line of the song.

"You know we love you, and I am very impressed with your planning," said Lauren, as DJ Steve pretended to pick an apple, breathe on it and then buff it up on his shoulder, "but we're changing our song today."

His shoulders dropped with disappointment.

"We're going to take it up to the next level and take on the real divas."

"We are?" said Briony, unsure of what Lauren was planning.

"Today, Matthew . . ." Lauren continued, leaving a pregnant pause, as if she were appearing on the '90s talent show *Stars in Their Eyes*, ". . . we are going to be Whitney and Mariah and sing *When You Believe*."

"Oh, I love that song!" Briony almost buckled with excitement, but it didn't take long for reality to set in. "It's very high, though." She creased her nose up.

"Ah, don't sweat it," said Steve. "It'll be a breeze. After all, you've got miss 'I-sing-on-cruise-ships' here to help you."

"Why, thanks for the confidence boost," Lauren chuckled, wrapping her arms around Briony. "I know you can do it," she said to her. "I wouldn't have suggested it otherwise."

Briony looked into Lauren's eyes and could see that she truly believed in her ability to sing the song. "You really think I can do it, don't you?"

"I know you can. DJ Steve, we'll be up as soon as you can get us onto the stage."

He confirmed their choice with a nod of his head and proceeded to lift one headphone to his ear and concentrate on his sound system. He pointed to the stage and then rifled around with his spare hand for two microphones, which he handed over to Lauren. "You're starting the show tonight."

Briony looked up at the clock on the wall. "Fuck!" she said. "When did it become seven o' clock?"

Aware that she was procrastinating and trying to distract herself from the pending performance, Lauren ignored Briony and handed her a microphone.

"Good evening, Red Lion. How are we doing on this fine May evening? I'm DJ Steve, and I welcome you to another Friday night karaoke."

The hubbub paused for a moment, as the punters turned to see who was speaking. But once they realised it was just the regular DJ, they returned to their conversations and his voice became white noise in the background.

"Song selection slips are scattered around the room, so just jot down your name, the tune and its number and then get it up here to me."

He took a moment to gauge his audience to see if he'd actually attracted anyone's attention, but there weren't any obvious candidates. He was aware though that the night was young and that intoxication levels were currently low.

"So, we're going to kick it all off tonight with some familiar faces and the voices of Briony and Lauren!" At this point, some of the regulars did look across to the stage. "They're taking on a different number tonight. So, girls, the stage is yours."

Lauren didn't need to be told twice; singing live to an audience was what she did for a living. Well, it had been until recently. Briony was more hesitant, so Lauren took her hand and pulled her to the centre of the mini stage, which was only a foot off the floor.

Briony breathed a silent sigh of relief when Lauren started to sing Whitney's part, but on second thoughts, she realised that meant she was Mariah. As she silently panicked, Lauren's crystal-clear voice filled the room as she gently sang the first couple of lines of the song, building a passionate and dramatic atmosphere. The bar staff stopped working while the patrons held their breath.

Briony looked into Lauren's bright eyes; it was clear to her and everyone watching that she was really enjoying her performance. Briony's stomach was eating itself with nerves, her palms were sweaty, and her mic was slipping in her hand; it was getting closer to her part. The music dropped a bit lower, and she knew it was her turn.

Lauren squeezed her free hand. "Oh-oh-oh, mm mm, yeah," she began.

Lauren carried on into Mariah's part without taking her eyes off Briony, encouraging her to join in. Briony took a deep breath and raised the mic to her mouth just in time to begin singing her lyrics. Lauren, sensing that she just needed to get her out of the starting block, carried on into the second verse with her. She knew full well that nerves dissolved once you really got into it.

Briony didn't know the song off by heart, so she read the neon blue words trailing across the TV screen and sang the verse with Lauren. Before long, she was singing all by herself, unaware that Lauren had taken a backseat. Her perfect timing and tone brought tears to Lauren's eyes, and she wiped them carefully, so as not to smudge her mascara. Then she brought her spare hand to the mic and clapped against it, encouraging the pub to support Briony. As they applauded, Briony looked from Lauren to her audience, clearly enjoying the recognition. Her growing confidence was clear to see as she built up to the chorus, which the girls sang together, turning back to face each other and singing as if no one was watching. The entire pub was in awe of the powerful performance coming from the mini stage and erupted into applause once it had finished. Lauren raised Briony's hand and then brought it down again, leading her into a joint bow. Briony noticed the tears in her eyes, and her heart almost burst as she threw her arms around her neck. Lauren accepted the hug and squeezed her tight, but with an eye on the crowd. She could read an audience like a book and smiled in their direction. "For those of you who were here last week, this is the end of our performance. No extras." She winked, aware that some punters were probably hoping they would make out on the stage again. Briony laughed knowingly.

Barbie resembled Goldie Hawn as she strutted across the

dance floor towards the girls as they stepped down from the stage. "That was amazing," she said. "You are both so blessed to have such amazing singing voices. I can't even sing Happy Birthday in tune."

"Barbie, you are the stunning cake at the party that everyone is mesmerised by. We're just the entertainment," Lauren flirted.

"Lauren's right, everyone wants a piece of you," Briony added.

Barbie fanned away the compliments.

"Has Mr S said anything more about Mani?" asked Briony, immediately bringing them down from the high they were all on.

Lauren rolled her eyes at her.

"Ah, don't be like that, I'd just prefer the cards to be on the table, you know, so I don't have to tiptoe around worrying I'll say the wrong thing."

"Try not to fret, doll," said Barbie. "It'll all come good in the end." Lauren nodded in agreement. "In the meantime, let me get you both a cocktail. Hopefully, that'll help put things to the back of your mind."

"Thank you, Barbie, maybe that'll work. There's certainly no harm in trying." Briony raised her arms, her palms facing up, and tried to relax. Everyone else seemed chilled, so why shouldn't she be? "I'd love a cosmopolitan."

"Of course, darling, and I'm guessing the same for you, Lauren?"

"Yes, please!"

"I'm just going to pop to the ladies'," said Briony, as they all headed to the bar. "All those nerves from singing."

"Too much info!" Lauren laughed, as Briony disappeared to the bottom of the bar, where the nearest toilets were located. She walked down the long corridor towards them, which was also the way to the cellar. Already, she was reminiscing about what had taken place down there with Lauren. Her heart was still as full now as it was then. Maybe even more so. She was still smiling as she reapplied her lipstick, tidied up some smudged mascara and her hair and exited ready for a sweet cosmopolitan with her friends.

"Bri, I think we need to talk."

She stopped dead in her tracks. The smooth American voice coming from behind made her shudder, as if someone was walking over her grave.

An extremely slow ten seconds passed before she turned to see Mani casually leaning against the wall. At that moment, she so wanted to feel Lauren's hands slide around her waist, and to be fuelled by her strength, but she was all alone.

"Did you follow me? What do you want?"

"Yeah, I did. I wanted to chat to you on your own, without Lauren. Look, it's all got a bit fucked up here, but can't we just be cool? We had awesome sex in the kitchen, then you came to Dad's and Lauren set me up, and—"

"Stop right there. Lauren didn't set you up. You invited her to your father's *Downton Abbey* room and asked her if we'd have a threesome with you. She didn't make you do that."

He appeared to be thinking over her words. "But look at the two of you!" he eventually proffered. "I was only enquiring, just like any red-blooded man who had two beautiful women at his house – one with whom he'd already had wild sex – would."

Briony couldn't help but feel a little bit sorry for him. His big act had failed, and she was now the one with all the power.

"Yeah, OK, thanks, but don't you get it? That's not OK. I'm your employee, and we would have had to work together knowing that you had asked my best friend to have a threesome. It's not cool."

Mani ran his hand through his hair and stepped closer to Briony. She could smell his sexy aftershave and was starting to feel most uncomfortable. Wasn't Lauren wondering where she was?

"I have a thing, which I'm having therapy for."

Briony put her hand up to stop him coming any closer to her or revealing any more. She looked into his eyes but couldn't work out if it was the drink talking or whether he really did feel compelled to open up to her.

"My mom disappeared when I was a kid. I never knew why, and I haven't seen her since. I'm having to learn that not all women are like my mom. When I start to have feelings for someone, I end up making dick moves because I don't know how to behave."

"Whoa, there!" She looked into his puppy dog eyes and could see that he was really trying. Maybe it had been a bit mean of her and Lauren to tease him in the kitchen. She remembered one of the quotes that was forever popping up on her Facebook page: *Be kind, for everyone you meet is fighting a battle you know nothing about.*

"Oh God, Mani, I had no idea. I'm really sorry about your mum and I apologise for the way Lauren and I treated you."

He stepped even closer, and Briony could feel the heat of his body. "I don't want to sound like a needy douchebag, but thanks, I really appreciate it."

They laughed a little and some of the tension between them dissipated.

"You know that Keith told Dad, though?"

"Yeah. Barbie informed us earlier. She said Mr S wants to do me for sexual harassment."

"Ah, no, don't worry about that. I'll smooth things over with Dad. I just really wanted to talk to you without Lauren. You're different when you're with her."

"No, I am not! You don't know Lauren like I do, and I'm no different now than when we're together."

Mani stepped back and threw his hands up in surrender.

"OK, I'm sorry. I guess I meant that I couldn't have had this conversation with you if she'd been here. Don't bite my head off."

Briony didn't want to admit it, but she silently agreed that three would have been a crowd in this conversation. She loved Lauren and she loved how she always made her feel safe and protected, but Mani wasn't exactly being a dick right now and she thought she'd handled the whole thing pretty well on her own. She smiled at him. He wasn't a bad guy, and evidently, he had his own issues to deal with, which he'd been open enough to discuss with her. He stretched out his arms, inviting her for a hug, and she saw no harm in returning the gesture. At that moment, and completely out of the blue, he pulled his hands up and cupped her face, before ploughing his tongue into her mouth.

"Briony! What are you doing?" Lauren's pained voice called from behind them.

With two hands on his pecs, Briony pushed Mani off with all her might, before vigorously wiping her mouth with the back of her hand, as if he'd coated her lips with paint. While she scrubbed her mouth, she missed Mani pulling a smug, pleased-with-himself face at Lauren, as he pushed past them towards the bar.

Briony turned to look at Lauren and her heart fell to the pit of her stomach. The dazzling lights that always shone from her soul were suddenly missing. Her shoulders had caved forwards, her head was low and Briony could see the sparkle of tears forming behind her eyes. She tried to envelop her in her arms but was promptly pushed away.

"Please, Laur, he did that on purpose."

"You didn't stop him, though."

"What do you mean? He literally stuck his tongue into my mouth as you arrived. I hadn't even processed what he was doing."

Tears fell down Lauren's cheeks. "After I just sang that beautiful song with you. After everything we've been through over the last few days. You're just another straight girl. I'll never learn!"

Briony was shocked by the utter devastation pouring out of Lauren. She shook her head. "No, don't do that. I'm nothing like any of your straight-girl conquests. I love you. I love *you!*" She held Lauren's face and leaned forward, so that their foreheads were touching.

Lauren shook her off again. "I don't know, Bri. You're fucking gorgeous and this is probably going to happen a lot, and then there'll be that one guy."

Briony grabbed Lauren's hand. "No, stop this." She pulled her down the now familiar corridor and the staircase to the cellar, where she sat her on an empty barrel and pulled up another, so that they could sit facing each other, their knees touching. "A bit familiar, huh?" Briony was playing the cute card, hoping to bring Lauren back to the point when they'd admitted their true feelings for each other, in the exact same place as they were now.

"Oh God, I love you so much, Bri, and to see you kissing Mani actually broke my heart." The pain was written all over her face.

"But I didn't kiss him! I didn't! He stuck his tongue in my mouth and I pushed him off."

"Yeah, but you only did that because I called out your name."

"No, no, it wasn't like that at all. Do you really think I want to kiss him? Especially, like you said, after we sang that beautiful song together."

Briony felt like she was a trapped tiger trying to claw her way out of the four walls surrounding her, yet she knew she hadn't done anything wrong. "I don't want to kiss him. I only want to kiss you."

She leaned forward and awkwardly lunged towards Lauren, who turned her head. "Nah, thanks, you've got him all over your lips, and I don't want to taste him."

"Well, I'll fucking wash him off, then."

Lauren watched Briony aggressively push the barrel backwards and search for something to clean her lips with. They were in a pub cellar, so they were surrounded by alcohol.

"You want me to taste nice? Take your pick." Briony spun around with her arms wide open, urging Lauren to choose something.

At that moment, something clicked in Lauren. She could see the flames behind Briony's eyes, and despite the fact she was angry with her, she was also finding her aggression a turn on. "OK, sit down, let's talk."

"You don't get to dictate this," said Briony. "I feel like shit, and I can't bear to see you hurting. If the only thing I can do to prove that I didn't want his kiss is to wash him off me in front of you then I will. I don't want you tasting Mani either, so pick a drink!"

Lauren raised her eyebrows, sucked in her cheeks and looked around the cellar. "OK, so I don't think he deserves alcohol, and I do rather like the taste of J2O Orange and Passion Fruit."

"Well, that's it, then." Briony followed Lauren's gaze across the cellar to where the soft drinks were stored. "What, this one?"

Lauren nodded. Briony ripped into the cellophane around a pack of twenty-four J2Os and pulled out a glass bottle. "So, this is how much he means to me." She placed the edge of the bottle top on the side of a metal shelf and hammered the heel of her hand against it. It didn't come off. "It's so much more romantic in the movies," she sighed.

They both laughed, before Briony tried again, and again.

"Do you want a hand?"

"No, thank you." And with one last bash of her hand, the bottle top flicked off and the girls heard it clatter on the cold concrete floor. Briony swigged the drink, swished the liquid around her mouth and gargled, before spitting it into an empty bucket. She then covered the opening of the bottle with her fingers and tipped it upside down, until she had some of the drink on them, which she wiped across her lips. Surely, there was nothing of Mani left on her now.

Lauren secretly questioned why she had reacted so venomously. *Oh, man, the jealousy Briony sparks in me is something else*, she thought to herself. She wrapped her arms around Briony's waist, before reaching up to her stomach and then cupping her breasts. "Oh God, that really was the worst, and I had no control over my words or anything. I've never met that part of myself before."

Briony locked eyes with her and they paused for a moment, before passionately kissing.

"Mmmm, you taste good," Lauren managed as their mouths moved together. Despite the coolness of the cellar, things were certainly heating up.

Briony then pulled away, just enough to talk to Lauren yet still be in full contact with her. "Let's get out of here. I want to take you home."

Lauren kissed her. "Oh yes, let's go."

Holding hands, they walked up the stairs and past the toilets.

"Oh shit, we'd better go and pay Flo for the J2O." They giggled like schoolgirls as Briony's conscience got the better of her.

"Oh, she'll be fine about it, Bri, especially if we tell her why we ended up down in the cellar again."

Briony nodded. At the bar, the sound of a WhatsApp notification rang from her handbag. She took out her phone and looked at the message. "It's Nat," she said.

Chapter Twenty

Before Briony could read her friend's message, Mr Schwartzberg came barrelling down the stairs from the top bar. "Miss Greene, can I have a word, please? In private!" He lifted his eyebrows in the direction of Lauren, who thankfully wasn't looking.

"What is it this evening?" said Briony under her breath. "Why don't people want to talk to me and Lauren together?" She was unnerved by Mr Schwartzberg's serious expression. His eyes had reverted to the tiny, dark, toad-like ones she'd associated him with before getting to know him on a more personal level. "Yes, of course, Mr S." She quickly turned her attention back to Lauren. "Babe, please can you pay for the J2O and explain to Flo what happened. Mr S wants to talk to me in private."

Lauren nodded and went to find the landlady, while Mr Schwartzberg led Briony to a quiet corner. She felt timid as his giant form towered over her.

"What I'm about to touch upon is a very sensitive subject," he began. "But I have to admit that I am most disappointed in you, especially considering the generosity I have shown you of late."

Briony tucked her hair behind her ears and had a feeling she knew exactly what Mr Schwartzberg was referring to. Not one for confrontation, she let him continue.

"Emmanuel has raised a grievance of sexual harassment involving you and Lauren. I won't go into detail, but I can't have my company's name smeared with such an accusation, so we need to come to an agreement."

Briony gulped, despite the fact her mouth was bone dry. "I don't know what to say, Mr Schwartzberg, I . . ."

"So, you're admitting liability, Miss Greene?"

"Oh God, no sir, no! Well, there is an element of truth, but it's not so cut and dry. I'm not sure what Mani has told you, but I feel he may have missed out some significant details."

On balance, she was pleased with her response.

"I don't like the sound of this at all, Miss Greene, and I may have to rethink my offer of continuous employment at Schwartzberg Finance Ltd."

The blood drained from Briony's face. This was really serious, and she couldn't see a way out. Of course he was going to believe his son over her.

"I am so very grateful for your generosity, Mr Schwartzberg, and I don't want the good name of your company smeared with such an accusation, either. But I refuse to respond until I know exactly what I am being accused of."

Mr Schwartzberg nodded his approval. "I agree, Miss Greene, we need to discuss the finer details so that we can all agree on an outcome. Come to my office at nine on Monday morning and we'll deal with the issue. It would be beneficial if you could provide some concrete evidence to support your defence."

"I'll be there," Briony replied.

"OK, now, where is the restroom?"

Briony was surprised at the sudden ending to the intensity of the conversation and pointed her boss in the direction of the men's toilets.

"OK, thanks, Miss Greene. Despite the circumstances, the Red Lion has been good to us, and I agree with you that the cheese and bacon baguette is outstanding."

"Lauren, where the fuck are you?" Briony said out loud, as she watched her boss waddle off. She couldn't see her anywhere and decided to ring her. She still had her phone in her hand from when she'd noticed that Natalie had sent her a WhatsApp message. Unlocking the device, she went into the app and read Natalie's words.

Bri, I need you and Lauren. I think Martin has killed himself.

Briony felt sick to her stomach as she processed the shocking message. She immediately called Natalie, but there was no answer. Next, she clicked on Lauren's number. She answered after a couple of rings. "Where are you? Nat needs us. She thinks Martin has taken his own life."

"What? I'm just in the cellar cleaning out the J2O bucket. I'll be right there."

Seconds later, she was back in the bar with Briony, who showed her the message. "Shit," she said.

With no time for goodbyes, they ran from the pub straight to Natalie's house. They saw her through the living room window. Illuminated by the lamplight behind her, she looked as pale as a ghost. Briony waved her arms, trying to attract her attention, but though she had her eyes fixed on the front garden, she didn't appear to notice her visitors. They charged through the unlocked front door and joined her. Still, their friend didn't move.

"Nat, we're here," said Briony softly, but Natalie just continued staring out of the window. Briony looked at Lauren and they nodded at each other before moving towards her and gently pulling her into a group hug. They felt Natalie exhale. "The police haven't long been gone," she said. "They think Martin jumped in front of a train this afternoon."

Natalie's voice was unrecognisable. It was croaky, as if she had a forty-a-day cigarette habit, yet she was also so matter of fact. Both Briony and Lauren's eyes glistened with fresh tears, but Natalie could shed no more.

Briony gently tucked Natalie's hair behind her ear and cupped her face. "We love you and we're here for you," she said, before turning her attention to the practicalities of the situation. "Where are the kids? Do they know?"

Natalie shook her head. "They're upstairs asleep. Thank God they were in bed when the police arrived."

As she felt Briony and Lauren encompassing her, Natalie couldn't deny that right now, she needed the touch and comfort of her friends. Even so, the constant gnawing feeling in her stomach wasn't something anyone could soothe. "There's going to be an inquest!" she announced. "Are they going to lock me up? What's going to happen to the kids?"

"Nat, babe, why on earth would they want to put you in prison?" asked Lauren.

"Wouldn't the inquest just be to formally establish how Martin died?" said Briony. "Wait, it might not even be him, right?"

Natalie shook her head. "I know it's him, and I made him do it! If I hadn't been with Jason and then that Jake in London he wouldn't have jumped. So, I'm a murderer. They're going to put me away for life."

Lauren manoeuvred Natalie to the sofa and sat her down.

"Honey, you didn't make him jump," said Briony. "I can't

believe we're having this conversation, but if he did this, he did it by himself. You're by no means responsible."

Stubborn at the best of times, Natalie simply replied, "Yes, I am."

"Sweetheart," said Lauren, as she took a seat next to Natalie on the sofa. "You didn't murder anyone."

"I bloody did. I may not have physically pushed him, but mentally I made him jump."

"No, no, no, you didn't!" Briony pressed.

"But I did. I told him I wanted a divorce."

This was news to Briony and Lauren, and they simultaneously took a deep breath.

"And that was the last thing I said to him, ever."

Her words hung in the room like stale air.

"Right," Lauren eventually said, taking charge. "We're staying over with you tonight. Which one of these is the sofa bed?"

Natalie ignored Lauren and got to her feet. "I need a wee," she said, marching out of the living room.

Briony sat with her head in her hands. Lauren knelt in front of her and took her hand. "Look, this isn't about us or how we feel," she said. "We've got to be strong for Natalie. We can cry when we get home, but right now, it's all about our friend. Now, I think I've worked out which one is the sofa bed."

As Lauren rummaged behind the sofa for the duvet and pillows, Briony remembered how not so long ago, when she jogged past the house, Bethany and Milo had told her that Martin was sleeping downstairs because of his 'snoring'. Briony figured that this was probably the quilt he'd used. Was it going to smell of him? She had to change it. "I'm just going up to the airing cupboard to get some fresh linen," she announced.

"Why?" asked Lauren, who recoiled when Briony explained. "OK, babe, I love you."

Briony hadn't realised just how much she needed to hear those words. "I love you so much more," she replied. She proceeded quietly up the stairs, aware that it was the worst possible moment for the kids to wake up.

Meanwhile, Lauren decided to look for Natalie, who still hadn't returned from the toilet. She found her in the dining room with a bottle of Mr Sheen and a yellow duster. She was polishing the table as if her life depended on it. "Honey, what are you doing? Why don't you leave that and come and sit with us?"

Lauren tried to take the cloth away from her, but Natalie batted her away. "This is where Martin was smoking his weed," she said. "He got ash everywhere. I need to get rid of it."

Lauren put her arm around Natalie and gently tried again. "Right, lovely, give this to me," she said. She pulled the duster from her friend's clutches like she was performing a magic trick. As she did so, Natalie's arms slumped to her side, as if the air had been let out of her.

"OK, OK, I've got you," said Lauren, as she clung onto her friend, who was like a lifeless rag doll in her arms. She guided her back to the living room, where Briony had already made up the sofa bed with a fresh duvet cover, sheet and pillowcases. When she was on a mission, nothing could slow her down.

When she saw the state Natalie was in, she went rushing over to her. "Sweetie, we're here and we love you so very much," she said, hoping her words might ease a little of Natalie's pain. Lauren lowered her gently onto the side of the sofa bed and Briony coaxed her head to the pillow and lifted her legs so that she was lying on the mattress. Closing her eyes, Natalie promptly fell asleep. Briony and Lauren kissed her cheek and set about making her comfortable. Briony removed her socks and jeans and pulled the duvet up to her neck. Lauren took off her make up using some products she'd managed to find in the bathroom. The girls hugged, so grateful to have one another.

"I want to knit Natalie into this," said Briony through her tears, as she pointed between her heart and Lauren's. "I want her to feel the strength and support I have from just having you here."

"I know, babe, me too. I was just thinking the same thing."

Briony looked deep into Lauren's glistening eyes. "You really were, weren't you?"

"I really was," Lauren nodded, not having the space in her head to consider whether it was more than a coincidence. "Let me take your face off, too," she added, "and then we can try and get some sleep."

Lauren set about taking Briony's make up off and then repeated the routine for the third time that evening on her own face. Briony brought in three glasses of squash and snuggled in close to Natalie, with her arm across her friend's tummy, holding her tight. Lauren turned out the living room light and used her phone's torch to direct her to the free side of the sofa bed. She snuggled into Briony and pulled the duvet up to her shoulders.

"Night, Nat," said Briony, leaning over and kissing her friend on the cheek. "Night, Laur."

Lauren affectionately cupped Briony's face and ever so gently planted a kiss on her lips. "I hope you manage to get some rest," she said, knowing she wasn't the best of sleepers. Tonight, especially, her mind would be racing.

As Briony slipped back into position holding Natalie close, she felt Lauren's familiar hand and arm slide across her tummy and pull her in. She could tell that Natalie was deep in sleep as she wasn't moving, and her breathing was slow and heavy. It didn't take long for Lauren to drop off, too, and she could feel the warm air of her breath brush across her shoulders. She didn't believe she was ever going to fall asleep, but somehow the rhythmic sounds of her friends' breathing provided enough white noise to lull her into the world of dreams.

Chapter Twenty-One

Natalie woke with a start, as if she were under the command of a hypnotist. The lounge was still dark, so she realised it must be early. She untangled herself from Briony's embrace and ran up the stairs to Bethany's bedroom. She was flooded with relief when she found her sleeping peacefully, but what about Milo? She headed to his bedroom to find that he'd kicked his covers off in the night. Carefully, so as not to wake him, she covered him back up again. Fortunately, he didn't stir. She then moved across the landing and walked into the bedroom she shared with Martin. The curtains were wide open, so she figured he must have gone into the office. He often caught up with paperwork on Saturday mornings.

She didn't like the anxious, out-of-control feeling inside, but she reasoned that at least Martin had made the bed before leaving. But why on earth was she still wearing yesterday's knickers, bra and top? She took her dressing gown from the hook on the back of the bathroom door and wrapped herself up in it.

As she reflected further, she wondered why she'd felt the

need to check on the kids. Of course they were asleep, she'd put them to bed the night before. After using the bathroom, she went down to the kitchen and began making herself a cup of coffee.

Stirred by the sounds and light from the kitchen, Briony and Lauren woke up at the same time.

"Where is she?" Briony asked, and they promptly jumped out of bed to find their friend.

"Babe, how are you? Did you manage to get some sleep?" Briony asked gently.

"Not bad, thanks, how about you? And you, Laur?"

Lauren and Briony exchanged looks. Considering that she'd just learned her husband may have taken his own life, Natalie seemed way too calm.

"Do you want a coffee? Three sweeteners for you, Bri, and you're the same, aren't you, Lauren?"

Briony and Lauren moved over to their friend in sync and rubbed an arm each.

"Nat, do you remember what happened last night?" said Briony.

"No, I don't. I must have drunk a lot and fallen asleep because my mind is blank, and I have a bit of a fuzzy head."

"Are you sure about that?" said Lauren. She was mightily unnerved, because as much as her darling friend was standing in front of her, she was clearly somewhere else.

"Oh God, what did I do? You know I can't handle a lot to drink. We didn't do shots, did we?"

"OK, let's leave the coffees for now," said Lauren. "We'll get them in a minute. Come and sit down with me and Bri."

She and Briony each took a hand; Lauren pulled from the front while Briony led her from behind, towards the table she had ferociously polished the previous evening.

"What is this, maypole dancing?" Natalie protested. "You're getting me all spread out, like the ribbons before the dance and plaits." She spun around to face Briony. "We did this at school, remember?"

Lauren pulled out a chair for Natalie and Briony guided her to sit down. Although Briony wasn't religious, she found herself looking towards the ceiling and asking for help. She sent out a silent prayer that Martin would walk through the door and that this had all been some sort of sick joke. But who would be so cruel to play such a prank?

Lauren got chairs for her and Briony and they sat either side of Natalie, their knees touching. They took a hand each as they prepared to deliver the devastating news her brain had somehow blocked out.

"Well, if it isn't Maypole, then it's gotta be, 'Light as a feather, stiff as a board. Light as a feather, stiff as a board . . .'"

Both Briony and Lauren got their friend's reference to the '90s movie *The Craft*, in which three friends believe they are witches. Briony had seen it many times with Lauren, whose celebrity crush was Neve Campbell.

"No, babe," said Briony, inhaling to give her time to prepare her next words. "The police were here last night—"

"Honey, they think Martin took his life yesterday afternoon." Lauren finished the hardest part of Briony's sentence.

"No, you're wrong. He wouldn't do that!"

Briony intertwined her fingers with Natalie's. "Yes, that's what we're hoping, too."

Natalie got to her feet and headed for the living room. Briony and Lauren chased after her, seeing her clutching her phone.

"Who are you calling?" said Briony. "It's still dark outside."

"Mart left early this morning," Natalie replied. "He even made the bed; he knows how much I hate leaving the bed unmade."

Both Lauren and Briony knew that the bed hadn't been slept in because Martin hadn't made it home.

"Well, the bastard has his phone turned off now," Natalie continued. "Actually, I bet he's on the Underground. There's no signal down there."

Witnessing her friend's pain, Briony welled up. She quickly wiped away her tears before Natalie noticed.

Then Lauren had an idea. "Honey, do you really not remember the police coming round last night? Bri, give me your phone. You sent a message to us when we were at the pub, asking us to come over."

As Briony started looking for her phone, Natalie got up and went back to making the coffees, trying to block out what was happening. Briony scrolled through her phone and found the message. She rubbed Natalie's arm and saw the petrified expression on her face. It was obvious that deep down she did remember, but she was in the midst of some sort of denial.

Briony read Natalie's message out loud and the kitchen fell silent. Then Natalie's legs gave way and she fell to the floor, dragging Briony with her. As she cried and heaved, Briony and Lauren felt some relief that at least now she was acknowledging the tragedy.

"Of course I fucking remember," she sobbed. "I was just trying to hold it together for the kids."

Briony was taken aback by Natalie's aggression.

"OK, babe, OK." Lauren rubbed Natalie's back in an attempt to calm her down.

"You've been treating me like I'm fucking mentally unstable since you got here," Natalie hissed. "I don't know why I messaged you in the first place."

It was as if their friend had been replaced by the devil.

"What? Nat, please don't turn on us," said Briony. "We love you and we're here for you. We're all in way over our heads right now, and we're doing the best we can. If the way we've been responding has upset you, we are very sorry."

Natalie looked from Briony to Lauren and then stared in the direction of the dining room, unable to look at them as she spoke. "I don't know what I'm feeling, but what I do know is that I can't control any of it. It's real, it's not real. He's here, he's not here. It's my fault, it's his fault. Would he have done it if I hadn't mentioned getting a divorce? Did he not think about the kids? Could he not see his worth? All these thoughts are crashing through my head at such a pace that it's like a rollercoaster. I tried to be the emotionless one and take it in my stride, I tried to be the oblivious one and ignore it, but you two have made me realise that the only way to face this is as me. And it hurts so bad."

Briony sobbed and Lauren joined her and Natalie on the floor and engulfed them in a hug. They were going to get through this, the three of them together.

Chapter Twenty-Two

Briony and Lauren waved at the back of the brand-new Audi Q8 as it disappeared up the road. Natalie had insisted on driving Bethany and Milo to a last-minute playdate, and who were they to try and stop her? She'd called a mum friend and asked her to look after the kids for a few hours due to a family emergency. Thankfully, her friend had been more than willing to help, with no questions asked. The morning had been a strain on the adults, as they pretended Martin was out and that everything was hunky-dory. The kids were beyond excited that Auntie Bri and Auntie Lauren had been on a sleepover at their house.

"I think Nat was right in keeping the news from them," said Briony. "I mean, there's still hope."

"I don't know, babe," replied Lauren, who didn't share her optimism. "The Old Bill has good reason to believe it's Martin, or else why would they deliver such news?"

"I know, I know, and you're right, but until it's confirmed, I'm going to live in hope that he will walk through that door. I'm worried for Nat, though."

"Yeah, me too," Lauren agreed.

"The way she detailed the pace of the thoughts going through her head was unsettling. And there were moments this morning when the Natalie we know just wasn't there."

"Thinking about it, she's never had much shit to deal with in her life," said Lauren, "so I'm not sure how good her coping mechanisms are."

"Since when did you become Dr Newland?" Briony retorted sharply.

"Oh, come on, please don't fight with me. I know you're hurting, but our beautiful friend has pretty much had her fabulous life handed to her on a plate, without much effort on her part. But before you start, I'm not for one moment suggesting that she deserves this, I'm just worried that her shoulders aren't as strong as ours."

"But this isn't her fault."

"No, you're right, it isn't. It's just so shit. Clearly, Martin was struggling, and I don't think any of us realised how much."

"Yes, you're right. I just wish we could have recognised the signs."

Both Briony and Lauren became lost in their own thoughts and the silence of the house. It wasn't long until Natalie flew through the front door. Breathing heavily, she plonked herself down on the bottom step.

"How could he do this to me and the kids? I do love him, but I'm also so fucking angry with him. Am I allowed to feel this way, or does it make me the world's most hideous person?"

"In these circumstances, I don't think there is a right way to feel, so don't beat yourself up about anything," said Briony.

"Nat, honey, do you think you should call your mum?" suggested Lauren.

Natalie jumped to her feet. "God, no, she knows about the pregnancy and Jason. She'll blame me!"

"And what about Martin's family? They're going to start wondering why they haven't heard from him."

"I can't tell them, either. They always thought Martin was too good for me, and it turns out they were right."

"Nat, please stop blaming yourself. It's not your fault."

Natalie didn't appear to hear Lauren. "I just want to go to bed. Shut myself away for a while," she said.

"Perhaps that's a good idea," said Briony. "You've got to listen to your body. I'll wake you up when it's time to pick up Bethany and Milo."

Natalie looked like she'd seen a ghost, and it took a few seconds for her to reply. "Shit. What am I going to tell them?" The pain shot through her like a dart, and the reality of breaking her children's hearts felt so unbelievably unfair. Why did *she* have to tell them? She marched up the stairs, shut the bedroom curtains, climbed into her side of the king size bed and closed her eyes. Briony, who'd been following close behind, shut the door behind her and then jogged back down the stairs to Lauren.

"I probably shouldn't say this, but I'm furious with Martin for leaving us with all this to deal with," she said. "Plus, I've got my meeting with Mr S on Monday. I'm pretty confident it'll go OK, but it'll be bloody serious if Mani decides to play dirty."

Despite the glorious spring sunshine that was pouring through the lounge window, the air in the room felt icy. "My gut instinct is telling me that for now I just need to concentrate on breaking the news to Paula and Ted and Martin's parents, Mike and Jill," said Briony. "Can you stay with Nat while I do that?"

"I know how much you like to do the right thing all the time, but I don't think this is actually up to you," said Lauren. "Please don't hate me for saying this, but breaking this kind of news won't be easy."

Lauren's words resonated with Briony, but she still felt a pang of wanting to help. "I know my do-gooder ways get on your nerves sometimes," she said, "they get on mine, too, but I can't help the way I am. Right now, protecting Natalie is my driving force. She's in no fit state to do this herself, and I don't think it would be fair to do a ring round."

Lauren ran her hands through her hair and looked out of the bay window into the front garden and Natalie's quiet crescent. "It's such a gorgeous day," she said, "and yet what we're dealing with is so terribly dark. I want to protect Nat, too, so hear me out, as I have an idea. We can run it past Nat when she wakes up. Why don't we get on the phone and get everyone to the pub this evening? It may sound inappropriate, but I've read that people need to talk at times like this, and it could be healing to have all Martin's nearest and dearest together. I'm sure Flo would cordon off the bottom area of the bar for us, like she does for the poker night lot."

Briony gazed at the bright blue sky outside; there wasn't a cloud in sight. As she contemplated Lauren's words, she realised that she was, as usual, bang on. "You always seem to pour confetti over the trail I have dug out, creating a pretty path rather than a muddy track to the same destination."

Lauren smiled at the analogy.

"I have Paula's number on my phone," said Briony, "but I don't have any contact details for Martin's parents. Why would I? Nat has her mobile with her upstairs, so maybe we could ring from her phone, which would ease the blow a little, as it won't be a stranger calling. Why don't we grab a coffee, let Nat rest for another half an hour or so and then ask her what she thinks?"

"I have an even better idea," said Lauren. "Let's get the sofa bed back out."

Briony scrunched up her face.

"No, not like that. Let's set our alarms for half an hour's

time and have a power nap. It'll help us feel more alert than a coffee will."

It sounded like a perfect idea to Briony, who was feeling incredibly weary. "I will want spooning," she said.

Together, they got into bed and pulled the covers over their shoulders. Briony set the alarm on her phone and enjoyed the familiar feel of Lauren's hand moving across her tummy and pulling her in close.

When they woke to the sound of the alarm, they realised they hadn't moved and were shocked that half an hour had passed so quickly. They both felt more prepared for what was to come.

Briony followed Lauren up the stairs, and they gently opened the door a fraction, not wanting to disturb Natalie if she was still sleeping.

"She's not here!" said Lauren, pushing the door fully open. The bed was made, and light was streaming through the window.

"Oh my God," said Briony. "Where is she?"

Chapter Twenty-Three

After climbing into bed, Natalie heard Briony patter down the stairs and start whispering to Lauren. She lifted the covers to muffle her own voice. "Mart? Was the 'D' word the weapon I used to kill you? I never meant for any of this to happen, and now here I am in our bed with your blood on my hands, and I can't wash it off. You've tainted me. You've condemned me to a life sentence without even giving me a chance to defend myself. I'm no angel, but then neither are you. I'm no killer, either. You know me, I can't even squash a spider, but somehow . . . somehow, I have managed to kill you."

She searched the room to check no one was listening and fidgeted, as if every part of her skin were itching. She pulled the covers up again to mask her voice. "Your blood is like paint, and it's stuck to me. Everyone will know what I did. Everywhere I go, people will see me and whisper, 'She's the one who killed her husband.' Do you know how angry I am with you? Do you? I'll show you how fucking angry I am."

She flung the covers fully off her and then froze, concerned that her sudden movement may have alerted her friends downstairs. Slowly, so as not to make a sound, she got out of bed and tidied the pillows and covers. Then she drew the curtains, flooding the room with light, and leaned out of the window, like a bird ready to take flight. After a few seconds' thought, she pulled the laundry bin under the windowsill, climbed on top of it and swung her legs round, so that she could sit with her feet dangling outside. She enjoyed the freedom and the peace until she felt something hard beneath her feet.

"Thank God you never put things away, Mart," she said out loud. Turning to face into the room, she reached out her foot and rested it on the ladder that a few weeks ago her husband had been using to remove the ivy that had started to wind its way around their bedroom window. The metal had been warmed by the sun and was unusually hot to the touch. Quickly, she climbed down the ladder until she was in the back garden. Fired up by adrenalin and emotion, she ducked under the window and into the abyss down the side of the house, where the monumental rubbish pile never seemed to get smaller. Underneath the household crap, the cardboard and the weeds, she could see the shiny object she was after. The spikes from the greenery prickled her skin as she pushed aside all manner of things until she got to the old golf club. Avoiding yet more windows along the side of the house, she opened the gate and hurried onto her neighbour's driveway and then out of the crescent, while swinging the golf club in time to her steps. For the first time that day, she managed a smile and took a deep breath, pulling the warm air into her lungs and enjoying the sun on her face. Then, as if a switch had been flicked, she picked up her pace and completed the one-and-a-half kilometre walk to the train station in no time, her heart skipping a beat when its red and white sign came into view. She walked past the opening to the ticket office and looked towards the platforms.

"How dare you leave me, leave your children and leave the blame on me?" she shouted. The commuters looked away as she walked past, turning a blind eye to her obvious distress, fearful of the air of danger surrounding her. She walked past the vehicles parked outside the station and made her way into the newer, multistorey car park, where, providing he parked before nine am, Martin had an allocated space.

Then the thought hit her. Martin hadn't left early yesterday, because he'd had that young PT over . . . the one he'd been hoping to go to bed with.

"What happened to your fucking pride, Martin?" she said out loud, as if the gloomy space before her could provide an answer. "Did you actually drive after smoking all that weed, you absolute dickhead? What if you'd hit someone?"

Tears poured down her cheeks as she held up the golf club and then brought it down on the cement floor. The impact reverberated up her arm, aggravating her elbow. "Stupid thing!" she screamed at it, before carrying on through the car park, her gaze flitting between the vehicles either side of her. She continued this way up to the fourth floor, trying not to touch anything in the urine-stained, stinking stairways. Despite how fit she was, she was sweaty and red-faced by the time she reached the top floor. Her dark hair hung lankly down the sides of her face, and there were dark rings under her make-up free eyes. Finally, she spotted the familiar silver Audi A8 parked near the back wall, its nose poking out of the space. She stormed over to it and pulled the handle on the passenger door, but the car was locked. "Of course, why would it be open?" she said. "You obviously needed to take the keys with you. Just where were you planning to go next?"

She swung the golf club behind her shoulders and gave the passenger door an almighty whack, creating a huge dent. She looked at her handy work and was pleased with how hard she'd managed to hit the car. Then the alarm started to sound, with the indicator lights flashing on and off in time with it. She looked over her shoulder and realised she didn't have a lot of time. The space next to Martin's car was available, allowing her the room to freely swing the club even further behind her. She wasn't fazed by the alarm; if anything, it intensified her attack, and she hit the passenger window. She heard a crack and pounded it again and again until it finally shattered. Shards of glass covered the passenger seat and sprinkled across the car park floor. Now she could start looking for Martin's phone.

In truth, Natalie wasn't totally sure why she even wanted to see it. It was something Martin took everywhere with him, so if he'd left it behind in the car, then this would be further proof that he'd known exactly what he was doing when he headed to the train platform. He'd have known he wasn't coming back. He usually kept the phone in the storage compartment inside the armrest between the two front seats, so she stretched her hand through the window to try and open the door from the inside. Broken glass tore through her bare arm, cutting it to shreds, but even with blood oozing down her pale skin, she didn't feel a thing. The blood caused her hand to slip as she pressed down on the handle, but eventually the door opened. Glass crunched underneath her calf-length Nike leggings, piercing even more of her skin, as she kneeled on the seat and pulled up the lid to the compartment.

As expected, there was Martin's black iPhone in its familiar blue case. Her blood smeared all over it as she picked it up. Wiping it on her top, she saw that the screen was blank. She pushed the power button, but nothing happened. "Dead," she said, "just like you." Then she curled up on the passenger seat, the phone cradled to her chest, all that was left of her husband, and began to wail.

Chapter Twenty-Four

"Where has she gone?" said Briony, sitting on the top step by Natalie's front door with her head in her hands. "Did she sneak out while we were sleeping? Do you know what we've done? We've let her down when she needed us the most."

"No, sweetie, we haven't let her down at all, we just need to find her," Lauren calmly replied. "Look, this isn't how she would normally behave, is it? She would have at least left us a note."

"Exactly! She's not behaving like herself, and she's most probably in shock. She needed us and we were snuggled up asleep. She must have felt so lonely seeing us together like that."

"We've got to think like Natalie," said Lauren, wearing her detective hat once again. "Where would she go?"

"She'd come to the flat," said Briony. "But clearly, we're not there, and I really don't know where else she would go. I'll have to phone her mum. What else can I do?"

Paula picked up after a couple of rings.

"I've got some news," said Briony, bypassing the formal greetings.

"Thank God," said Paula. "Where are you? Is Lauren with you? I've just had a call from the police."

Briony quickly switched the phone onto speaker so that Lauren could listen in. She swallowed hard, bracing herself for what she was about to hear. "Is she OK?"

Lauren took the phone from Briony and rested it on the windowsill so she could put her arm around her.

"She's in hospital. She was found in the train station car park covered in blood after smashing up Martin's car."

"But she's OK?"

"Yes, according to the policewoman I spoke to, but she has lost a lot of blood."

"Paula, I didn't want to have to break the news to you like this, but Martin killed himself yesterday," Briony said.

"Oh, my word, please tell me that's not true."

Briony struggled to continue, so Lauren took over. "I'm afraid so. The police visited Natalie last night."

"What . . . what did he do?"

"I'm so sorry that you've got to hear this from us, but he jumped in front of a train."

"Do the children know? Why didn't Natalie call me?"

"No, she hasn't told Bethany and Milo yet, and they're with a friend of hers right now. I think she's in shock. She rushed a WhatsApp message to us last night after the police left, and we stayed with her."

"We were keeping her safe," said Briony, feeling the need to explain herself. "But we fell asleep, and when we woke up, she'd gone. I'm so sorry."

"It's not your fault, dear," said Paula. "Do you want to meet me at the hospital?"

Briony nodded at the phone.

"Paula, Briony is nodding," Lauren explained.

"Yes, we'll be there as soon as we can," Briony said. "We'll come in Natalie's car because it's still here and looking at me from the driveway. She must have walked to the station car park."

Once Paula had hung up, Briony grabbed hold of Lauren's hand and pulled her into the kitchen. "Thank goodness you are here and not on the ships," she said.

"I know, I'm so glad I am here, too. I have my savings, but it won't cover all of us. If I need to, I will find work to support you, Natalie, Bethany and Milo."

"You really would, wouldn't you?"

"Yep, I really would. Now, let's find the car keys and get to Nat."

The two of them promptly got busy searching drawers, cupboards and Natalie's selection of handbags. Deflated, Briony came down the stairs thinking hard about anywhere they might have forgotten to look. Her eyes fell to the console table by the front door. "For goodness sake, what a pair of dozy tits we are!"

"What?" said Lauren, from Natalie's bedroom.

"They're right here, with her house keys," said Briony. "She left without taking any of them. Let's go."

Lauren came up behind Briony on the stairs and grabbed her round the waist, stopping her in her tracks. "Hurry up, then," she teased.

"Don't pass me on the stairs," warned Briony. "It's bad luck."

"I don't think anything worse can happen," Lauren quipped darkly.

Briony put on her shoes as Lauren locked the back door. "Did you notice the ladder going up to Nat and Martin's window before?" she asked.

Reading Lauren's thoughts, Briony replied, "Surely, she can't have climbed down from her bedroom window?" But even as she said it, she had to admit that considering her friend's current state of mind, anything was possible.

Chapter Twenty-Five

P aula texted Briony with the details of which ward Natalie was on, and the unmistakable hospital smell hit her as soon as she walked into the building with Lauren. Together, they blindly followed Paula's directions, going up some stairs, down a seemingly endless corridor and turning left, right and left again until they finally located Natalie's bed.

"Babe, what happened? Are you OK?" said Briony, as she took in the troubling sight of her friend. Her right arm was tightly bandaged, and her pretty face was covered in gashes. She was hooked up to a drip and brightly coloured readings danced up and down on the machine next to her bed.

"I don't know what happened," said Natalie, as Briony pulled the curtains around the bed to give them some privacy. She tried to raise her arms and then winced in pain, obviously momentarily forgetting her injuries. "I just feel so stupid for losing control."

Besides the cuts to her face and arms, Natalie's shins were shredded like pulled pork. She was relieved they were hidden from view under the sheet and weren't adding to the shit show her mum and friends were currently having to witness.

"At least you're OK, honey, and it's so good to see you," said Lauren. Her warm words echoed the sentiment of everyone else.

"The police told me that a woman dialled 999 after finding Natalie on the fourth floor of the multistorey," Paula explained. "She was drifting in and out of consciousness because she'd lost so much blood. Apparently, she took a golf club to Martin's car and beat the living daylights out of it."

As her mum spoke, Natalie stared out of the window and focused on the branches of a tree, as birds landed and departed from them. She may well be the centre of the story, but she didn't remember any of it. In fact, she couldn't even recall waking up that morning. She decided she preferred to keep it that way. "The doctors are a bit worried about me, so they have given me some mood-enhancing drugs," she explained.

Briony and Lauren could feel their friend's discomfort, as Natalie had never understood the need for people to take so-called 'happy pills' before. She felt it was a sign of weakness.

"My GP prescribed some for me," admitted Briony. "After Nanna and Papa died and I was feeling really low. I'm not sure you knew that?"

Natalie shook her head.

"I didn't know either," said Lauren.

"I didn't say anything because you were at sea, Lauren, and Nat, you had your kids. Neither of you needed my drama on top. I guess in some way I was embarrassed, too, but they helped me through a pretty low time and I'm grateful I took the doc's advice. You won't be on them forever, Nat."

Even though what Natalie had experienced was on another level, Briony's honesty about her own difficulties somehow made her feel more normal. "Don't make me cry," she said, "it seems that's all I've done since finding out about Martin. Tell me something funny, please. I want to laugh and get some of my natural happy drugs firing."

Briony racked her brains trying to remember a suitable joke, but her inability to remember any punchlines frustrated her efforts. Suddenly, she felt Lauren tugging on her denim skirt with such force that it slid over her hips and landed on the floor. She hadn't been home since the date in town, and without the chance to put on some clean knickers she was still commando. As she struggled to cover herself, gentle sniggers gave way to full-blown laughter.

Briony tried to laugh along, but her face was bright red. Unable to bend over and pick up her skirt without revealing even more of herself, she remained extremely still, as if she were in the stocks.

"Oh, shit, sweetie, I am so sorry. I forgot you didn't have any knickers on," said Lauren, coming to her rescue. "I was just trying to bring a smile to Nat's face."

"Yeah, right." Briony was fuming, but as she looked over at Natalie, she could see a genuine sparkle in her eyes. She decided her humiliation was worth it if it had managed to cheer up her distraught friend.

"No, honestly, I did forget," Lauren protested. "Paula, please let me apologise for my immaturity and lack of consideration. I thought it would be censored naughtiness but instead you got full-frontal nudity."

"Briony, you have a lovely body," said Paula. "What I wouldn't give to be thirty years younger and look like you. What Lauren just did was immature, but it was also absolutely hysterical."

"Thanks, Lauren," said Natalie. "I've never wanted to see Briony's tutu, but clearly today it was something I *needed* to see." Everyone laughed, including Briony this time. "I won't ask why you're going commando," Natalie continued, "and I definitely won't ask how you knew, Lauren." She grinned knowingly at her friends.

"Oh, no, hun, nothing like that," said Bri. "It's a long and boring old story."

"Please just talk to me as if we were in your flat or down the pub," Natalie replied. "I'm craving some normality."

Briony pulled up a chair close to Natalie's bed. "Well, you know me, I'm not one to shy away from talking about myself." Natalie and Lauren looked at each other and rolled their eyes in unison. "It all started after London, when we decided to go on our first official date together—"

"Paula, shall we go and get some drinks?" interjected Lauren.

"You read my mind," Paula replied. "We'll go and get some brews from the café. Briony, that should give you enough time to explain to my daughter why you haven't got any underwear on."

Briony blushed. It felt like she was getting told off by her best friend's mum for not wearing any knickers, which, in effect, she was. Lauren raised her lips in a 'sorry-not-sorry' smile and shrugged, before linking arms with Paula.

"White coffee, three sweeteners, please," said Briony.

"A hot chocolate with tons of sugar, please, Mum," Natalie added.

Once they were out of earshot, Lauren squeezed Paula's arm. "How are you doing?" she asked her.

"I'm OK, love, how are you?"

"This isn't about me. How are you *really* feeling?" She squeezed her arm a little harder. She'd learned from living and working with hundreds of staff on the ships that to really get to the crux of how someone is, you must ask them twice.

"I'm not sure."

Jackpot! She let Paula speak.

"There is so much to take in. Martin's dead, Natalie's a

mess." She looked into Lauren's sympathetic eyes. "At least she's still with us."

Lauren stopped in her tracks and gave Paula a big hug.

"Thank you, Lauren, you really are a good friend to Natalie."

Lauren hugged Paula tighter to let her know she appreciated her words. She loved being able to offer comfort to people and was grateful that as well as giving her the chance to see the world, her job had allowed her to really see and accept herself. Living away from home for so long was lonely at times, but it was during these moments when she learned the most about herself, including how to enjoy her own company and support herself in happiness and in pain. She felt that it was these lessons that had given her the strength and confidence to help others.

Not so long ago, she'd been lucky enough to stay in an ocean villa in the Maldives for two weeks by herself. It had been a fortnight of growth, where although she had felt incredibly blessed to wake up amidst such natural beauty, she had also never felt so alone. It was during this holiday that she was able to finally acknowledge the gaping hole in her life and accept that she both wanted and needed to share her life with someone. It was a time for finding the delicate balance between light and dark. She remembered lying on the beach and looking across at her villa, which stood tall and strong over the water. That became her go-to image whenever she needed strength. She envisioned it now. "We'll get Natalie through this," she said to Paula, with utter conviction in her voice.

Paula grabbed Lauren and kissed her cheek. "You're right, we will," she replied.

When they arrived back on the ward with the drinks, Natalie's eyes were wide.

"What have you heard?" Lauren asked.

"I can't believe Briony's boss is accusing her of . . ." Natalie looked at Paula. "Mum, close your ears, please." She paused to give her mother time to respond to her request. "Sexual harassment after the fake threesome in the work kitchen."

Paula smirked and looked away, pretending not to hear but secretly transfixed by the wild lives of her daughter's friends.

"Things didn't quite go to plan, did they, Laur?" Briony said.

"Please don't worry, babe, we've got Barbie on our side. It'll all be fine."

Paula snorted. "I tried not to listen, but I'm sorry, girls, a fake threesome and a woman called Barbie?"

Everyone laughed. The plot of this current chapter was admittedly amusing from an outsider's perspective.

"Paula, I am sorry," Briony said.

"Oh, don't worry, hun, as long as you're all OK, that's what's important."

Their laughter subsided as Briony and Lauren each reflected on the more serious situation facing their friend. Could they have done more to help her? The silence was broken by the arrival of a dark-haired, female doctor wearing funky, zebra print glasses.

"Good afternoon, everyone," she said, before turning to Natalie. "How are you feeling, Miss Stevenson?"

"Please call me Natalie. If you want to know the truth, I feel like a complete idiot." It was the release she needed. She was like a can of cola shaken up ready to explode upon opening. "I don't know why I did what I did, and I can't even remember doing it. Thank goodness that woman called an ambulance. I could have bled to death." She raised her bandaged arm and once again winced in pain at the movement.

The doctor smiled warmly, reminding Natalie that she was

somewhere safe. "There's no need to worry," she reassured her. "Even if help hadn't arrived when it did, you wouldn't have died from your injuries, but what I am concerned about is that you weren't aware of what you were doing. For that reason alone, I want to keep you in overnight."

Natalie agreed. "That's the scary thing," she said. "What if I go there again?"

"Don't worry about that for now," the doctor said. "Just get some rest and we'll review things in the morning."

"But I've got two children," Natalie replied. "How am I supposed to care for them if I can't care for myself?" Her stress levels began to rise fast, as her gaze flitted between the women around her. "And I killed their dad! I can't be a mother to them anymore."

Everyone could see the change in Natalie; she'd disappeared again. The doctor perched on her bed and looked her in the eye. "Your mum has told me that she will pick up Bethany and Milo from their playdate, and then they can have a few sleepovers at nanny's house."

Paula was impressed by how the doctor had remembered the names of Natalie's children from their earlier conversation.

"Nat, we'll move in, won't we, Laur?" said Briony. "We'll stay with you."

"Yes, yes, of course we will," Lauren replied enthusiastically.

Natalie felt overwhelmed by the love and support of her mum and friends, but still the idea of being alone with Bethany and Milo terrified her. She'd killed their father and no longer felt deserving of them.

Chapter Twenty-Six

B riony enjoyed the sweet purr of the Audi Q8 as she started up the engine and pulled out of the parking space towards the hospital's exit. She looked at the box where she needed to insert her prepaid parking ticket and then put her foot down on the brake. "Bollocks, I've lost it," she said, frantically searching her pockets.

"I've got it here, babe," said Lauren. "You asked me to look after it so that you wouldn't lose it, remember?"

Briony rolled her eyes, recalling their earlier conversation. "It's been a long day," she said, taking the ticket and watching it get sucked into the box. The yellow barrier rose, and they wordlessly listened to the radio all the way back to Briony's flat.

Once inside, the home she'd occupied for over a decade felt unusually alien to Briony. She went into the kitchen and put the kettle on, so preoccupied by her thoughts that she didn't even notice Lauren coming up behind her. She nearly fell over when she turned around and they banged into each other. Coffee granules jumped from her spoon and bounced all over the kitchen floor.

"Sorry, I thought you knew I was there," said Lauren. "I just wanted to give you a hug."

Crunching the coffee into the floor, Briony threw her arms around Lauren. They clung on, enjoying each other's warmth and familiar smell. It was the medicine they both needed.

Briony pulled away first, but she knew that she could have stayed there all day. "It's weird, so much has happened since we were last here. I can't explain it, but this place just doesn't feel like my home anymore."

"I kind of understand that because I've never had a full-time home per se," said Lauren. "When I was singing, it was wherever I happened to be at the time. I learned to be happy in the now. But now my home is with you, and wherever you are. Home really is where my heart is."

Briony smiled. "Well, listen to you, Little Miss Romantic!" she teased.

"I've had a lot of time to think about the concept of home," Lauren replied, curling her index and middle fingers into quotation marks as she said the word home. "Where's my phone?" she added, before grabbing it from the worktop and asking, "Siri, what is the meaning of home?"

"Home is the place where one lives permanently, especially as a member of a family or household," responded the virtual assistant.

"Where one lives permanently," Lauren repeated. "Well, my head and my heart are with me permanently, and you are in my heart, too. That means, Bri, babe, that you *are* my home."

"How come someone so clever and so wonderfully emotionally intelligent ended up with me, huh?" Briony said, as Lauren crouched down to get the dustpan and brush from the cupboard under the sink.

"I had nothing to do with it," said Lauren, turning her head and looking up at Briony. "We have Mamma Universe to thank. She put us in contact all those years ago in drama class, and she has watched us grow knowing we were meant to be—"

"Together!" said Briony, completing Lauren's sentence before kneeling on the floor next to her. "Gosh, our connection is so powerful."

Lost in the thoughts provoked by their conversation, the two girls cleared the floor together before finally making their coffees.

"Alexa?" Briony waited for the light flash of acknowledgment from her countertop device. "Play my Britney Spears playlist, please."

But as *Baby One More Time* started to play, she realised the song was too much for her right now. "Alexa, off please!" Once silence had returned, she added, "I love you, Brit, but maybe not today."

She sat next to Lauren by the breakfast bar and took her hand. "I really couldn't have done this without you," she said. "Martin committing suicide and Natalie having what can only be described as a nervous breakdown really is a nightmare."

Lauren nodded. "As a unit we are stronger, and that includes Natalie. I had a chat with Paula earlier, and she said that she will take Bethany and Milo for as long as Natalie needs. She was worried because she and Ted don't have the space in their home for Natalie, too, but before she said anything else, I told her we'd move in with her."

"I couldn't have said it better myself," agreed Briony. "I don't want Natalie to feel rushed." She shook her head, as if trying to evict some bad thoughts from her brain. "I've got that bloody meeting on Monday with Mr Schwartzberg. It was driving me crazy, but you know what, now I'm not even bothered what happens."

"OK, good," said Lauren. "Now, let's get our shit together and pack for a few days."

Lauren and Briony escorted Natalie to the living room, where she was greeted by a rainbow of balloons arching over the mantlepiece and a big sign with hearts and kisses and "Welcome Home!" printed on it in purple. Two vases containing tulips and daffodils had been placed on either side of the arch, and their summery fragrance filled the room.

Natalie moved awkwardly. She was still covered in bandages and the wounds beneath them were sore. "I was only in hospital for a day and a night," she said. "I mean, thanks, but it's all a bit overkill."

"We wanted to make a fuss of you," declared Briony.

"Where did you two sleep?" Natalie enquired.

It struck Briony as a strange question. "Down here on the sofa bed," she replied.

"I was thinking I could sleep there," said Natalie. "I don't want to go in my bedroom; the sheets still smell of Mart and there's all his stuff in there, too."

Briony had anticipated Natalie's reservations. "We've changed the sheets and had a tidy up," she said. "It's proper uncomfy down here. Do you remember all three of us sleeping on the sofa bed on Friday night? We were thinking that maybe we could sleep upstairs with you on your fabulous orthopaedic mattress?"

"Hmmm, I'll think about it," Natalie replied. "I don't actually remember sleeping down here with you two, but you're right, it is a bit small."

Briony and Lauren were happy to let their friend call the shots for as long as she needed to. It was mid-morning, so they sat in the garden drinking coffee and enjoying the late May sunshine. The birds were singing and Natalie's cats, Ant and Dec, were sunbathing on the patio.

"I'm just going to pop to the Co-op and get us a French stick for lunch," said Lauren, rising from her chair.

Shielding her eyes from the sun, Nat looked up at her. "You two really don't have to fuss around me," she said. "What happened yesterday was a blip. I am a grown up and fully capable of looking after myself."

As she spoke, Natalie looked agitated, and Briony realised that maybe they were smothering their friend a little. She was right. She was an adult, and if she needed some alone time then that's what they would give her. "I know that," she said. "It's just that you've been through a lot, and we want to take care of you whilst you recover."

"Yes, and I really appreciate it. I love you both so much, but I actually enjoyed the peace and quiet I had at the hospital. Do you understand? I just need a bit of time at home by myself."

Briony looked over at Lauren. Neither of them was convinced that it was a good idea to leave Natalie alone, but for now she was the boss and they had to respect her wishes. "That's fine, sweetie," she said. "Why don't Lauren and I get out of your way and then we can reconvene in an hour? Laur can go and pick up that lunch for us and I'll go up to Bethany's room and use her desk to prep for tomorrow."

"Ah, that thing at work. Do you think everything's going to be OK?"

Briony didn't want to bother Natalie with her own problems. Lauren shot her a warning look, too, reminding her not to make a big deal of it. "It's going to be absolutely fine," she said. "It's just a formality; I'm not really in trouble."

"Ah, OK, phew," said Natalie, accepting Briony's somewhat fabricated version of events.

"I tell you what, I'll walk to the shops," said Lauren, deliberately changing the subject. "That'll give you some more time to yourself, honey."

"Thanks so much, girls, I love how you totally get me."

Lauren and Briony both leaned over to kiss Natalie's cheek, aware that a hug might further aggravate her injuries. They left her in the garden and headed into the house.

"Babe, can you pick me up a notebook from the shop?" Briony said to Lauren. "I'm pretty sure there'll be something to use in Bethany's room, but when I was seven, I would have been extremely cross if one of Nan's friends had tucked into my stationary."

"Yep, me too," agreed Lauren. "I'll add it to the list."

As Lauren headed out, Briony used the upstairs loo and then locked herself in Bethany's bedroom.

Out in the garden, Natalie was feeling warm, as her bandages added an extra layer of insulation. She went inside in search of her stand-up fan, figuring that she'd keep out of the sun and sit in the dining room instead. She found the fan in its usual place in the cupboard under the stairs. As she went to plug it in, her attention was drawn to the framed wedding photos of her and Martin on the wall. They had been there for years, but she hadn't properly looked at them for ages. She laughed a little about how young they looked. In one photo, Martin was standing behind her as she signed their marriage register; in another, they were gazing into each other's eyes looking completely smitten. Instead of finding the image cute, it created a rumble of boiling lava inside Natalie's stomach.

"Was it all a load of bullshit?" she said to her groom. "I thought you loved me. You know what? I don't want to see your face in *my* house anymore. You took that privilege away with you!"

Natalie spoke with a deep, fractured voice, as if the volcano inside her was beginning to steam, and the smoke was affecting her vocal cords. Ignoring her discomfort, she pushed a chair close to the wall and clambered awkwardly onto it, pulling the picture frames from their hooks before flinging them onto the dining room table. The velvety material on the back of the frames stopped them from smashing or making too much noise. She needed to be quiet, as no doubt Briony wouldn't agree with what she was doing. Looking at the spaces where the pictures had hung, she could see how filthy the walls had become. The rectangular shapes looked much brighter than the rest of the paintwork.

"You're like a bad stain," Natalie said, continuing her tirade. "Are you going to keep tormenting me for the rest of my life? I need you out of here. I can't look at you!"

In the living room, Natalie winced as the bandages pulled on her cuts and gashes, whilst she scooped from the wall and shelves any photographs featuring her dead husband. As best she could, she tiptoed up the stairs and did the same with the pictures that trailed up the wall either side of them. Then she crept back downstairs with her unbandaged arm filled with frames. In the kitchen, she cut out Martin's head from any of the photos of them with Bethany and Milo. She wanted to keep the memories of their children.

Next, she wrapped the glass sheets from the frames in paper and put them in the recycling bin. In the garage, she cleared a space around their recently purchased terracotta chiminea and hauled it into the garden. Her wounds ached from the strain, but she carried on, cramming the photos and frames into the pit. Then she doused them with petrol from the jerry can they used for the lawnmower and tossed in a lit match. As the flames roared into life, Natalie felt a flicker of excitement, as nature mirrored her emotional state. Thick, black smoke rose into the clear blue sky, accompanied by a strong chemical smell from the burning plastic. Oblivious, Natalie watched Martin's smiling face melt, grinning to herself as the edges of the photographs curled up and turned into ash. She took a seat and continued to watch her husband's metaphorical cremation.

Upstairs, Briony was listening to *Capital FM* through her phone and headphones. She felt like she was putting a good case together for tomorrow's meeting and had lost track of the time. She needed to remember to get the video footage from Lauren of Mani accosting her in the Downton Abbey room, and it would also be wise for them to have two copies. She lifted her head and smelled something burning. She was just trying to place whether it was wood or not when the wail of the smoke alarm downstairs cut through the song she was listening to. Tearing out her earphones, she shot up like a rocket and went to investigate. While it didn't appear smoky on the landing, the smell out there was certainly stronger. She charged down the stairs, the alarm seemingly getting louder with each step. Was Natalie trying to cook something? She couldn't see her, so she grabbed a tea towel and wafted the smoke away from the alarm. Even with the help of a wooden spoon, she'd always been too small to reach the reset button, which is why it was useful when the much taller Lauren was around.

"Nat?" she called breathlessly, panting as she jumped up and down, putting her whole body into getting the smoke away from the alarm. Natalie came in from the garden, seemingly unconcerned. "Oh, Bri, thanks so much. I was hoping it wouldn't get inside."

When the alarm finally stopped and Briony could cease hurling herself about like a mad woman, she ran over to Natalie. "Why is there smoke?" she said. And then she looked out into the garden and saw the flames raging inside the chiminea, which was frighteningly close to the garden furniture. "Shit! What are you doing?"

Natalie remained surprisingly calm. "Don't panic, I'm just having a clear out," she said. "I haven't set the house alight, have I."

"Exactly what have you been clearing out?" Briony asked. "You're supposed to be resting."

"I know, but I couldn't, so I decided to declutter instead, and that has been good for my soul."

Briony sensed that something wasn't quite right. Natalie wasn't exactly the spiritual type, and the word soul wasn't part of her usual vocab. She went outside and got as close as possible to the chiminea, prodding the elements in the fire to see if she could figure out what was in there, but she could only see ash and bits of wood.

"Nat, what did you burn?"

"Just some stuff. Would you like a coffee now that the alarm has stopped?"

Before Briony had a chance to reply, Natalie started getting the mugs out of the cupboard. She investigated the chiminea again to try and figure out what was burning.

Just then, Lauren bounded through the front door armed with a long French stick and a Co-op bag full of groceries. "Oh my gosh, what on earth happened here?" she asked. "Why's it so smoky and where have all the photos gone?"

Natalie carried on making the coffees, either oblivious or employing selective hearing.

Briony joined Lauren in the hallway and followed her gaze up the stairs, where there were bare screws where once all Natalie's precious photographs had hung.

"Fuck, I ran down the stairs and didn't even notice," said Briony. "The smoke alarm was going off and it was all a bit crazy." She followed the bare walls down the hall and into the lounge and dining room. "Nat, babe. You haven't burned *all* your pictures, have you?"

Natalie was busy filling the mugs from her boiling water tap. She turned around, and both Briony and Lauren were surprised by how serene she was compared to earlier, yet there was still a weird energy about her.

225

"Yes, I did. Well, come on, he didn't want to be here anymore, so I don't want to keep looking at him. It just reminds me of what he's done."

She was so matter of fact that for a split second Briony agreed with her logic.

Lauren gently took the mug Natalie was holding and put it on the counter. "I think we should make these sorts of decisions together from now on," she said. "Unless you've kept copies on your computer, those photographs are lost forever."

"Good!" Natalie replied.

"OK, so let's make some lunch and then maybe we can find some new pictures to hang up," Briony suggested, trying to calm the growing tension in the room.

"I burned the frames, too."

The silence that followed was palpable. Briony and Lauren were on territory they'd never traversed before. The fire was still simmering, and the smoke hung in the air as a constant reminder of what had just taken place. While Natalie was certainly acting out of character, the sneaky side of her behaviour was altogether familiar.

"Nat, babe, you didn't burn the pictures of Bethany and Milo, did you?" Bri asked.

Natalie seemed shocked by the question. "No, of course I didn't. I want to be able to look at those, but I don't think they should see me."

As she spoke, her shoulders dropped, as if the shame she was carrying weighed her down physically.

"Oh my gosh, Nat, that's ridiculous," said Lauren, taking her into her arms. "Why on earth can't your children see you?"

"Because . . . because I killed their father!"

As Natalie spoke, Lauren let go of her and took a step back, shocked by the tone of her voice.

"And because I'm clearly not fit to be their mother," Natalie continued. "They're not here anyway, so I'm assuming the authorities are arranging more suitable accommodation."

"Bethany and Milo are safe with your mum and dad," Briony reassured her, desperately hoping her words would get through. "The authorities aren't involved, and they never will be."

"Mmmm," said Natalie. "That may be fine for now, but it won't be long until they find a wonderful Julie and Steve, or maybe a Steve and Steve, to give them a better life."

There was no obvious way into Natalie's thought process. She doted on her children and speaking this way was no doubt killing her. But for now, at least, Briony and Lauren knew that she was beyond reasoning with.

"After lunch, why don't we all sit down and have a game of Cluedo?" Lauren said, surprising everyone with her board game suggestion.

"Such a good idea, but maybe not Cluedo, eh?" said Briony, raising her eyebrows at Lauren, who quickly realised that under the circumstances, a game about solving a murder really wasn't the ideal choice.

'Oh, yeah, that's right," she said, thinking on her feet. "I remember the last time we played there were some bits missing. Maybe a card game, then? I learned loads on the ships."

Without saying a word, Natalie went into the dining room and opened one of the sideboard drawers. She rustled around in it, moving paperwork, spare keys and all manner of other junk until she found a pack of playing cards. She sat at the table, shuffled the deck and started setting up for a round of Clock Patience.

Briony felt a tug of nostalgia, as it was one of the games her grandparents had taught her back in the '90s. "Do you want a hand with that?" she asked.

"No, thanks," Natalie replied, pulling a face that was an exact match of how Bethany looked when she wanted to be left alone. The resemblance was uncanny.

Briony put her hands up in surrender and walked away before she said something she would regret. "Actually, I've got a call to make."

In the kitchen, Lauren had already started preparing lunch. Briony headed into the garden to ring Paula.

After they'd eaten, they played a couple of games of Rummy before the Uno cards came out. Before they knew it, the afternoon had vanished. The games provided a brilliant distraction for all three of them, and it was the most normal they'd felt since being hit by the dreadful news of Martin's suicide. Briony's unabashed competitiveness, Lauren's poker face and Natalie's attempts to look at her opponents' cards inspired the familiar banter between the old friends, and it was just what they needed. Afterwards, they went out for a gentle early evening stroll before ordering a pizza and binging on episodes of *Tipping Point* and *The Chase* on catch up.

The smell of smoke had faded, but the walls still looked hauntingly bare. Briony and Lauren had worked out that Natalie was much better if they didn't mention anything about her recent episode, Martin or the kids.

When Briony managed to get a moment alone with Lauren in the garden, she filled her in on her recent conversation with Paula. "Apparently, Bethany has been asking to see her mum," she said. "She's worried that she will go down the same route as her dad."

"Bloody hell, poor kids," Lauren replied. "So, I take it Paula has told them?"

"Yes, she said it was the worst thing she's ever had to do, but it was surprising how well they took it. She thinks their anger will come out later, but for now she just wants to keep them safe."

Lauren nodded along, aware that Briony was leading up to something else.

"So, tomorrow, when I have my hearing with Mr S and Mani, and potentially a lawyer, too, a mental health nurse called Daniela is coming over to see Natalie. While I'd love you to support me at the meeting, we can't leave her on her own." Her voice lowered to a whisper. "Will you stay here with her while I go and sort out my mess?"

Lauren winked at Briony, before cupping her face and planting fairy kisses down her face and neck. "I have fallen in love with a smart, intelligent woman, who I know will be able to sort these men out," she said. "Of course I'll stay with Natalie, and if Mani is a massive dick tomorrow, just walk out."

Briony considered Lauren's suggestion for a moment. "Yeah, you're right, we've got enough to worry about without any added bullshit from him."

Lauren nodded. "It's not as if you're doing the job anymore, babe."

"Oh, but I will need the position back. You're not working now, and we can't survive on fresh air."

"Right now, that's the least of our worries," said Lauren. "On principle, I think Mani needs to own up to his dad and take responsibility for his actions."

Briony laughed. "You getting all authoritative is kind of hot," she said.

"What will be will be," replied Lauren, raising her eyebrows provocatively.

Natalie walked through the back door. "What will be?" she asked, suspicious that her friends were talking about her behind her back.

"Briony's presentation at work tomorrow. You know our overthinker here, she's trying to pre-empt the outcome."

"Following my questionable decisions of late, I'm in no

position to dish out any advice," said Natalie, "but do talk to me. If nothing else, I could do with the distraction."

Briony wasn't sure how to respond. Natalie was certainly unpredictable, but the evening had been calmer, and while she wanted to protect her friend from any further stress, she felt they were all on a more even keel. She admitted that the meeting was more than a formality and explained just how worried she was.

"Never mind," Natalie said. "It's not like you haven't got any other options. We're going to be personal trainers, remember."

Briony had forgotten all about the impending course they'd signed up to at the gym, but she knew that seeing Jason would only serve to remind Natalie of the events leading up to Martin's death. She clearly wasn't thinking straight still. "Mmmm, we'll see," she said. "Let's not think about that right now."

Chapter Twenty-Seven

Lauren and Natalie woke to the sound of the shower in the main bathroom flowing. It was getting light outside and on the chest of drawers next to the bed were two mugs of coffee that Briony must have put there. They swigged them down before they went cold.

Briony came into the bedroom with a towel wrapped round her head like a turban, and a larger one around her body. The combined scent of her shampoo, moisturiser, shower gel and lotion resembled a bowl of summer fruits and her face glowed from the application of her day cream. Based on her presentation alone, Lauren decided she was going to smash it with Mr Schwartzberg. She and Natalie left her alone in the bedroom to finish getting ready, and when she came down the stairs and into the kitchen, she looked stunning.

"Wow, Bri, it's like one of those shows on the telly – the big reveal after a major makeover," said Natalie.

Briony had selected a clingy black trouser suit that highlighted her peachy bum and dinky waist. Her hair was in a messy but stylish bun, with loose strands falling down the side of her face and brushing her shoulders. Make-up wise, she'd gone for a dark, liquid eyeliner, smoky eyeshadow and long, curled eyelashes, with just a tint of pink on her lips.

"You certainly look like you mean business today," Lauren added.

"Would you like another coffee?" Natalie offered, as Briony brushed the creases from her suit.

Briony shook her head. "No, thanks, hun, I don't want to be needing the loo in there. I'm going to leave now, so that I can have some time on my own to prepare and get into the zone."

They all looked at the clock; it was only seven, but they chose not to comment. They knew Briony was a performer and needed the time to get into character.

"OK, hotty, go get 'em," Natalie said.

"Thanks, Nat, I'll do my best. Don't forget that Daniela, the mental health nurse, is popping round at ten."

Briony could tell from the look on Natalie's face that she didn't like the sound of the visit. "Don't panic," she reassured her. "Lauren will be here, and your mum might come over, too."

Natalie didn't react, while inwardly realising that she couldn't fight this and had no other choice but to go with it. Maybe even her mum would bring the kids. She found some hope in her heart and could feel the tug from the invisible string that connected her to her daughter. The analogy came from a book that Bethany had brought home from the school library when she wasn't settling into reception class too well. It explained that no matter where you were in the world, there was an invisible string connecting your heart to the hearts of the people you loved. After Natalie had read the book to Bethany a couple of times before bed, she had left for school in a much happier state, knowing that she was attached to her mummy. Natalie hoped that she still had faith in that string, because today she was holding on tightly to her own.

Lauren grabbed Briony and Natalie's hands and pulled them in close. "We've got this, girls!" she said. It was the support and encouragement they all needed to hear.

"OK, I'm off," said Briony. "Think good thoughts for me, please."

As she sauntered to the door, Lauren patted Briony's bum. As she continued to admire her beloved's derrière, the green-eyed monster arose from the deep. What if Mani tried it on with her again? She mentally ticked herself off and told herself that Briony would be absolutely fine. With any luck, she'd be home by eleven – only four hours away.

Meanwhile, Briony closed the front door and stepped onto the driveway, sucking in a deep breath of spring air. She did some self-talk, too, reassuring herself that she didn't have to worry about Natalie, because she'd be safe with Lauren and Paula. All she had to do now was hold her shit together and be confident, honest and compassionate. She had nothing to hide. Even so, it worried her that if Mr Schwartzberg did keep his promise to let her return to work, things would be extremely awkward at the office from now on. But everything had changed, and she really did need a regular wage.

As she pulled into the car park, she was surprised to see that some eager beavers were already at the office. It had never once occurred to her to start work earlier than her official time. She obviously hadn't loved her job as much as she'd thought. She saw the gold Jag parked close to the door and a shiver ran down her spine. Apparently, she'd had a lift in the very same vehicle following her drunken date with Mani, but she had no recollection of it. The thought made her feel vulnerable, as these men had seen her in her very worst state. She spotted Keith walking about in the upstairs office and felt the pain of being stabbed in the back. It was such a shame he'd blown the whistle on her, because they'd once had such a great working relationship. Still, she should have been more wary, as he hadn't earned his title as the King of Office Gossip for nothing. Maybe he'd acted out of jealousy, or maybe this was his way of getting all the gossip in the first place. She wondered how she could be expected to carry on working as his assistant. He'd completely lost her trust, and he clearly had no loyalty towards her, either.

She watched Keith come over to the window and survey the car park. Was he looking for her? She was in Natalie's Audi, and she felt smugly certain that he'd be perturbed by her sudden upgrade from Gina.

The hour and a half she spent waiting in the car passed slowly. She watched people parking up and shuffling towards the building, ready for another day. She speculated how although she'd never actually seen Lauren perform on the ships, she couldn't imagine her starting a show with her body bent forward and her shoulders slumped. She decided that rather than being just another office drone, she'd emulate her showbiz persona: head up, shoulders back, boobs out and hips swaying. She brushed herself down, fiddled with her hair, adjusted her make up, adding an extra layer of lip gloss, and stepped out of the car.

Walk tall and confidently, with long strides, she told herself, performing her catwalk strut right across the car park. She switched her phone to silent and dropped it into her fake Louis Vuitton handbag; another gift from Lauren, no doubt acquired from a looky looky guy at one of the ports she had stopped at.

Inside, she was greeted by the sounds of a regular day at the office: phones ringing, the tapping of fingers on keyboards and people talking or listening to the radio. But despite the buzz all around, she felt completely alone. She popped to the downstairs toilet before heading up to the main, open-plan office. As she entered the room, she felt like the newbie at a group exercise class, with everyone looking her up and down.

If Keith had anything to do with it, she was sure most of the staff were aware of her pending appointment with the big boss.

Just then, her lovely friend Wendy, who worked at Schwartzberg Ltd as a cleaner, came flying over, her face full of concern. "Darling, what on earth is going on?" she said. "You know what the gossip mills are like around here."

Briony loved how Wendy always wore the perfume Anais Anais, which took her right back to the '90s. She reflected how Wendy was inadvertently responsible for her brief liaison with Mani, whom she'd first met after covering Wendy's Saturday cleaning shift so she could attend a matinee in the West End. Expecting to have the whole place to herself, she'd been shocked to find Mr Schwartzberg and his handsome son, who was over from the US, doing some weekend work, too.

"Oh, Wendy, who knows. You probably know more than I do, but to be honest, I don't really care. Natalie's not well and she's my priority right now."

Wendy noticed a dramatic difference in Briony's attitude. The last time she'd seen her, she was loving her job, but now she seemed nonplussed and unhappy to be in the office. She threw an arm across her shoulder. "Well, I hope your friend gets better soon," she said.

The way Briony had put it, Natalie could have nothing more serious than a cold, but she didn't have the heart to share the extent of her vulnerability with someone who didn't know her.

"Would you like a coffee, dear?" Wendy asked.

"I'd love one, ta," Briony replied, thinking how a caffeine hit was just what she needed. "But if you don't mind, I'll stay up here. I don't want to bump into anyone unnecessarily."

Wendy knew not to ask.

Just then, the door to Mr Schwartzberg's office opened inwards with such force that any loose paper was in danger of being sucked into his lair. Briony looked up at the towering man, reflecting how her feelings towards him had gone full circle. At first, he'd been Mr Toad of Toad Hall, then he'd been the kind man who'd rescued her while drunk, invited her to hang out at his mansion and offered her forever employment. Now he was back to being Mr Toad again, after accosting her in the pub and accusing her of sexual harassment.

"Miss Greene, are you here alone?"

"Oh, yes, Mr S. Sorry, Lauren couldn't make it."

"Oh, well, that's a shame. Follow me, we'll be having our meeting in the conference suite downstairs."

He stomped past and Briony's stomach lurched. While she'd peeked into the conference suite on many occasions – often just to catch a glimpse of Mani, back when she was madly in lust with him – she'd never actually been inside it. She walked slowly down the stairs, along the corridor and past *the* kitchen. When the door opened, she felt a flash of panic, but fortunately it was only Wendy.

"Oh, I thought you weren't coming down?" she said.

"Yeah, I know, but Mr Schwartzberg wants to see me in the conference room."

Wendy looked surprised. "Oh, OK, hun, don't panic. Everything will be fine."

Briony took the coffee from Wendy and thanked her, but right now she wasn't sharing her colleague's positivity.

"Let me help," Wendy added, opening the door to the conference room, which matched the decadent splendour of Mr Schwartzberg's mansion. The long boardroom table was made with dark, heavy wood, and the matching chairs were upholstered with sleek brown leather. Mr S clearly loved his expensive bling, so it was no surprise to see an exquisite chandelier hanging from the high ceiling, with the light from it enhancing the vibrancy of the royal blue carpet. Briony could understand why her boss was so successful, because even with her nerves, the opulence of her surroundings made her feel fabulous, and she would no doubt sign up to anything if it meant a chance of obtaining a piece of it.

"Miss Greene?"

Briony snapped back into the present and looked towards the terrifying triad that was Mr Schwartzberg, Mani and Keith. They were standing at the top end of the table drinking from expensive looking cups. She noted that there was no solicitor present and felt grateful for small mercies. She strolled over, feeling just a little inadequate with the *I ♥ NY* mug that Wendy had given her. She noticed Mani and Keith looking her up and down and tried to match her expression to the positive vibe her power suit was clearly giving off.

"Let's take a seat," said Mr Schwartzberg, signalling it was time for the meeting to begin.

Briony felt like she'd been thrown into the lion's den and wished Lauren was with her. Keith took a seat first, crossing his sparrow legs in his characteristic feminine fashion and getting ready with his wooden spoon for some serious stirring. "Shall I start the proceedings, Mr Schwartzberg?"

Briony gave him what she hoped was her dirtiest of looks.

"No, no, Keith, I'll come to you when or if I need to."

Briony struggled to conceal her pleasure at Keith getting ticked off. But not for the first time, she remembered that it was her poor judgment of his character that had got her into this mess in the first place. She imagined herself sat in the dock in an orange jumpsuit ready to stand trial. And for the first time that morning, she was ready for the ride.

Chapter Twenty-Eight

"Miss Greene, I must admit that I have never before found myself in a situation like this one," said Mr Schwartzberg. "So let me begin with how I managed to find myself in this position.

"I had a meeting with young Keith here, and he informed me that you smuggled Miss Newland into the workplace kitchen, where the two of you undressed in front of Mr Schwartzberg Junior and offered to perform sexual favours for him."

Briony glanced over at Keith, who looked as if he was going to wet himself from excitement.

"I am assuming this was for career development," continued Mr Schwartzberg, "but I think we can all agree that I certainly didn't get to where I am today by employing this method."

His beady eyes were serious, but Briony swore she could see a glimmer of humour behind them and giggled. Keith kept his back straight, maintaining his pride as the whistleblower, while Mani had his head down, clearly conscious that he wasn't quite the innocent party.

"I'm really sorry, Mr Schwartzberg," Briony said, "this isn't a laughing matter, but I can assure you that I wasn't after career progression, I just wanted Mr Schwartzberg Junior to own up to treating me in a way I didn't deserve."

She had practised her defence in her head and felt she'd executed it well.

"That's interesting, Miss Greene, please tell me more," said Mr Schwartzberg.

It wasn't the reaction she'd hoped for. "Oh God, this is so ridiculous. Do we really have to go into detail?"

Keith seemed to feed off her discomfort. "I can tell you what she and Lauren told me, on the day it happened."

"For the love of . . ." Mani stood up, his attention fixed on Keith. "Dude, we are only here because of you. I don't know what you're getting out of this, you sad little man."

"Hey, hey, Emmanuel. Take a step back," said Mr Schwartzberg. "You will all get your say and then I will decide on a course of action."

Mani's outburst made Briony feel a pang of sympathy for him, which she knew Lauren would disapprove of. He'd been a dick, but everyone makes mistakes, and in their effort to teach him a lesson they'd clearly hurt his pride and injured his masculinity.

"Mr S, let me show you how this all started." Briony reached into her handbag and took out her phone. But as she scrolled through her videos, she realised that with everything going on, she had forgotten to ask Lauren to forward the footage of Mani suggesting the threesome. "Shit, shit, I haven't got it on my phone," she said. "I can message Lauren and ask her to send it?"

"Well, well, Miss Greene," said Mani. "Surely if it had been that important, you would have ensured you had the evidence ready before you came in?"

Mani went straight from Briony's good books right into total douchebag territory again.

"I do have to agree with Emmanuel," said Mr S.

Briony wanted to explode over the injustice, especially considering what she'd been dealing with outside of work, but she kept her lips sealed. What had happened to Natalie was none of these men's business.

"I'll describe what happened instead," Briony pressed on. "Around the time we were singing *Mack the Knife* at your house, Mr S, Mani ushered Lauren into your *Downton Abbey* room and asked for a threesome with her and me. That's why we left early. It wasn't because I was feeling poorly, per se, just sick to the stomach after discovering what little Mani thought of me. He approached Lauren without even bothering to enquire what my feelings were on the matter."

"Oh, hold on there!" Mani got to his feet again, while wiping the sweat from his brow. "You had sex with me next door," he said, pointing in the direction of the kitchen. "You came onto me!"

Briony reacted by slipping into actress mode. Mani was really pissing her off now. "You didn't need to act on it, did you? And you deleted the CCTV footage so your dad wouldn't find out. Surely, that's against company policy?"

"OK, everyone calm down," said Mr Schwartzberg. "Obviously, there are parts of this saga that I wasn't aware of." He turned to Briony. "What I can say is that neither Keith nor my son have acted at all gentlemanly here.

"Miss Greene, I have no desire to see the footage, so don't worry about that, but we do have a situation because I don't want this kind of awkwardness in my workplace. And Emmanuel, what is this about you deleting CCTV footage?"

Mani looked away, avoiding his dad's gaze. "OK, I admit that I did delete the footage of Briony and me, er, fucking in the kitchen."

Briony felt uncomfortable with Mani using the f-word in front of his dad, especially as it was something they'd done during worktime, but Mr Schwartzberg seemed unfazed.

"Yeah, I did lure Lauren away from the party to ask for a threesome," Mani admitted. "But, Dad, you know I'm having therapy for this kind of stuff."

Like a bomb detonating, Mani's words reverberated around the conference suite and altered the mood entirely. Briony looked at Keith, who for the first time since the meeting began looked as if he wanted the ground to open up and swallow him.

"So, anyway, the next day at work, Briony sent me a message to meet her in the kitchen, and when I got there, Lauren was there, too, and they started performing for me."

Briony fidgeted, as she remembered just what that performance had entailed.

Mr Schwartzberg obviously had images in his mind, too, but thankfully he kept his eyes on his son.

"We were just getting to the good bit," continued Mani, "when it all stopped, and Lauren said I had to pay Briony a ransom of a year's salary, or else they would tell you what I had asked of them."

As he spoke, Briony felt desperately embarrassed, on her own behalf and Mani's. He was having to expose details of his private life to his father. It was clear that Mr Schwartzberg was uncomfortable, too, as he shed his jacket and loosened the top button of his shirt.

"Well, son, let's not delve too much into our personal business here; I am aware of your struggles." Mr Schwartzberg turned his attention to Briony. "As for the behaviour of you and your cohort, Miss Greene, I'm really not sure what to say."

Briony's stomach felt as if it had dropped to the floor; her body no longer had shape or a skeleton.

"I can't completely blame you," Mr Schwartzberg continued. "After all, you and Miss Newland were only responding to Emmanuel's first move, but going forward, I can't see how this type of behaviour fits into the foundation of a solid and productive workforce."

Briony wanted to respond, but she couldn't find the words.

"I think we should have a break now and reconvene in an hour," suggested Mr Schwartzberg. Briony looked at her watch. It was already ten, dashing her hopes of being home for eleven. She just wanted to be with Natalie.

She looked at all three men in turn, this time feeling sorry for Mr Schwartzberg. He'd only ever shown her kindness, and he didn't deserve to be in this difficult position.

The extent of Keith's vindictiveness had taken her completely by surprise, and she figured it would be no loss if she never saw him again after today. She couldn't imagine a way for them ever to be able to work together.

Then there was Mani, who seemed to be working through some major mother and women issues, albeit badly. Did he really deserve to have his sex life dragged through the mud before his dad? The prospect of a new career as a personal trainer was beginning to look like the best option. Maybe she and Natalie could go into business together.

She stood up and walked over to Mr Schwartzberg. "I'm really sorry it has come to this," she said. "In all honesty, it's mostly all my fault, so please cut my notice short and I'll leave right away. I really appreciate your offer of a job in the future, but we all know this could never now work."

In the background, she could hear Keith sighing with relief.

"My friend is having some problems, and I really need to look after her. In a way, maybe this was supposed to happen. Maybe Emmanuel and Keith's behaviour was to enable us to move forward in our own ways, and maybe I was meant to be available to care for my lovely friend full-time until she has recovered."

There was empathy in Mr Schwartzberg's eyes as he met Briony's, which were now glistening with tears. "Thank you, Miss Greene, your apology is appreciated, and despite everything, I am sorry to see you go. But it's true that your time at Schwartzberg Finance Ltd has come to an end. Your pay will cease from today, but I wish you all the best for your future. If and when you do decide to look for another job, I'll write you a glowing reference, because your standard of work has always been exceptional."

Struggling to find her words again, Briony looked around the room. Mani was slumped in his chair like a guilty teenager, and again she felt guilty for putting him through all this. Keith still had his back straight, but he couldn't bring himself to look back at her. "OK," she snivelled. "That's fair. Thank you again, Mr S."

She hastily exited the conference room, which, thankfully, was on the same level as the car park, reducing her chances of bumping into any of her now former colleagues. She hung her lanyard on the bottom of the banister and made her way to Natalie's Audi, reflecting on her words at the meeting. Maybe this *was* all meant to be. Once in the car, she snapped on her seatbelt and synced her phone to the vehicle's Bluetooth so she could ring Paula. She'd had an idea.

After their chat, she drove home without looking back. She didn't have the sense of loss she'd expected to experience. All she wanted was to get to Natalie's and see how her appointment with the mental health nurse had gone. She had a feeling that things were finally starting to look up.

* * *

At precisely three-thirty that afternoon, Briony watched from the bay window in the living room as Paula pulled into the driveway in her white BMW. She could see two excited faces in the back and felt a cascade of butterflies erupt inside her tummy. She went into the kitchen and stuck her thumb up at Lauren.

Natalie, who was busy making a brew, got suspicious. "What's going on?" she asked.

"Nat, please take a seat in the lounge," said Lauren. "Don't question anything, just do as you're told."

Natalie didn't appreciate being bossed around by Lauren, but she didn't have the energy to fight back. She heard the door open, and the flurry of shoes being removed. The sound was so achingly familiar that she could have exploded from all her pent-up love. Lauren had secretly connected her phone with Natalie's wireless speakers, and a familiar Spice Girls song began to play. As soon as Natalie recognised the tune, she was desperate to get up from her seat, but Lauren held her hand up to form a stop sign.

And then in walked Briony with Bethany and Milo. "Mama, I love you," they sang.

Natalie was overwhelmed by the unconditional love she felt for them, and the love they clearly felt for her. She gathered them into her arms and cried for how they'd loss their dad, and – to an extent – lost her, too. But she knew she was on the right path now to getting better, for herself and for them.

Lauren took Briony's hand and Briony took Paula's, and they joined in with the song, too.

"Yuck, let me out," Milo said, squirming out of his mother's embrace.

"Mum, where are all the pictures?" Bethany asked.

At that moment, Natalie realised the world was still turning, and that life had to go on. Her children hadn't changed. They loved her just as much as ever. "I'll tell you all about that later," she said to her daughter. "Why don't we do some painting, and you can decide on some colours for the walls? I think the house needs redecorating. What do you think?"

"I agree," said Bethany. "Just look at the difference between the wall and where the pictures were hanging. It's gross!"

Everyone laughed and Lauren thought of a way to keep the light-hearted atmosphere going. "So, who wants ice cream?" she said.

Her question was aimed at the children, but the cries of "yes, please," were unanimous.

They moved to the kitchen, where Lauren found some Raspberry Ripple in the freezer. She got an ice cream scoop from the drawer and took out two bowls from the cupboard, deciding to serve the kids first.

As she dished up, Briony rolled her eyes. "Flippin' heck, Laur, who's that for? Neither Bethany nor Milo are going to manage all that."

"Oh, Lauren, that's two scoops too much," agreed Natalie.

It was obvious that Lauren didn't have any children of her own.

"Give two to Milo, and three is plenty for Bethany," said Natalie. She paused for a second, reflecting on her words. "I guess three is enough for me, too. Natalie, Briony and Lauren."

She took some Hundreds and Thousands from the cupboard and sprinkled them over the ice cream. "With a scattering of Bethany and Milo, too.

"Not forgetting you, Mum," she added, taking two strawberries from the punnet in the fridge and placing them in the two bowls as well. "There you go, my perfect family."

Just then, Briony's phone beeped and vibrated on the

worktop. Lauren picked it up. "Bloody hell, babe, you're going to want to see this; it's a notification from your bank." She held the phone in front of Briony's face and then repeated what it said. "A deposit of thirty-two grand has just been paid into your account by a Mr Ellis Herbert Schwartzberg."

Briony felt overwhelmed by her former boss's unexpected and immensely generous act of kindness. Money may not buy happiness, but it could certainly buy her and Lauren time, which they could now devote to Natalie.

Acknowledgments

Thank you to Rich and Portia, and my fabulous family and friends, for your ongoing support, belief and encouragement.

Thanks so much again to Danielle, from Wrate's Editing Services, for all your help and everything you have done to make *Two Scoops, Too Much* a reality.

I would like to thank Sam for listening to my ideas and answering my nurse/medical-related questions on the school pick-ups. I really appreciate your help.

Thanks also to Police Constable John Belson, from the Joint Operations Unit at Thames Valley Police, for assisting me with police-related questions.

My additional gratitude to everyone who has read, enjoyed and reviewed *Two Scoops, Not Three*. Your words mean so much.